THE GIRL WHO LOVED GARBO

THE GIRL WHO LOVED GARBO

A NOVEL BY

RACHEL GALLAGHER

DONALD I. FINE, INC.
NEW YORK

Library of Congress Cataloging-in-Publication Data
Gallagher, Rachel,
The girl who loved Garbo: a novel/by Rachel Gallagher.
p.   cm
ISBN 1-55611-200-9
I. Title.
PS3557.A411558G5   1990
813'.54—dc20   89-46031
CIP

Manufactured in the United States of America
10 9 8 7 6 5 4 3 2 1

Designed by Irving Perkins Associates

G

This book is dedicated to my mother
Ethelyn

ACKNOWLEDGMENTS

For their continued assistance and encouragement of me during this project my profound thanks to my agent Angela Miller and her assistant Suszanne Dooley, and my editor Susan Schwartz.

Also, deep appreciation goes to the following: Jessica Abbott, Laura Biscotto, Richard Gallen, Brijid Leary, Deborah Liebman, Anne and George Nelson, Holly Romero, and *Tantaleh* Lillie Andreasen, for the variety of help and support each provided me throughout.

A very special thanks to my uncle, Harry Tarzian, and to Ashby Meek whose humor and example served as a constant source of inspiration.

I also wish to pay tribute to Cara McCarty, Assistant Curator, and Marie-Anne Evans, Administrative Assistant, of the Department of Architecture and Design of The Museum of Modern Art for their help, and also the fine staff and work of the Department of Film, and all my pals in Special Events (past and present): Joan Howard, Cathy Lehman, Andrea Stone, Phyllis Bell, Aileen Kelso, Maggie Edmonston, and Nancy Fitzgerald including those *hostai exemplar*, Maria Martin, Catherine Grimshaw and Peggy Schneider.

Of my colleagues in the Department of Film, I owe a particular debt of gratitude to Mary Lea Bandy, Director, for her unwavering generosity and unfaltering patience, and for providing me with the time to write; Stephen Harvey, Associate Curator, for his unflagging encouragement, tutelage, and "commiseration"; Mary Corliss, Assistant Curator, and Anne Morra, Curatorial Assistant, for their astute and ready advice; Charles Silver and Ron Magliozzi, Study Center Supervisor and Assistant Study Center Supervisor, for their tireless research assistance; Eileen Bowser, Adrienne Mancia, Larry Kardish, Curators, Jytte Jensen, Curatorial Assistant, Robert Beers, Assistant, and John Johnson, Sr. Cataloguer, for keeping the faith; Marilyn Mancino, Assistant, for trekking to California to retrieve the Hollywood maps; Sally Berger and Laurie Rigelhaupt, Assistants, for their insights, and for listening; Sarah Eaton, Film Publicist, for her guidance, and last but not least, Museum projectionists Charles Kalinowski, Tony Tavalacci, and Greg Singer for providing endless hours of enjoyable film-viewing.

A particular debt is owed to the fine staff and work of the Departments of Film, and Architecture and Design of The Museum of Modern Art.

To the following authors I wish to express my appreciation: John Bainbridge, *Garbo*, Holt, Rinehart & Winston, 1971; Cecil Beaton, *Cecil Beaton: Memoir of the 40s*, McGraw-Hill Book Co., 1972; Kevin Brownlow, *The Parade's Gone By*, Alfred A. Knopf, 1968, and Leatrice Gilbert Fountain, *Dark Star*, St. Martin's Press, 1985.

BOOK
ONE

CHAPTER ONE

Dinnertime is when I miss Eddie the most. My ex-live-in, he and I have been separated for nearly a year. When you live alone people become obsessed with your mealtimes. What they're really asking is, "How can you stand to eat all by yourself night after night?" The more appropriate question for me would be not what I eat, but where? I eat all over the house; once even in the bathtub.

I live on the top floor of a brownstone on a quiet, tree-lined street close to Central Park. It has a stoop, and a vestibule, and a nosy landlady who lives on the first floor with a bulldog named Bruce. The hallway has been painted dark maroon with matching carpeting and contains a narrow stairway flanked by shiny wooden banisters that smell of furniture polish. The stairs creak. The creak alerts the landlady, Mrs. Wallace, who likes to monitor the traffic in and out of the building. There are only six of us, five with Eddie gone, but I suppose we keep Mrs. Wallace busy enough.

Mr. Hennessy, who lives below me, is an elderly man who shuffles in and out. He tips his fedora whenever a female is within ten square feet of him. B. B. Ottermeyer lives below Mr. Hennessy. She is a tall, thin, quiet woman of indeterminate age who works in "the Arts." I've never seen her before 8:00 P.M., and suspect she may be a vampire. The Feldstone-Kleins are newly-weds who occupy the ground floor apartment. Each is studying for a doctorate in psychology. Sometimes they come up for air and take long walks in the park. The husband is a curly-headed cherub, far prettier than his plain-faced wife, who is friendly and smiles a lot.

We found the apartment through an ad in the New York *Times*, a fact which nobody believes at first. "You found *this* through an ad?" people exclaim when they see the apartment: four large, sunny, rent-stabilized rooms, including a sit-down kitchen and a working fireplace, all for $898.26. They want to know, How much did we pay in "key" money? Who did we have to kill to get the place? Believe it or not, except for one month's security, we didn't have to spend a dime, or murder a soul. Eddie has that kind of luck. He looks like Tom Hanks, only taller, thinner, and more boyish, if that's possible. My father says he's "full of the blarney."

Initially, Mrs. Wallace was reluctant to show us the apartment. "It's taken," she said. I would have given up, but Eddie cajoled her into letting us take a peek. He flattered her, made her laugh, reminded her of her son, she said. By the time Eddie was finished with Mrs. Wallace, she not only gave us the apartment, but provided free cable plus the name of reliable yet inexpensive movers.

The landlady senses something is wrong between Eddie and me, but she's not sure what and has made it one of her life's goals to find out.

A couple of days after Eddie moved out, Mrs. Wallace cornered me on my way home from work.

"I haven't seen that nice young man you *live* with," she said, reminding me of Granny Peck, my mother's mother, who thinks my morals loose. "Has he been away?"

Mrs. Wallace is as subtle as a stench.

"He went to California on business."

"Oh? Will he be gone long?"

"Not long."

Mrs. Wallace comes up to my navel, but she would have made a good Philadelphia linebacker. Her chunky body blocks my passage. She is dressed in her usual smock, with wadded Kleenex stuffed into the pockets. She is always housecleaning so I figure the smock protects the loud, print, Forties-type dresses she favors. Her wiry white hair lies coiled, ready to spring, around her head. Bruce is sniffing around my feet. It's funny how people begin to resemble their pets. A major difference between Mrs. Wallace and Bruce is that she doesn't drool. Nor does she hump my shin.

"Brucie!" she says, wagging a pudgy finger at him. "Bad doggie. Bad. Come away from her." She tugs hard on his collar. Reluctantly, Bruce disengages from my leg.

"Excuse me, Mrs. Wallace," I say. "I think I hear my phone ringing," and sprint up the stairs.

"He's such a nice young man," she calls after me. "I hope there's no trouble between you two."

Frantically, I fumble for my keys, which are lost in the bottom of my shoulder bag.

"I'd hate to see you lose a nice boy like that."

The raspy sound of Mrs. Wallace's voice gets closer and closer. My God. She's coming after me. Where are my damn keys?

"Listen," she raves, heaving herself up the stairs. "I know how it is. My Robert lived with a girl, not the one he's married to now, of course, but another girl, and the problems they used to have . . ." She pauses. "You young people these days think you can get away with anything, but let me tell you, you can't. Do you know the Ten Commandments?"

Out of frustration I dump the entire contents of my purse on the floor. My keys spill out, but it's too late. I'm trapped. She's practically on the landing, with a wheezing Bruce not far behind.

"The Ten Commandments. Do you think Moses made them up? If everyone followed the Ten Commandments what a nice world this would be."

Breathless, but triumphant she arrives, her beady black eyes gleaming. Frantically I throw stuff back inside my purse. Bruce sniffs and growls.

Inserting the key into the lock, I say, "Excuse me, Mrs. Wallace. But I've had an exhausting day at work. I'm very tired."

"You tell Mr. Geary that I was asking for him," she calls through the closing door. "Tell him I've baked some of that apricot strudel he likes so much."

"I will," I say, closing the door in her face. I feel sorry for Mrs. Wallace, who is a lonely widow, but I dislike more than pity her. All her vulgar nosiness and false cheer make me want to do is scream and flee.

There is a message on the machine from Mom. "Hi, honey. I know you're not home from work yet, but I just wanted to alert you to the package I sent. It should be arriving by parcel post today or tomorrow. Call me. Dad and I are worried about you."

Mom always worries about me and my younger brother, Brad. It's her career. At first she looked askance at Eddie's and my living arrangements. It went against her antebellum notions of proper decorum for a lady. Valerie Burgess Peck—of the Bristo, Tennessee/Virginia Pecks—is a template of Southern femininity, and petite. Dad is tall—taller than I am, but not by much. I am my father's daughter, that's for sure.

I often find myself wandering the four rooms fondling objects that remind me of happier times with Eddie not that I'm unhappy. Sometimes time and space enshroud me, creating my own special world, which I kind of like. It takes getting used to.

My stomach growls and all thoughts turn to dinner. The refrigerator reveals a couple of cartons of week-old Chinese; a half-empty container of yoghurt, some moldy bread, and a can of tuna. The cupboards hold several boxes of cereal and some cans of soup. What's the coffee mug doing here? Every time I see the mug I vow to throw it out. The handle is broken, so it's useless. I gave the mug to Eddie in college and suspect that he left it, and a lot of other sentimental junk, behind on purpose to remind me of him. The mug is decorated with line drawings of fornicating octopuses, which always makes me smile.

In college, Eddie was one of my many suitors. Since I was one out of five girls taking engineering courses his interest was less

6

because of my irresistible beauty than that the odds were over-whelmingly in my favor. Other guys I dated were smoother, cooler, better dressers, dancers, drinkers, even kissers than Eddie. But he made me laugh, especially in bed. Neither one of us was too experienced sexually, and if the rest of our bodies had mated as ardently as our bony joints and long limbs, we would have filled a house full with children by now. Making out with Eddie was like being embraced by a giant octopus. Affectionately, I dubbed him "Octaman," and it became our private joke. After our freshman year we moved in together and began collecting junk with the octopus theme.

The Ping-Pong ball that lives inside the mug is another useless object I can't bring myself to part with. Written in bright red nail polish on its surface are the words I LOVE YOU. Another gift from me to him. In our sophomore year Eddie developed a fetish for Ping-Pong balls. Not the game, just the balls. He wanted to describe life inside one of them for an expository writing class. He bought a whole box and drilled holes of varying sizes through the tops. We'd sit in the campus library studying together. Eddie'd peer through the little holes in the balls, holding them up to the light.

"What's it like in there?" I asked one night.

He focused his large, round, brown eyes on mine and said, "Lonely."

I think I fell in love with him at that precise instant.

Describing life inside a Ping-Pong ball tickled Eddie in ways I'll never quite understand. Everybody else in the class wrote papers describing their rooms, or cars, or closets. He got an A − on the paper. The minus was because he'd chosen an "inappropriate" subject; the A because he'd done such a fine job.

I read the paper and had to agree with the prof. Eddie had tackled the assignment brilliantly from both a physical and meta-physical angle, but the subject was bizarre.

We used to fight constantly over his choice of a major. When he dropped out of architecture to take up business I told him he was acting like a dork. He said it was none of my business and slammed the door on his way out. Eddie is a big door-slammer. I wondered if the switch of majors had anything to do with the fact that I pulled better math and engineering grades?

Selling things comes easy to Eddie. Before wine, he'd sold shoes, men's haberdashery, pots and pans, household appliances and medical supplies to help pay college expenses. Peddling prostheses and wheelchairs challenged him for a while, and he got a job with a New York–based company after graduating from college. He did well, and when the California job offer came, off he went. There was a lot of door-slamming going on around this time, so it was a welcome break for us both. We needed a change—from each other, and ourselves, our lives together. I felt I couldn't breathe. It was around this time that I developed my obsession for Garbo.

Eddie says that he passes the house where Garbo used to live every day on his way to and from work. He's switched majors again: instead of medical supplies he now sells California wine. Drinking wine has always interested Eddie. He and a few of his friends got together once a month for a "tasting." Oenophiles are a weird bunch. If you ask me, wine tastings are just an excuse for a bunch of guys to get together stag and get drunk. The one and only time Eddie brought me along I got so drunk by the dessert wine that I passed out.

Eddie is doing well in California, well enough to talk about buying a condo on the beach. He wants me to come out.

Every so often I put all the stuff that reminds me of Eddie—the cup, the Ping-Pong ball, the E.T. doll, the stuffed penguin—into a box and put the box in the trash. But I always retrieve it at the last minute.

"Shit or get off the pot, babe," my friend Cara said when I told her about being unable to throw the junk away. Frankly I hate that expression. Life cannot be reduced to a biological function.

"Crap," Cara insisted, "you just don't want to grow up."

Garbo's worst critics accused her of being "childlike," so I guess I'm in good company.

The Shelstein's kitchen sounds and smells like an old-fashioned country hearth, but it's equipped with every high-tech culinary gadget invented. Both Cara and Shel cook. He makes great Chinese, especially chicken wings, and she does nouvelle-vegetarian.

I love to eat at their house, but am always bothered by all that fancy and expensive kitchen equipment. Something in me resists the excessiveness of gadgets that waste energy to perform tasks that can be accomplished with an economy of effort and a simplicity of tool whose purity of design cannot be improved upon. Cara, Shel and I spend hours arguing about the merits of the automatic can-opener/knife-sharpener versus the manual "miracle" can-opener. You know the kind: it's made out of metal. The can rim is held between a cutting blade and a turning gear, which with pressure applied by squeezing two handles and rotating the can by turning a winged key, opens it. From a design point of view the object is sheer perfection. It is utilitarian, inexpensive, cost-efficient, portable, durable—plus, it burns calories and is good exercise.

One night after we all downed a few of Shel's Mega-Margaritas, the Shelstein's challenged me to a can-opening contest: my "miracle" manual against their latest yuppie kitchen porn. At first they were winning, but by the fifth can the machine was acting up, from wear and tear or a mechanical glitch. I won by a landslide. We dumped all the contents of the opened cans into a huge pot and made an inedible stew.

Before Cara and I became friends I used to see her wheeling her shopping cart at the neighborhood supermarket. She studied the labels of cans and packages like she would be given a pop quiz at any second. Her hair was a wild mass of black curls. She wore a lot of black and favored high-heeled shoes and tight designer jeans. Not my type, I'd think, barrelling down the aisles in baggy corduroys and sneakers, carelessly tossing cans, boxes and bottles into the basket.

"There was always so much junk food in your cart I thought you had a houseful of kids," Cara confided after we'd become friends.

I am always on the prowl for tastier cereals and review this particular section of the supermarket with a devotion bordering on reverence. One day while in the midst of seriously debating whether to go for chocolate-covered corn flakes or a healthier, sugarless all-bran type, I heard a voice behind me warn, "Don't do it."

I turned and saw Cara.

"Why not?"

"It's poison. Here," she said, handing me a box of imported granola. "This tastes good and is better for you."

Cara's coal-black eyes watched me with amusement. I didn't know whether to blow her off as a pest or follow her advice.

"What the hell," I said, "I guess it won't hurt."

Thereafter, whenever we'd bump into one another at the market we'd say hello and stop to chat. She'd ask me to retrieve items from high shelves.

"How I envy you your height," she said one day.

"It's been no picnic, believe me."

This got us going.

"Oh yeah? How would you like to spend your life looking at things from the perspective of people's navels?"

"At least you're not mistaken for a redwood tree."

"You don't have to shop in the children's department."

"You don't get cramped legs at movie theaters or in airline seats."

"You don't have to fear being trampled on in crowds."

"You don't have to worry about bumping your head all the time."

On and on we bandied, rolling our carts down the aisles.

"Did you ever consider modeling?" she asked on another day.

"Passionately, when I was a teenager. My mother used to laugh and call me Cyclops, because my eyes are a tad too close together. And my brother and I have a slight case of scoliosis, curvature of the spine. She'd call us Quasimodo 1 and 2. Somehow that squelched my modeling plans."

Cara let this pass. "Believe it or not, that's all I wanted to be.

I used to hang from tree branches and ask my girlfriends to pull on my legs in an attempt to stretch myself. I ate so many vitamins my mother thought I'd overdose. I drank milk, exercised, stayed away from artificial stimulants and chemical substances, but all in vain. Nothing worked. So I did the next best thing. If I couldn't be a model, I'd be a model's booking agent. Sure you're not interested?"

"Positive. But thanks anyway."

I'd select an item and toss it in my cart. She'd replace it with one containing fewer additives or preservatives or dyes. I didn't even know Cara's last name until one Saturday, after grocery shopping, she invited me home with her for lunch. Her husband Shel was there, vacuuming.

He turned off the vacuum, and she introduced us. "Nice to meet you," he said, firmly shaking my hand. A sexy bald man, I thought. Bedroom eyes. Kind face.

"Back to work," he said, resuming his task.

"Don't mind him," Cara said. "Vacuuming is his meditation. Shel says it relaxes him. It makes the cleaning girl happy, and Shel happy, and when Shel's happy I'm happy. What can I offer you to drink?"

Cara and Shel have become my best friends, and her large homey kitchen my sanctuary. Eddie and I used to double with them on weekends—for dinner, movies, a show. The Shelsteins miss Eddie more than I do. Together the four of us formed a happy quartet. Now we're an odd trio.

In a scene from *Queen Christina* Garbo walks around the hotel room fondling objects sensuously, much to the delight of John Gilbert, who is falling in love with her. I have nearly rubbed the nail polish off the Ping-Pong ball with my thumb. I drop it back into the cup. The problem of dinner still looms. Cereal no longer appeals; pizza does. Eddie and I would order out, but I'm hesitant to do it for myself. That's what you bump up against constantly when you live alone: yourself.

Overcoming my own inhibitions, I pick up the phone and order one with everything, surprised at how easy it is. No one accused me of acting selfishly. No one denied me the pleasure of eating a whole pizza by myself. Often I eat with Garbo. She's hanging on the wall opposite my bed, or a large still of her is. The film still is from *Grand Hotel*. In it, Garbo is holding onto Barrymore, or Barrymore is holding onto Garbo, it's hard to tell which. Eddie hated the still. I remember the day I carted it home. He said, "Either that goes, or I go."

I didn't think he was serious. I've spent hours staring at the photograph, transfixed, trying to figure something out. Garbo and Barrymore are locked in a romantic embrace, each holding onto the other, staring into one another's eyes. But who is in whose arms? Who's surrendering? Even in a man's arms, she looks self-possessed. How does she do it?

Garbo is a conundrum I am anxious to solve.

The phone rings, and I screen the calls: one is from speak-of-the-devil, Eddie, and another from my mother: did I receive the package? She doesn't trust the mail anymore. It's an expensive item, and although it's insured, she'd hate to have it lost in the mail. That's Val for you. If she doesn't have anything to worry about, she'll invent something.

This must be my night. Next, there's a cheery message from an old college friend who's recently moved to the city, and who wants to get together. Right after her, there's another call. Recognizing the voice, I hold my breath. Should I pick up? Better to let him state his case. I can't believe it. Joel Holdesky. Mr. Retro himself. After he's finished, I replay the message. Would I like to catch the Garbo flick at The Museum of Modern Art with him on Sunday?

My heart starts pounding, and I feel nauseous. Is this love, or do I have indigestion from the pizza I just ate?

I dial Cara's number. "Joel called."

She's waiting for more.

"He wants to take me out."

"Great." Then, "What's the problem?"

"I don't know. No problem. I just had to tell someone."

She laughs. Cara's laugh is husky, like her voice.

"Eddie called, too."

"What did he say?"

"Just to call him."

"A good idea. Good night, babe."

"Night."

Sleepy, I decide to call Eddie and my mother tomorrow, from work. I've been avoiding them, and as guilty as that makes me feel, I can't help it. In their different ways both my boyfriend and my mother are forcing me to confront things I don't want to deal with. Just thinking about marriage and mortgages makes my chest constrict and I can't breathe.

The room feels stuffy. I get up to open the bedroom window. I can hear Eddie's voice saying, "Close it." He hated to sleep with open windows. Maybe he thought vampire bats would fly through the gates and feed off of us as we slept? I used to comply, but not totally. I'd always leave one open a crack or two. He never knew the difference, or if he did, he kept quiet about it. Now I can open the windows as wide as I like for as long as I like, but I'm all alone with my triumph.

Crawling back into bed, I think, "It's the little things that count," except that the big things get more press and hog the limelight. I'm not entirely sure where open windows fit into Eddie's and my future together. That and a thousand other subtle shifts created by his absence make me avoid returning his calls, responding to his demands. I just want to be left alone, to have time to figure it out—but I'm afraid I'll get my wish; I scheme up ways to postpone and sustain the relationship simultaneously.

Yawning, I decide to put off calling Eddie until tomorrow night. As for Mom, I'll wait until after I receive the package to call her. It's probably another frilly scarf or pouffy belt or dainty handbag. Poor Val. She's determined to turn me into her idea of Southern womanhood if it's the last thing she does.

CHAPTER TWO

Y ou'd think the vast marble lobby of The Museum of Modern Art would be a great place to wait for somebody; but not for me. The Museum holds too many memories of Eddie, whom I half-expect to see lope through the revolving doors. We used to spend a lot of time here together. He loved the old movies, and although I do too, my primary passion was and still is the Museum's permanent Architecture and Design collection.

When I was in grade school our art teacher, Mrs. Iacuzzi, rented a bus and took us on a field trip to The MoMA to view some popular painting exhibit. On the second floor of the old museum there was a section with glass-encased objects in it. Curious, I wandered over to take a peek and accidentally discovered a whole new wonderful world of sleekly designed vases and glasses and bowls. Objects that you'd see around the house being showcased behind glass and considered "decorative art" was a new concept.

Mrs. Iacuzzi had thought I was lost and got angry when a guard found me sequestered in the A&D collection, ogling the Mies van der Rohe Barcelona chair. She yelled at me in front of all the other kids, but it was worth it. I'd just experienced some kind of epiphany, an apotheosis of the mundane, and my head was aspin with visions of Useful Objects, Good Design and Machine Art.

That night, thinking I looked feverish, my mother felt my forehead.

"She's burning up," she said.

For two delirious weeks I stayed in bed, spending endless hours sketching and resketching eggbeaters and staple-removers and flashlights and blow-dryers in a frenzied attempt to improve upon their form and function, their *design*—the union of art and machinery and objects produced for mass consumption. One day I awoke from my torpor and announced, "I'm going to be an industrial engineer."

Mom stared at me for a while, blinking rapidly, then said, "That's nice, honey. I'm glad you're feeling better."

To Mom the only kind of design worth considering is fashion, or jewelry, and she constantly bemoans the fact that I chose my father, who owns a chain of hardware stores, and not Paloma Picasso, to emulate.

I have a few minutes before Joel's arrival and take the escalator to the fourth floor, where the design collection is housed. From the fourth floor you can see the top of the AT&T Building. One night when Eddie and I were at the museum, we were admiring Philip Johnson's tower. The top of the AT&T Building resembles a Chippendale highboy crown, and at the instant that Eddie and I were discussing Johnson's reason for this bit of architectural whimsy, the full moon appeared, cupped within the crown of the building as though it had been designed for that very purpose. Eddie and I looked at one another and laughed. The idea of Johnson designing for such a sentimental notion as framing the full moon struck us as funny. But I've been haunted by the image ever since and want to recapture it.

It's too early for a risen moon; I'm not even sure what stage it's in, but I stare at the crown of the AT&T Building, imagining a full moon at its center, turning the monolith into a modern Stonehenge; a place of magic and mystery where prayers might be heard and answered. What do I wish for? A promotion at work, more money; for Eddie and me to get together; world peace, harmony and understanding. The end of war, of starvation, the New Millennium. Without the moon, the AT&T Building is just another totem to modernism. No prayers will be answered here.

I'm late. From the escalator to the lobby I see Joel waiting for me. He never stands still. Some part of him is always moving. He glances at a watch that he pulls from his jeans pocket—a pocket-watch. A relic of his father's or grandfather's? Joel's contradictions impress me. He's in his punk mode: jeans, white T-shirt, black leather jacket. His hair grows in little perky spikes on the top of his head, sort of like the way Charlie Sheen wears his. The pocket-watch doesn't fit in.

"Sorry I'm late," I apologize, "but I was up on the fourth floor praying for a full moon."

Joel chortles. That's right, he's remembering, I'm with the Garbo freak, the nut.

"Have your ticket?" he asks.

"Nope."

After negotiating two tickets at the information desk, we take the escalator down to the theater. Joel looks me over, grinning. "Lipstick," he says, "a miniskirt," he says, "I'm flattered."

"Don't be. My best friend Cara is inside this body. I'm at home in jeans and sneakers watching Star Trek, The Next Generation."

"I should have figured you for a Trekkie."

A surly security guard clicks us in. We are among the last. It's a full house. Joel and I have to sit in the front row. My skirt slides up. He surveys my legs. I survey him surveying me. I could eat a plate of spaghetti off the top of Joel's head. We are an odd-looking couple, even sitting down, but I find him sexy. He's small, but trim and compact, with a certain kind of agile grace like an athlete or a dancer.

"Where'd you get the pocket-watch?" I ask.

"I bought it. I collect them."

He's looking over his shoulder. "Program notes," he mutters. "Be right back," he says, running up the aisle.

Seconds later he hands me a program note.

"Thanks," I say. The lights dim.

"Ever see this one before?" Joel asks.

"No."

"This is Garbo's first film with Gilbert," he stage-whispers.

"I know."

The curtains part.

"You're gonna love it," he says, grinning. Then, "Hey, it's nice to see you."

"It's nice to see you, too."

The pianist strikes a chord and begins to play. From the moment Garbo appears on screen I am captured. Her magnificent face appears in close-ups throughout the film. While watching her I always have a sense of reassuring myself that I am not making her up, that she is real, or as real as the play of light and shadow and moving images projected onto a giant screen will allow. Aware of her seductive beauty, the camera reveals her face by moonlight, the lighted match, the flickering fire, uncovering depths of female beauty and desire that I didn't know existed. Gilbert in his white makeup and dark eyeshadow looks bug-eyed and clownish to me. But together they exude a palpable sexual chemistry.

Joel's thigh presses against mine. The spot where we touch is no bigger than the palm of my hand. I feel the heat of his body being transfused into mine. I can't remember feeling this self-conscious with a boy since I went to the movies with Billy Berkshire and it took him nearly forty-five minutes to put his arm around me. I can't breathe. If I breathe I'll fall apart. If I move I'll fall apart. My leg cramps and I have to move.

I can't believe Garbo and Gilbert's open-mouthed kisses, and how hot the sex scenes were, how erotic. I tell Joel so. We're standing outside the museum. I should be starving but I'm not. I want to drape myself over a chaise lounge with Joel lying at my feet, in a frenzy of desire. I want to howl at the moon. The moon! It's full!

"Come on," I say, grabbing Joel's hand and tugging. "I want to show you something."

Back on the fourth-floor landing I point to the AT&T Building, but it's too late. The moon is above it, listing to the right.

"At the right moment," I explain to Joel, "the crown cups the moon in its hands."

"Kind of like a crowned jewel," he says, "or packing a giant snowball, or holding a giant basketball for the last shot of the game," he suggests. "I always hated that building, until now. C'mon, Duffy," he says, jumping on the escalator. "I want to show *you* something."

He hails a cab outside the museum. "Pier 83," he tells the driver. "At the end of West Forty-second."

"Where are we going?" I ask.

"Ever taken the Circle Line tour?"

"No."

"That's what I thought."

"What if I had?"

He shrugs. Pays the cab driver. Buys two tickets. We board the boat.

"Hungry?" he asks, veering off toward the concession stand. Joel, I decide, is a native New Yorker. He reminds me of people I work with. They definitely march to the beat of a different drummer. While the rest of the world is cruising along in slow motion, New Yorkers are off and running. Their reflexes and responses are faster, as though they were running out of time. Everything is sped up. He orders four hot dogs with sauerkraut, and two draft beers. What if I were a vegetarian?

When I ask Joel this he laughs. "Are you?"

"No."

"Then what's the problem?"

The hot dogs are delicious. Better than the "dirty waters," I tell him, the kind you buy from the street vendors.

"Dirty waters," he says, trying it on for size. "You make that up? I like that. If I had time I'd take you to Nathan's in Coney Island. Best hot dogs in the world. Maybe next time."

"Maybe next time," I repeat to myself.

It's a beautiful night; full moon, starry, a little chilly—but a chill that hints of summer, not fall. The tour guide announces points of interest as we head up the Hudson. Manhattan is prettier to look at from a distant shore than to live on. I feel a buzz from the beer.

"How'd you like the film?" Joel asks. He's leaning on the railing, smoking a cigarette. I am reminded of every shipboard romance movie I've ever seen.

"I loved it," I say. "I loved her, with him. You could tell they were in love. The movie was so . . . hot," I conclude, feebly.

Joel looks at me. Our eyes link and I feel a little thrill. He has this way of seeing through me, like he knows things about me I don't know.

"First movie love scene filmed in a horizontal position," he says.

"Really?"

"Garbo and Gilbert didn't know anybody else existed. When the director, Clarence Brown, yelled 'Cut!' during the love scene, they kept at it, oblivious to everyone else. Brown said to hell with it, and walked off."

"How do you know so much about Garbo?"

"She's my neighbor. I also studied acting."

"You did? Where?"

"Shh," he says, motioning me to be quiet. The tour guide is talking about Sutton Place, which we're passing. "The big brown apartment building by the water is the home of Greta Garbo," he says.

Joel smiles, and I realize that this is why he wanted to take me on the Circle Line.

"Do you think she's home?" I ask.

"She's not half as interesting as you think," Joel says.

"You've told me that before." Why does he have to spoil it?

"When I was a waiter, working this fancy East Side French restaurant, I used to wait on her. She'd come in alone. Her table was always waiting, no matter how crowded it got, on the off-

chance that La Garbo might appear. Sometimes she'd come with
a friend, but mostly alone. The meal was on the house, and she
could really eat, and drink, packed it in. After she was finished,
either the owner or the maître d', depending on who was there,
sometimes both, would rush up to her table and attend to her.
Pull out her chair, help her on with her coat. Tell her what a
pleasure it was to see and serve her. She accepted it all, graciously, like she had it coming. To me, she'd say a special,
'Thank you.' That was it. That was the tip. 'Thank you,' " Joel
said, lowering his voice in imitation. "For a while I coasted on it.
I was like you, smitten by the Great Garbo.

"But then I began to 'tink' about it. What were her thank-yous
to me? Did they pay the rent? Help me pay for acting classes? Put
food on the table? Could I package them and sell them? No. But
thinking like that gave me an idea.

"Perhaps she'd be so kind as to autograph a menu for me, one
per meal. Maybe she'd write, 'To Joel. Thank you, Greta Garbo.'
Now that would be something. So one night I beat the fawning
owner and maître d' to her table, and asked her politely if she'd
autograph the menu. Her eyes flashed. I'd insulted her, but it was
too late. Her manner changed completely. Became like ice. She
left in a huff. I was fired."

"Fired?"

"Fired." He flicks his cigarette into the swirling water below. "I
heard that she'd asked about me one night, a few weeks later.
'Where is that nice boy who used to wait on me?' she said. The
owner told her I had been let go. 'You shouldn't have done that,'
she said."

"You shouldn't have done that," Joel repeats to himself.

I'm not sure what I am supposed to do with the story, or how
to react. I want to tell him about the time I saw Garbo, fleetingly,
rushing down the street. I want to share my insight into her
loneliness with him when he leans over and kisses me.

Joel's lips are full and sensual, kind of like Tom Berenger's. I
like the way they feel pressed against mine. At first he tastes like
tobacco, but his breath is sweet. He smells of aftershave, and

some kind of powdery substance, like talcum powder, or, is it? I can't believe it—baby powder. I don't know whether to mother or molest him. Our bodies do not touch, only our mouths. His is open. The kisses become deeper, wetter, wilder. I pull away to catch my breath. We gaze at one another in a daze and kiss again, and again, each jolted by the novelty of who it is we are kissing, and where. I haven't really wanted anyone since Eddie. Being celibate was part of my being alone.

I am aware of our fellow ship-boarders staring at us, but I don't care. It makes it more romantic, somehow, and I feel like the star of my own movie. Is this what Garbo felt while kissing Gilbert on the set?

We disembark, Joel puts me in a cab, says, "I'll call you" and waves goodbye. I fall asleep thinking of him, and awake thinking of him. The next day at work I replayed the scene in my mind over and over again. Images of *Flesh and the Devil*, of Garbo and Gilbert, of Garbo kissing Gilbert and Gilbert kissing Garbo cascade around my brain. Joel becomes Gilbert and I become Garbo. The line between fantasy and reality begins to blur. After a while my memory of the evening seems phantasmagoric, unreal, but potent and haunting, like a dream you can't forget.

"Sounds like you're falling in love," Cara says, above the whir of the Vegematic. She is stuffing raw vegetables into its mouth for a "cocktail."

"Where'd you go afterwards?"

"Home."

"His place or yours?"

"Neither."

"You mean, you went to the movie, took a Circle Line tour so he could show you some old apartment house, kissed a few times, and then went home? *Alone?*"

"Um-hm." I am scooping peanut butter with my fingers from the plastic container. It's the sugarless kind that Cara buys in the health food store.

"I prefer Skippy's."

"And I prefer that you either eat that spread on a cracker, or not at all." Then, "Did he take you home?"

"He put me in a cab." I replace the lid and wash my hands in the kitchen sink.

Cara is looking at me with a cocked eyebrow.

"He offered to pay for it."

The eyebrow arches higher.

"I refused."

"Oh," she says, "that makes it okay."

"Caaa-ra! You're missing the point."

"What point is that?"

I don't really know so I remain mute.

"You're acting like a virgin."

"Like a vir-gin," I sing, in my best mock-Madonna, "for the ve'ry first time."

Cara laughs and places a glass of puke-green liquid before me. "What's this?"

"A vegetable juice cocktail. I just made it. Fresh."

I cannot drink slime-green concoctions from which I think strange creatures will crawl.

"One sip," Cara coaxes.

"Needs salt."

"Tell me about Eddie."

"What about Eddie?"

"What did he have to say when you called him back?"

"I didn't call him."

"What are you waiting for? An engraved invitation?"

"He's just going to hound me about coming to California." I feel restless, anxious to leave. "I've got to go," I say, jumping up.

"Stay for dinner. We're having fresh pasta, with pesto."

"Thanks, Cara, but I'm not hungry. I didn't sleep very well last night."

She gives me a quizzical look.

I buss her cheek goodbye and jog home.

I'm anxious to get home for another reason; to see if Joel has called.

There are two irate messages from Eddie, one from my mother, and another from the old college chum who wants to reunite. After a hard day at the studio Garbo took long, hot baths. A good idea. I disrobe all around the apartment.

There's a knock on the door.

"Just a second." I throw on a bathrobe.

Mrs. Wallace hands me a package.

"Thank you," I say. "My mother has been worried about this."

The landlady rolls her eyes. The gesture summons profound empathy for all mothers everywhere who are abused daily by their inconsiderate and ungrateful children.

"Is it your birthday?"

"No, nothing like that. Well, thank you, Mrs. Wallace."

"That's nice. Sending you something for no reason. I used to do that for my Robert, before he got married."

Bruce is getting ready to hump my shin.

"Well," I say, shaking Bruce off my leg, withdrawing. "Thanks again."

"Don't mention it."

She's put off, but I don't care. I have this feeling that she is standing outside my door, her ear pressed to the wood, for most of the evening.

The package turns out to be a Hermes scarf with a delicate floral print, very pretty, very feminine, very Val, but not Rebeccah. I need something with a bigger and bolder design— chain links, equestrian gear. I'll call her later, but first things first.

Submerging myself into the pine-scented bathwater, I feel the tension seeping from every pore.

The phone rings. Thinking it may be Joel, I leave a trail of water from tub to telephone.

"Hello."

"Rebeccah!" Eddie says. "Why the hell haven't you called? Didn't you get my messages?"

"Eddie. Hi. Yes, but I've been busy. I'm sorry. I was going to call you tonight."

"What's wrong? Why are you out of breath?"

"I was just soaking in the tub. I'm dripping wet. Let me get a towel.

"Hi. I'm back."

Silence.

"Eddie?"

"I'm here. Thinking. About you. Naked. In the bathtub."

Distance has improved Eddie's and my sexual fantasies about one another. The tub is a large, white porcelain number with feet. Once we tried to make love in it, with disastrous results.

"God, how I miss you," he says.

"I miss you, too." And at that precise moment it's the truth. But I don't always.

"That's what I'm calling about. I want you to come out here. Can you come within the next few weeks?"

"It'll be tough. A slot has opened up at work. I've applied for the job. They're giving me a hard time, for the usual reasons. Everything is still up in the air. I have to put up the good fight. It wouldn't be a good time for me to leave now."

"I found this fabulous apartment on the beach. Two bedrooms, one with a balcony overlooking the water. Rebeccah, you won't believe this place. It's like something out of a Le Corbusier nightmare, on the inside. On the outside it's a modernist wet dream. I can't wait for you to see it. You've got to come out. I'm about to close the deal. I want you with me."

"What do you need me for? Can't you close without me?"

Exasperated, he sighs.

"Eddie, I need more time."

"We're three thousand miles apart," he yells. "I haven't seen you for nearly a year. How much time do you need?"

We compromise: I book a flight for the last two weeks of the month. I don't know what it's going to solve, really. Eddie is cherishing the belief that the intrinsic problems between us will dissolve in the California sun. Maybe he's right?

The bathwater has become tepid, but it feels good to surrender myself to its amniotic fluid. Val will be delighted that I'm going to see Eddie. Cara will want to go shopping for the trip. Closing my eyes, I try to imagine Eddie wearing baggy bermuda shorts and eating seaweed. Isn't everyone in California health-conscious? Why do I pull away from him? I know I love Eddie, but is that enough? Why don't I just marry him and be done with it? What am I afraid of?

Squeeze-sponging the water over my face feels good. My mind wanders. I recall last night with Joel and experience a deep, pleasant contraction in my uterus. Almost as good as sex. I think of kissing Eddie, of making love with him. Nothing. Just a pleasant memory, no physical side effects. Thinking of Joel makes me think more of Joel, and less of Eddie.

Cara says I have the seven-year itch. She'd read an article saying that restlessness during a long-term relationship is not only natural, it's part of our ancestral brain patterns. I wish I could be as sure of the world as Cara is. I have no answers, only questions. I feel a yearning that echoes a longing I can't name and don't understand.

I want to talk to somebody. Not Cara. Much as I love her, she'd only lecture me about my reluctance to grow up. Mom might understand what I was talking about, but her overriding need for me to conform to her ideas of propriety would overrule her sympathy. My father is a possibility, but it's impossible to get to him without going through my mother first. I could call him at work tomorrow, but the need is immediate. Joel. I want to talk to Joel.

I'd written his number down somewhere.

A woman answers. "Hello. Hello? Who's there. Who is this?" I hang up.

So Joel has a girlfriend. I should have known. She had some kind of foreign accent, and sounds sexy. She probably lives with him. Suddenly, it all clicks into place—except for one little detail. Why did he ask me out? Why didn't he go to see *Flesh and the Devil* with her? Above all, why did he kiss me like that?

"Maybe she works Sundays," Cara says. "Maybe she hates Garbo movies? Maybe he's just a good kisser."

Maybe, a thousand maybes.

I am not a happy packer. Clothes are bundled, balled and squeezed into my suitcase. To tell the truth, I'm glad to be going away.

Mrs. Wallace greets me at the foot of the stairs bearing gifts: an apricot strudel, wrapped in brown paper, for Eddie. She wishes me luck in Yiddish and kisses both my cheeks. B. B. Ottermeyer, wearing her gossamer smile, slips past us, out the door. Now where is she going at 10:00 P.M.? Mrs. Wallace calls after her. B. B. Ottermeyer smiles and waves.

"Such a nice girl," Mrs. Wallace crows. I don't get it.

The cab is late. Mrs. Wallace talks to me from the top of the stoop, in her loud, booming voice. They can hear her in Park Slope.

"My Robert used to live in California," she says. "In San Francisco. I visited him there once. So beautiful," only it comes out "be-uuu-tiful."

Joel is standing before me handing me a bouquet of anemones. I hadn't heard from him since our last outing, weeks ago.

"What are you doing here?" I blurt.

"Is that any way to greet a pal?"

The taxi pulls up.

"Going somewhere?" Joel asks.

"California."

"California? Where in California? California's a big state."

"Los Angeles."

He sidles next to me in the cab. Mrs. Wallace cranes her neck with curiosity.

"You give my love to Mr. Geary," she shouts.

"Who's that?" Joel asks. "Dorothy and Toto?"

"Still looking for Kansas," I say.

"Joel," I explain, "I'm on my way to the Newark airport."

"I love Newark. Some of my best memories are of Newark, and of Los Angeles. Two of the country's more happening cities. What's in Los Angeles?"

"A friend," I tell him. But he's not interested. He's acting very manic, hyper, up. En route to the airport he explains why he hasn't called, interspersed with tips on places to go and people to see on the West Coast. He hasn't had a moment to himself. After a nightmare of both legal and financial hassles, he's finally opening his own restaurant. He's been thinking about me, and wanted to invite me to the opening night party personally.

"Congratulations."

"What day are you coming back?"

"The fourteenth."

"That's the night of my party. What time?"

"Around midnight."

"Good. The party will still be going strong. You can make it."

The airline ticket agent tags my luggage, checks me in.

"Joel . . ." I begin.

"Who is this friend in California?" he interrupts.

"Who's the woman with the sexy accent?"

" . . . ?"

"The one who answers your phone?"

"A friend."

We're even.

My row is announced. Time to file through the boarding gate.

"I have to go."

He kisses me, long and lingeringly, and for one wild instant I consider *not* boarding the plane. His smell, the smell of baby powder, intrigues me. Where does he put it?

Three flight attendants, standing at the plane's entrance, watch us, grinning. "Better hurry," one says.

Joel calls out the name of his restaurant. "Holdesky's. On the corner of Hudson and Barrow. Be there."

"I'm not sure . . ."

27

"I'll look for you."

The steward asks me if he can put the flowers in water?

"No. That's all right. I want to hold them."

"I don't blame you, sweetie," he says, winking.

Throughout the entire flight I imagine swabbing Joel with baby powder all over his body. My stomach erupts volcanically the whole time. It's obscene.

CHAPTER THREE

Eddie is never hard to spot in a crowd. He towers over everyone. Put Tom Hanks's head on a young Jimmy Stewart's body and you've got Eddie. He sees me and begins yelling.

"Rebeccah!" he calls, waving both arms frantically, as though I could miss him. The sight of him welcoming me so eagerly turns me into a pile of mush. All of the love I've ever felt for Eddie erupts. I am crying, kissing and hugging him all at the same time.

"Eddie," I say.

"Rebeccah," he says.

"Eddie."

"Rebeccah."

We sound like a TV perfume ad. I'd forgotten how well our bodies fit. Being with Eddie is like coming home from work and changing from high heels and panty hose into a soft, loose robe and slippers. It's familiar, comfortable, warm and safe. For some strange reason I expect him to smell like baby powder.

"It's so good to see you," he says. "You look great. A little thinner, and pale. People from New York look like they've just been let out of the dungeon. The natives here should hand out oranges and giant tubes of suntan lotion, free. God," he exclaims, holding me at arm's length and looking into my face, "it's so damn good to have you here."

We hug and kiss our way to retrieve my luggage, and the car. "You can't get lax about LAX," Eddie says, as we wend our way through what has to be the world's largest parking lot in one of the world's largest airports. Eddie is talking a mile a minute. "I've got a system," he explains, rambling about how to beat the airport crowds, the lines, the endless waiting. I'm not really paying attention, but doggedly follow where he leads, noticing how good he looks: healthy and trim, like he's been working out. He's sporting a California tan. The kind you get from driving around hilly roads with an open sun roof, not the kind you get from laying on the beach for days baking in the sun. He can't wait for me to see the condo. Once inside the car I fumble in my shoulder bag for a Kleenex and rediscover Mrs. Wallace's apricot strudel.

"Oh, I almost forgot," I say, handing it to him. "Guess-what from guess-who?"

He sniffs it, and grins. "Apricot," he says. Then, "How is Mrs. Wallace, the old broad? And Bruce? Are his balls still scraping the floor?" Eddie eyes the flowers. "Who're they for?"

I'd forgotten the anemones which have become surgically attached to my hand. Joel and my New York life seem like a million light years away.

"They're for me."

Eddie is as eager as I am to depart the cavernous L.A. airport. We're driving around and around.

"Who gave them to you?"

"No one you know."

A teenager in a big four-wheel-drive truck passes Eddie, narrowly missing us. "Shit!" Eddie yells, veering and braking. "The kids out here are something else. They're born with tiny silver spoons in their noses and steering wheels in their hands."

He straightens the car, and asks, "So who gave you the flowers?"

"A friend. His name is Joel."

"Joel? Joel who?"

"He's just someone I met."

Eddie looks at me quizzically. He holds his head to the left side and begins to chew the inside of his mouth. He's deliberating. "Okay," he says to himself, then grins at me with a hint of mischief in his eyes. The subject of dating other people is something we've never discussed. I can't imagine that Eddie has spent the last year celibate, but I also can't imagine that he hasn't. I am returning his stare, and something is moving between us telepathically, but I'm not sure what. He reaches out one of his Octaman limbs and pulls me closer. It's difficult to nestle in bucket seats, but I do my best.

"Okay," he says again, as if talking to himself. "Okay."

I'm glad he's decided not to pursue the subject.

"Where'd you get the shirt?" I ask.

"Like it? I got one for you, too. Identical."

I'd never seen Eddie in anything but oxford-cloth, Izod, and sweatshirts. The Hawaiian shirt, his manner, his mood are all changed, and I wonder if it's something in the air here, this mystifying Los Angeles melange of metropolis and suburbia, mountains and desert, ocean and coastline. Maybe it's got something to do with the subconscious thought that at any minute the Big One could happen, and it's all over.

When I was a little girl I used to love sitting next to my father in the car while he drove. If my mother came along I was relegated to the back seat with my brother. Eddie drives like my father, with one arm leaning out the window and the other casually propped on the steering wheel.

He keeps squeezing my shoulder with his hand.

"We'll be home before you know it," he says, glancing at his wristwatch. "Less than an hour."

Back East you measure distance in miles, out here in the time it takes to get from one place to another. Back East a two-hundred-mile drive represents at least three to four hours on the road and is considered a lot. Here it's nothing.

So far California is runways and freeways, car fumes and exhaust, smog, concrete, signage and freaky palm trees that look like they've seen better days.

"What do you think of it so far?" Eddie asks.

"The color of the air matches your shirt."

Bad answer. He grunts, shifts gears and swerves the car onto another grid of the freeway. He negotiates the maze of freeways like a true Angeleno. He must spend more than half of his life in this jeep-like car, which is equipped with air-conditioning, a compact disc deck, and a cellular phone. The back is filled with cartons of wine labelled Napa and Sonoma. He's decided to take the scenic, seacoast route—101 west to 405, then south to Santa Monica.

"Like, this," he says in imitation of a Valley Girl, "is, like, the Valley. Birthplace of silicon and a whole new language. Want your nails done, your hair, your car? Like, no problem. On your right is a genuine orange grove. You can get the best goddamn screwdrivers anywhere in the world in the Valley. 'L.A.'s bedroom,' it's called," Eddie says like a tour guide. "There are more single-story, ranch-style homes per capita in the Valley than anywhere else in the world."

The uniformity reminds me of the suburbs outside of Pittsburgh. Suburbs fill me with a Kierkegaardian sense of dread. As a kid I loved playing whiffleball on the lawns, and climbing trees, but by puberty I couldn't wait to leave. *Halloween* and *Murder on Elm Street* could only be set in the suburbs.

"You're awfully quiet," Eddie says.

"I'm overwhelmed." It's the truth.

Eddie turns left on the San Diego freeway, the seaside route that hugs the California coastline all the way from the Pacific Palisades to Tijuana.

He turns off the air-conditioning, opens up the sun roof.

"Smell that," he says, inhaling deeply. I smell the ocean, feel the sun, melt into the bucket seat.

"Great, huh," Eddie says, like he'd put the Pacific there for my benefit.

"You're nuts."

"I tell you, Rebe," he says, sincerely, "I've never felt so good. You're going to love it out here. Did you know that Santa Monica is named after poor Saint Augustine's mother, who cried tears of joy when her wayward son embraced Christianity?"

"Thanks for telling me."

"We'll do the pier some other time," Eddie says, swinging past it. "But I just wanted you to get a taste."

A pretty girl and boy wearing earphones roller-skate past us. So far everyone I see has the body perfect. The men are so built their necks are beginning to disappear between their broad, muscular shoulders.

"Do you skate?" I ask.

"For sure. I'm just an average California kind of guy: I skate, surf, smoke a little dope. Venice is the place for skating. Nobody walks in Venice. I know a great little dive in Venice that serves the best margaritas in the world. I'll take you there."

Pretty soon we're cruising around a maze of apartment complexes on a hill that overlooks the ocean. He points the car towards a cluster of stark white, cubed buildings, placed one on top of the other in rows of pairs, all with monopitch roofs. It looks like a cluster of Citicorps skyscrapers transported and miniaturized by a mad futuristic architect.

"Eddie!" I exclaim. It's not, it can't be? This nonfunctional nightmare is not what he calls home?

"Patience, Rebel, patience."

The condo complex is a study in purism, function and design: flat roofs, flat walls, no color. I imagine the inside of Eddie's condo: pure white rooms stripped of all the little trappings that I'd grown to love in our classical Upper West Side apartment: casings, crown moldings, pilasters, mantelpieces, high ceilings, wide hallways and all the other emblems of bourgeois extravagance that the modernists have come to regard as anathema.

I was by now sitting up and paying attention.

"Isn't it beautiful?" Eddie exclaims. "It's perfect. I couldn't believe this place when I saw it. It had to've been designed by an oddball, maybe a dropout, like me. It's the kind of place I would've designed if I'd stuck. But I would've gone this guy one further, and thrown in a few moldings around the doorways,

33

maybe even added a cornice or two, you know, just as a tease. I can't wait for you to see the inside. It's going to blow you away." There was the old enthusiasm. And I felt a great pang of regret. Eddie had changed after he dropped out of architecture. He was angry, bitter. How in love with his own ideas for buildings he used to be. "Housing for the masses," he called it. By evening, after a grueling day of classes, he'd drag himself home riddled with self-doubt, his enthusiasm dampened by the professor whose criticism of his "sophomoric" (i.e., antimodern) ideas had defeated him. It tore me apart to see Eddie quit, and we argued about it constantly until he said, "No more." But my disappointment lay between us, unspoken. Now he's going to make it up to me. Maybe he didn't design it, but he can buy it. Eddie's love affair with consumerism and Southern California suddenly crystallizes.

"Just you wait," he repeats, parking the car and grabbing me by the hand.

Inside the box is a pleasant surprise: one of the living room walls is curved, as though the box had distended itself in a burst of liberation; natural wooden beams traverse the high ceilings; there's a fireplace with an elaborate marble mantlepiece; both the kitchen and bathroom walls are inlaid with Spanish tiles; plaster moldings outline the master bedroom walls; the ceiling is papered in an abstract pattern resembling cirrus clouds in a powder-blue sky.

I must look idiotic with my mouth hanging open, but from the moment I stepped off the plane my senses have been assaulted. I haven't gotten used to Eddie in a loud print shirt yet. Next he's going to pull out a joint and ask me if I want to get high?

He shows me the spare bedroom which he's turned into a study. It's a large, spacious room crammed with a desk, a convertible couch, and bottles of wine housed in metal wine racks.

Eddie is either living beyond his means or dealing drugs, or both.

"What can I tell you?" he says when I ask. "I'm a happening kind of guy." Then he switches gears: "You're going to love it here, Rebel. I know it. Wait till you see the tennis court and the swimming pool."

The sound of women's laughter comes from the landing. Two apartments occupy Eddie's floor: his, and one shared by "two girls by the name of Sharon and Karen" whom Eddie swears are a couple of call girls. One of them drives a British racing-green Jaguar, and the other a bright red Mazarati. Neither seems to work. They keep odd hours. Men come and go. Maybe Eddie is right. He's leering at me.

"They're probably budding actresses, with trust funds," I say.

"Yeah, and I am the real Anastasia."

The kitchen is small, but well-stocked and clean.

"No cucarachas," Eddie says, reminding me of our early New York apartment problem.

I am ready to believe in the miraculous; in California's restorative powers; in its ability to inspire instant lifestyle conversion— but the transformation of Eddie from a slob who drops his dirty socks and dishes wherever they may fall, into an anal-retentive neatness freak tries my credibility.

"Who does the cleaning?" I ask, opening and shutting cabinet doors. "Do you have a vase?"

Joel's flowers are wilting in my hand.

"A woman comes twice a week. Maria. She's the love of my life. Next to you."

He's standing behind me, pressing up close, squeezing me in one of his all-encompassing octa-embraces. "Let's play tonsil hockey," he says. "It's so good to have you here."

He wants to make love. So do I, but not in the kitchen, and not before I've cleaned up. Accidentally, I spill water on him.

"Put those damn things somewhere, will you," Eddie says, glowering at Joel's flowers.

There's a glass-topped coffee table in the living room in need of life.

"Come on, Reb, snap out of it," Eddie complains. "You've been acting like a buzz crusher ever since you got off the plane."

I'm not sure what a "buzz crusher" is, but I damn well know

what a button-pusher is. Nobody pushes my buttons like Eddie does. All of the hurt and anger of the past year's separation from him erupts.

"I need time," I say, "to get used to you, to this . . ."

"Since when do I need getting used to?"

"Since you moved."

He sighs. It's tough on him too. "Why don't you freshen up?" he suggests.

Without thinking I head toward the study bathroom.

"Where're you going?"

"To my room." I look around. "Where's my suitcase?"

"The suitcase is still in the car, which I was going to retrieve to put in *our* room. What is this *your* room shit? Since when do we distinguish between *my* room and *your* room?"

"Since you left me!"

"I asked you to come with me."

The stem of one of the anemones is broken, and the head of the flower is sadly flopping over the lip of the glass. I try to repair it, but it won't hold.

"Jesus, Rebeccah. Do you think you're visiting an old friend? This is me. Eddie. *Octaman*. Remember? We've lived together for over seven years. In some states that makes us common-law husband and wife. We're practically married. We're lovers. At least I think we're lovers. I don't know what we are anymore."

He flops on the tan leather couch, crossing his limbs in a body language that even a child could read. He looks like an eight-year-old when he's angry.

"Eddie, give me a break. You slammed out of the apartment nearly a year ago, remember? *You* left *me*. I'm not even sure why anymore. Then you buy this place and hustle me into it like some kind of June bride, like there's no question now, since *you've* made up *your* mind that I should just drop everything in New York and fly out here to set up house. I don't even know if I like *California*. Everything here is so . . . new," I say, lamely. "I need a few minutes to catch my breath. To sit down and say, 'Hi, how are you?' To feel my way around. You seem to misinterpret everything I say or do. So I don't want to say or do anything. I just want to take a bath, and a nap."

He unravels himself, and leans his head on the back of the couch.

"Take your bath," he says to the ceiling. Standing, he faces me. "Take your nap. Take your time. I have to go out. Get some stuff for dinner."

"Fine."

He hesitates, then says very slowly, with effort, "Would you prefer to eat in or out?"

"I . . ."

"Because," he says, interrupting me with exaggerated consideration, "if you want to go out, that's fine. I'll take you anywhere you want to go. But I had wanted to cook for you tonight. To make a special dinner for the two of us. But there I go again, being presumptuous."

Hawaiian shirts, Bauhaus run amok, hot tubs, neatness, and now cooking? "Since when do you cook?"

"Since I've been living alone."

For the first time since I got off the plane I feel like I've landed. Eddie and I stand revealed. No armor; nothing to hide behind except the naked truth. Being alone has had positive and negative effects on us both. In many ways I feel like I'm meeting a new Eddie, although the old one is still very much in evidence. The old one liked to do things his way and insist it was best for us both. We used to refer to one another as "my better half." If one was around, the other wasn't far behind. We shared everything, including likes, dislikes, tastes. The separation has revealed new parts of ourselves to ourselves, but not yet to one another. What other talents has Eddie's distance from me provoked?

"Let's eat in." I want to make a joke about his cooking, but his standoffish manner deters me.

"Good," he says. "I'll see you later. Dress is optional."

That's the last I remember. I awake, as if from the dead, four hours later to the smell of cooking. I can hear him rattling pots and pans in the kitchen. This I have to see.

Cara had talked me into buying a long, red, silky peignoir for "lounging around the house," something other than "torn T-shirts and ripped jeans," and now I'm glad. I spritz myself with perfume, and even rouge my cheeks and gloss my lips.

"What smells so good?" I ask.

"You do," Eddie says. "You look beautiful."

"Thanks." I wander over to the oven, and peer into various pots and pans: lobster tails, cream of mushroom soup, radicchio salad.

"You. Made. This?"

"Careful, careful," he warns. "You are about to insult the chef."

"I expected reheated pizza, or Chinese takeout, not *this*," I say with a sweep of my arm.

There's champagne and ice cream in the fridge. The table is set with a linen tablecloth and napkins, sparkling flatwear, crystal and cutlery. At any second I expect the hostess, the woman Eddie must be living with, to appear and welcome me.

Eddie reads my mind. "Relax," he says, pulling out my chair. He lights the candles, pours the wine. It's not just that Eddie cooking is a marvel to behold, but he's a good cook, a happy cook, and I keep pinching myself to make sure I'm not dreaming.

I hear movement in the apartment. It's only 7:30 A.M. I feel like I have to talk-to-Ralph-on-the-big-white-phone, or at least I think that's how you say throw up in California teenagese.

"Eddie," I whisper, nudging him in the back with my elbow. "Eddie. Someone's in the apartment."

"Ishmaria," he mumbles.

Oh. The cleaning lady. I plop back in bed and try to doze back off, but it's impossible. Not because Maria is blasting Dolly Parton on the stereo, but because I am wide awake, remembering last night: after dinner we stripped and did the hot tub. Then we did the heated jacuzzi. Most of all we did each other. Octaman was in his cups last night. I was enveloped by tentacles of love, of lust, of mutual need. Eddie held my breasts and said, "These used to live with me." He worked his way down my body speaking to different body parts, saying, "You used to live with me."

Afterwards, during pillow talk, he spoke to me of his loneliness during the first six months; how he'd almost called it quits and came home.

"Dating is pure hell," he said. "I don't know how anybody does it, and what's even more mysterious is how anything good ever comes out of it."

There was one girl he liked, someone he'd met in his cooking class, but she turned out to be involved with someone else and was playing games, using him to make her boyfriend jealous.

I didn't tell him about Joel. What was there to tell? That I'd met some guy who got fired because he asked Garbo for her autograph? Last night I couldn't stop thinking of Joel, of imagining what it would be like with him. Joel kisses better than Eddie. I'm not sure I can explain why. Eddie kisses with just his lips, Joel with his whole body, with all of him.

I have to pee. I also want my toothbrush which is in my purse in Eddie's study. En route I bump into a short, dark girl in high heels and a tight, red leather mini-skirt. *This* is Maria? She looks me up and down.

"You must be Rebeccah," she says.

I nod, dumbly, wrapping Eddie's bathrobe around me.

"I'm Maria."

"Nice to meet you," I mumble, sidling past her. "Excuse me, I have to . . ."

She understands. Maria is no more than twenty, or possibly thirty; she is an exotic mixture of Spanish and Indian, or Spanish and Asian, I can't tell which. She is one of the most beautiful women I've seen. Instantly, I move all of my stuff out of the study and into *our*, Eddie's and my, bedroom for the duration.

CHAPTER FOUR

After my encounter with Maria, I jump back into bed. This time I initiate all the love-play. Eddie doesn't have a chance. When we awake, Maria is gone. With the exception of the bedroom, where I had held Eddie captive, the place is immaculate; there is no sign of the mess from last night.

"Where'd you find her?" I ask Eddie.

It's like old times. We're hanging around the day after in our bathrobes, munching on whatever we can find to eat and reading magazines.

"She found me. Knocked on my door. Said she cleaned apartments. Not the girls next door. Those are "putas," but others in the complex. Was I interested?" Groaning, Eddie lifts his long body from the couch, reties the sash of his terry cloth bathrobe and shuffles into the kitchen for more coffee.

"She should be a movie star," I comment. I'm lying on my stomach on the floor leafing through a glossy magazine with a feature story about future garbage.

"Don't you think we should get married?" Eddie calls from the kitchen.

"Don't you think it's odd that a woman as beautiful as Maria is cleaning houses?"

"She has four kids, two of them are twins," Eddie says. "Her

40

husband works odd jobs. He's a drummer for a rock band that thinks they're the next Menudo. Did you hear what I just said?"

Of course I heard him. How could I not hear him? The entire time I've been in California, slightly more than twenty-four hours, Garbo has not entered my mind, not once, until that precise instant. John Gilbert was always asking Garbo to marry him, and she was always saying yes, and then reneging at the last minute. She jilted him at the altar. Do people still jilt people? The phrase has such an old-fashioned ring to it.

I once saw a picture of Gilbert taken on the day that Garbo had stood him up. It was a group shot of the wedding party. Gilbert's friend director King Vidor was marrying actress Eleanor Boardman. Gilbert had asked Garbo if she'd like to make it a double wedding. To everyone's surprise, she'd said yes. In the photograph, Gilbert was standing in the back, behind Vidor, glaring at the camera. His brows were knit. He looked angry, miserable, bereft. Staring at the photograph, I felt sorry for him. How could Garbo do something like that? Deliberately hurt and humiliate someone she had claimed to love?

Part of me wants to say, "Yes, Eddie, I'll marry you," and part of me wants to change the subject. Part of me quite easily imagines living happily ever after with Eddie in our bright, sunny Mies-box on the sea, part of me never wants to marry and wants to remain in New York City. That's the part that's winning this round.

"Let's play the Bean Game," I say.

"Grow up," Eddie says, re-entering the livingroom holding a steaming mug of coffee.

I toss the magazine aside and flip over on my back. Everyone is always telling me to grow up—except Joel, who will probably get around to it eventually.

In college Eddie and I played this game for hours, naming our imaginary children after beans. But we aren't in college anymore.

"How about Garbanzo," I suggest, ignoring him. "It's fitting. Especially if we live out here."

"Is that a yes?"

"I'm kind of fond of Chickpea, too. One of our kids should be called Chickpea, don't you think?"

"A garbanzo *is* a chickpea." He's miffed.

"Well, Chickpea can be little Garbanzo's nickname. What's the feminine of Garbanzo? Garbanza?"

Eddie is rolling the morning newspaper into a tube and peering through one end at me, like it's a telescope.

"How about Mung?" I say.

"Garbanzo isn't a bean, it's a legume," he says, swatting the coffee table, wishing, no doubt, that it was my rear end.

"All beans are legumes, but not all legumes are beans," I retort.

Nobody hates a smart ass more than another smart ass. Before I know what's happening, Eddie is lying on top of me, pinning my arms and legs with his body. He becomes aroused. I'm not, but he doesn't care.

Before Eddie there was a boy in high school. He'd been my first. I was crazy about him. Jay had the patience of Job. He introduced me to sex. We used to rent a motel room and sit on the edge of the bed, and he'd teach me how to fondle him. I remember the first time he placed my hand between his legs. I pulled it back like I'd touched a hot iron. Patiently, he put it there again, and again. I finally got the hang of it. Jay had become an addiction. When he broke up with me, toward the end of our senior high school year, I had become like a zombie. My mother got the name of a psychotherapist. Luckily college intervened, where I met and dated other boys, including Eddie. One of them, a cute Southern boy by the name of Ward, got carried away one night. We'd been drinking. And after a certain point I couldn't push him off. I felt then as I did now a mixed sense of helplessness and rage. The more I fought Ward off, the more insistent he became.

My best friend from high school, Deirdre Holland, and I used to talk about sex for hours. One day we made a list of all the words that described sex. Most of them were four-letter words that are commonly used to describe copulation—fuck, bang, ball, bone and slam. But it seemed one-sided. None of the words came close to what we felt was the *experience* of female sexuality, especially in the vernacular. We compiled lists. Technically, men penetrate. Okay, then what do women do? Surrender and yield? At first maybe. Watch any Garbo movie. Sexually she's the aggressor. Men are happy to surrender to her embrace. Jay often liked to let me do all the work. But why weren't there any words for this in the English language?

Deirdre and I got out a thesaurus: we tried out some words to describe female sexuality: envelop, encompass, enclose, enwrap, embody, ensphere, encircle; circumambient, ambient; inclose or enclose, infold or enfold; girdle, or begird. We laughed over the idea of "begirding." I wanted to begird Jay the very first chance I got. We wondered, is a woman penetrated or does she enfold? Men possess women just as they penetrate them. Do women possess men in their ambient embrace?

We never could figure it out, at least on paper. Men turn violent in their pain and rage. This is a side of himself that Eddie usually keeps under wraps. I feel his hurt and his need clash with mine in a conflagration of wills. I feel myself yield, but without consent. I feel myself surrender, but not relinquish. I refuse to struggle, yell or cry. For an instant, I think that I deserve what I'm getting. This thought is more upsetting than the act itself.

Eddie pants, groans, stiffens and collapses on top of me. I roll out from under him and just lay there gasping for air. I feel scored, shot and skewered, like a kabob on the spit. I feel staked, claimed and mounted, like the piece of rock the soldiers stuck the American flag on at Iwo Jima.

"Are you okay?" Eddie asks, reaching out to touch me; an act of contrition.

I can't look at him. I want to take a walk.

At first the sun hurts my eyes. I feel like a creature crawling out from beneath a rock. Santa Monica reminds me of the Hamptons gone tropical. The air carries warm ocean breezes and gently laps my skin. I want to strip and run barefoot to the sea. I want to languish here, and realize that that's exactly what I'd do: languish. A cleaning woman is walking down the street. Must be a bus stop on the highway. Except for her and a gardener, the streets are empty of people. No one walks in the suburbs. They drive their cars to gyms and fitness centers to work out on machines.

I hear the splashing of pool water; the laughter of children. That reminds me: I have to buy a pair of goggles and a sunhat.

I walk for miles and return hot and thirsty, bumping into two leggy blonde women in dark sunglasses who must be Sharon and Karen.

"Hi," they say cheerily.

"Hi," I say back. They look at one another and giggle. I have the feeling they know who I am. One of them wears her hair in dreadlocks, like Glenn Close in *Fatal Attraction*. They are heavily made up and outfitted in spandex workout clothes.

I find Eddie in his study, pouring over his latest baseball obsession, the L.A. Dodgers. He's swapped his most treasured pennants for a lot of Dodger memorabilia, especially relics of their Brooklyn days. I think the narrowing of Eddie's baseball fetish to one team is a good sign. He promised to take me to a game before I left. I said I'd go on the condition that he go with me to a Garbo movie. Why do we constantly stalemate one another?

"Hi," he says. "Where've you been?"

"Just wandering. I bumped into Sharon and Karen. I think you're right about them. What's for dinner?"

"It's the chef's day off," he says. "Let's order out."

We stuff ourselves on tacos and enchiladas and turn in early. Eddie has to hit the road tomorrow. Neither of us mentions this morning. Eddie doesn't say so, but every movement is an apology. He's solicitous, and treats me like a fragile piece of china. It's comforting, but it doesn't mask what lies beneath the reason. I fall asleep cradled in his arms, thinking about Garbo. It's far more comforting to ponder her problems than my own.

"Why do you have to ruin it, Yacky?" she'd say to Gilbert after he begged her to marry him.

What did she mean by that? Why did she think marriage would ruin things? Why did she tell Gilbert yes, finally, and then humiliate him by not showing up? What changed her mind?

"Is there someone else?" Eddie asks before we drift off.

I don't answer him. I don't know how to explain that it isn't a someone so much as a something.

By the time I awake the next morning Eddie is gone. There's a manila envelope with my name on it on the kitchen counter. Inside are a bunch of sightseeing brochures accompanied by a note from Eddie. He didn't want to wake me. He won't be back until tomorrow evening. There are instructions, including a detailed map, on how to get to the nearest car rental place. He even left me one of his credit cards, and the cellular-phone number in case I need him.

At first I'm crestfallen. What will I do all day without him? But then I remember my hidden agenda and feel rejuvenated.

My driving is a little rusty, but after a while I'm tootling around like a real Angeleno. There are so many motorcycles and vintage automobiles on the road that I feel like I stumbled into the Fifties. I like the idea of time travel—my plan is to retrace Garbo's steps on the day that she stood up Gilbert. Maybe I grew up watching too many Star Trek reruns? Or maybe there's something in this California air and sun that plays with your head? A little voice inside, which sounds awfully like Cara's, says, "Crap, Babe. You're the same on the West Coast as you are on the East."

I miss Cara, and make a note to call her later. But first things first. I need a map of where the old stars used to live. This isn't as easy to find as it sounds. Maps of the homes of the new Hollywood stars abound, but not the old. Finally, I find one in a drugstore in Westwood Village. If Santa Monica is the Hamptons-on-the-Pacific, Westwood Village is a Cannes-cum-California Shopping Mall. Burial place of Marilyn and Natalie, home of the UCLA campus, and mecca for movie mavens, everywhere you look in Westwood there's a first-run movie theater.

I study the map, searching for Garbo's name. Unbelievably, I can't find a listing for her. Gilbert is on it, so is Marion Davies, but no Garbo. And no King Vidor. I recall that Gilbert had lived on a hill above Vidor, and the wedding took place at Davies's Spanish hacienda in Beverly Hills. They all lived within a stone's throw of one another. But how was I going to find out where Garbo moved after she left Gilbert?

Larry Edmunds Bookstore is a cross between New York's Gotham and Strand: dusty, musty, cluttered and spilling over with thousands upon thousands of secondhand books. The place is chockablock with artifacts from America's movie heritage. I feel at home here and wonder if I look as pasty-faced and in need of citrus as the rest of the clientele. I find what I'm looking for within minutes: an out-of-print Garbo biography. She lived in Beverly Hills. I'm practically in her backyard.

A roly-poly salesclerk waddles towards me. His eyes twinkle, like it's Christmas and he's one of Santa's helpers.

"Can I help you?" he asks.

"Um, well, yes," I say, hesitating. How do I explain what I'm after? He glances at the book I'm holding.

"You're interested in Garbo?"

"Yes. And Gilbert."

"Ah," he says. "We have a fairly new biography of Gilbert, written by his daughter Leatrice Gilbert Fountain. Now where is it?" He rifles through a pile of books. "Here it is."

He hands me the book, *Dark Star*.

I don't want to buy the book, only to do some research.

"Will that be all?" he asks.

Something about this guy makes me want him to adopt me.

"Yes, thank you."

My eye catches a pile of old movie magazines. There are several Photoplays. Most of them are housed in Mylar bags. One features an article on Gilbert and Garbo, circa 1927. I can't believe my luck.

"I'll take this, too," I add.

Mr. Roly-Poly nods, like he understands, *completely*. In a place like Edmunds Bookstore, film fetishism is no big deal.

"You know, there's a Garbo movie playing just up the street. *Inspiration*, I think. It's listed in the paper. But you'd better park your car in a garage."

I thank him for the tip, but I'm not in the mood for a movie, even a Garbo movie. Armed with my maps, books and magazine, I sit in the car and plot my course. A homeless man taps on the window. Across the street what looks like a pack of gang members are eyeing me and the car. One of them catcalls; another whistles. "Hey, Big Red," someone yells.

It's time to head for the hills.

Hollywood resembles Times Square before the cleanup: seedy, downtrodden and dangerous. I didn't realize how late it was getting. Soon the traffic will be intolerable. Orange and violet hues of dusk canopy the city. I point the car west on Santa Monica Boulevard and rush home just one step ahead of gridlock. I have all of tonight and the next day to myself, and feel relieved that Eddie won't be home until tomorrow evening. I can't wait to hit the Jacuzzi and the books.

The doorbell rings. A young Hispanic boy hands me a dozen red roses wrapped in cellophane. The card reads, "You're full of Beans. I love you. Eddie."

I fall asleep on the couch reading the Gilbert biography. Eddie's call wakes me up.

"What did you do today?" he asks.

"I rented a car and drove around."

"I was going to ask you to come with me, but I'm breaking in new turf and it wouldn't have been much fun."

"How'd you do?"

"I put the bottles in paper bags and sold out."

I laugh.

"Do you have plans for dinner tomorrow night?" Eddie asks.

"Well, Jack called. He wants me to join him and Angelica for a weenie roast. Then I ran into Swifty. He and Mary are having a few people over . . ."

"There's someplace I want to take you. What did you eat for dinner?"

"Pepperoni pizza."

"You're hopeless."

"I had to borrow the yellow pages from Sharon and Karen, who were entertaining."

"See anything interesting?"

"No, but I got contact high from the smoke."

I'm staring at the roses. Somehow they make me feel sad. Joel's anemones look anemic next to them. I suppose I should throw them out.

"Eddie," I say.

". . . ?"

"Thanks for the flowers. They're beautiful."

"Like you."

"Now you're the one who's full of beans."

"How about Jelly?"

"How about Good Night?"

When morning comes I leap out of bed, eager to begin my adventure. I'm not sure what I'll find, but it's the journey that matters, not the arrival. At least that's what Cara tells me at least twice a day.

I feel a fondness for my tired but trusty old rental, waiting for me like a faithful horse. My father taught me how to read road maps when I was a child. Most cities have a heart, he explained, which is the hub, with main arteries leading to and from it like the spokes of a wheel. Yesterday I figured out that Los Angeles has no heart. It's just a sprawling, complex web of arteries and veins composed of interstate highways and freeways. It's not one city, but a continuous city embracing many hidden cities. Driving around L.A. induces an eerie sense of timelessness, which fits my mood perfectly. What was it Gertrude Stein had said about L.A.? There is no *there* there. But there is a funny kind of *here* here, too.

The plan is like this: I drive to the site of Jack Gilbert's house, then retrace Garbo's steps on the day of the Vidor–Boardman wedding over fifty years ago. Although Gilbert's house was torn down in 1983, the locale is the same.

Cara believes in spirit worlds, channeling and reincarnation; that other dimensions coexist simultaneously with this one. She has a large collection of mystical pornography that she's always quoting from.

"You sound just like Shirley MacLaine," I always tease her. I like to play devil's advocate, and give her a good argument. Schooled in engineering, I'm more comfortable with the material and tangible than the immaterial and intangible. But out here I'm ready to believe in the tooth fairy, flying cows and UFOs. I'm ready to believe that what happened in 1926 is replaying itself, an endless tape loop, in some other sphere. If I focus my attention enough I may be able to find it.

The hills of Beverly are sinuous and beautiful. What did Garbo think when she first came here? How did she react to the constant sunshine, the arid vegetation, the Santa Ana winds? According to his daughter, Leatrice, Gilbert had asked Garbo to move in with him during the filming of *Flesh and the Devil*. His house had a guest room like a monk's cell, complete with a crucifix and a prie-dieu. Gilbert hired a decorator to transform the room into a miniature Louis XVI boudoir, done in blue, ivory, and gold, with a black marble bathroom. But Garbo was no Marie Antoinette. She must have preferred the asceticism of the monk's cell to the excess of the renovation, and was too shy and polite to say so.

He called her *Flecka*, Swedish maiden. She called him Yacky. Eventually, he built her a cottage at the back of his property. Had she asked him to? Even then she prized her privacy above all else. Gilbert indulged her. He planted a pine grove because Garbo missed the sight and smell of her native trees. He built an artificial waterfall near the cabin, hoping that the sound of running water and wind through the pines would help ease her homesickness and insomnia. They both suffered from insomnia.

Garbo's great friend and mentor, the Swedish director Mauritz Stiller, was living in Santa Monica at the time. She tried to divide her time between the house on Tower Road and Stiller's place.

I suppose everything was fine until Gilbert started proposing marriage. But why would that spoil their idyll? He was the dashing movie idol of millions of American women who would have killed for such an offer. Marriage between Garbo and Gilbert seemed a natural. They were both young and hot, and the chemistry between them sparked both on and off camera.

I am going around and around in a mad carousel of thought and traffic. Better to concentrate here. I'm not sure where Gilbert's house was, but spot some pine trees that may have been the ones he'd planted for Garbo. Older, droopier, but nevertheless majestic, they are whispering amongst themselves in a strange, whooshing language I feel I can understand if I listen hard enough. Whispering pines induce trancelike states.

Once, Gilbert persuaded Garbo to elope with him. They drove to Santa Ana, to the very steps of the marriage license bureau. She bolted, ran to the hotel, hid in the ladies room, and—according to one version—climbed out the window and escaped.

Gilbert forgave her. With Garbo, Gilbert practiced patience and forbearance, two qualities he was not famous for. He knew what he wanted. He wanted Garbo, but she didn't know what she wanted. Or maybe she knew what she didn't want.

"Why do you have to spoil it, Yacky?" she'd say.

She wanted to stay together, but on her terms, not his. When she'd consented to make King and Eleanor's wedding a double ceremony, it seemed like she would really do it this time. She and Gilbert obtained marriage licenses under the names of their birth, not their star names.

The morning of the wedding was hot and clear. Is it sheer luck or coincidence that the morning I choose to retrace Garbo's steps is hot and clear?

According to *Dark Star*, Jack saw Garbo pulling out of the driveway without a word. This wasn't unusual. Greta often hopped in the car and disappeared. He must have been tempted to chase after her. He must have wondered where she was going. He must have feared that she was doing exactly what she was doing—pulling another disappearing act. He must have consoled himself with the rationalization that she was conforming to the custom of not letting the groom see the bride before the ceremony. But when did Garbo conform to any custom other than her own?

Turning the ignition key, I shift from park to drive. It's time to leave the phantom Gilbert in the phantom house—to dress, to worry and to ruminate on his marriage to the woman who would by the end of his career be more famous than he'd ever dreamed.

Slowly, reluctantly, I inch away, to go . . . where?

Where had she gone? What was she thinking? Wearing? Had she bought a dress for the wedding? Did she take it with her? Or was she wearing her usual slacks and men's slippers? Garbo considered herself one of the boys, a bachelor, but she also longed for a family. She used to tell Gilbert, "Let's run away together. Let's buy half of Wisconsin, and raise wheat and children."

If she went to Stiller's she must have headed south along Benedict Canyon to Beverly Drive and Santa Monica Boulevard. Geographically, little has changed in Beverly Hills. It reminds me of parts of Sewickly, where I grew up: big houses, landscaped lawns, long, circuitous driveways.

Someone behind me is honking wildly. I'm blocking his passage. I pull over to the side of the winding road. An old man in a brown Packard passes me. The Packard strikes a bell. Garbo once drove a secondhand Packard. This is a sign! Quickly, I follow the old man. His driving is a road hazard. He's barely making thirty miles-per-hour. We crawl south along Tower Drive, then he turns right on San Yasidro. He pulls into someone's driveway. No sign announces who lives there. After nearly a twenty minute wait I realize that this is the old man's residence. It's a dead end. Or is it? Did he know Garbo? Gilbert? He looked like he might have been a young man at the time of the wedding, one of their contemporaries. Maybe he was invited? Maybe he recently retired to California, and hails from New Jersey? Should I risk it? Drive up and knock on the door?

"Pardon me, but where were you on September 8, 1926?"

The road leads to a house hidden by trees. A dog barks. I see the Packard, parked outside a closed garage door. The place is a little ramshackle, in need of paint. I get out. The barking dog is quieting down. I hear a screen door slam. The old man is staring at me.

The gravel crunches under my feet. His lawn is littered with chunks of rusting metal. It takes me a few seconds to realize that the rusting metal is sculpture. By the old man? Is he an artist, or an eccentric?

"What can I do for you?" he says with a tinge of crankiness, but he's not hostile.

I feel like a complete and utter fool. "Can you tell me how to get to Lexington Drive?" I ask.

He stares at me through bright blue eyes. His chin is full of stubble, and his clothes are paint-spattered. He must be an artist.

"You go back the way you came, and take a left on Benedict and a left on Hartford. Can't miss it."

He turns to go back inside.

"I'm looking for Garbo's old house," I say.

He stops, but doesn't turn. "She lived on Chevy Chase," he says.

I have this strange feeling, not *déjà vu* exactly, but close enough.

"She doesn't live there anymore," he says.

"I know."

He's still poised to re-enter the house. I feel like Scheherazade. I have to keep him interested. I speak quickly. "She lives in New York. I'm searching for the past. The day she was supposed to marry Gilbert, and didn't show."

He turns and gives me his full attention. The dog yips. He lets it out. It's half-Chow, half–something else, old, like his master. It growls at me.

"Quiet Ben," the old man says.

The dog trots over to me, sniffs. Ben and I take to one another instantly.

"You're searching for the past, you say," the old man repeats. I nod. He laughs, shakes his head, like he'd thought he'd seen them all, then just when he thinks he has, one more comes around.

"You want a beer?" he asks.

"Sure."

He returns with two bottles of St. Pauli Girl. We drink them sitting on the porch steps of his house, which, I think, looks like it belongs in New Jersey and must be as old or older than its owner.

"Did you do those?" I ask, indicating the sculpture.

"No. My wife. She's dead. She knew Garbo."

I don't want to act overeager. "She did? Did you? How did she know her?"

"What's your interest?"

"I don't know. I'm not sure."

"She was a plain girl, shy, big-boned, clumsy. Except when she was in front of the camera. My wife worked as a set designer. Worked on some of Garbo's sets. She was no great shakes as an actress, according to my wife, who saw them all: Clara Bow, Theta Bara, Lillian Gish. Now there was someone, Miss Gish. Garbo admired Gish. Patterned herself after her. The Swede had good business sense, but she was like a fish out of water."

Did I hear him correctly? Did he say Garbo was "*plain*"? I can't hide my disbelief.

He's finishing his beer, losing interest.

"I want to show you something," he says. Ben and I follow him around the back. Sculpture litters the yard, but it's different. Like it's been spawned from its great, hulking parents on the front lawn. Still, it all looks like junk for the scrap heap to me.

The old man begins to hose down the sculptures. Then he flips on glaring klieg lights. The sculpture is transformed. Once I took acid and hallucinated spinning wheels of color in the sidewalks. They seemed so real that I bent over to touch the pavement.

That's what the sculpture reminded me of under the glaring focus of the lights.

"Looks better at night," he says. "The metal's special. Interacts with light and water. Kind of like Garbo with the camera."

Speechless, I trail after him to the front. "You won't find what you're looking for in these hills," he says. "C'mon Ben," he calls to the dog. "Time for our naps."

"Thank you," I say. He waves. The screen door slams. He's gone.

It's a matter of minutes from the old man's house to Lexington Drive, where Marion Davies's house is located. But I've lost interest in whatever it is I'm looking for.

Hunger gnaws, and my head feels buzzed by the beer. I want to go somewhere to eat, but I have a practically agoraphobic reluctance to leave the car. From the number of drive-ins in L.A., this fear must be prevalent. After wolfing down a burger, fries and a Coke, I am at a loss as to what to do next.

Memories of the strange old man haunt me. Who is he? Without thinking, I head back to the hills. At least I should see Garbo's old house before I leave, and I know Eddie won't take me there. About a year after Vidor's wedding, Garbo had promised to marry Gilbert again. This time the wedding was to be in the pine grove planted behind the house. She would wear a Swedish costume. She must have been humoring him. Friends of Gilbert's put Garbo down as selfish. They said that she took everything Gilbert had to offer, giving nothing in return. I don't believe it. I don't think Garbo knew what to do with the power, the force, she exerted on people.

Turning right on Wilshire, I wend my way to 1027 Chevy Chase Drive. I park the car across the street from the house, which is surrounded by a wall. Built by Garbo, or one of the myriad later tenants? Dudley Moore lived there while his house was being remodeled. So did David Puttnam during his quicksilver tenure at Columbia. I don't care who lives there now.

I wonder if the old man and Ben are really napping? I don't even know his name. What kind of metal would react to water

and light that way? Maybe the beer was laced with a hallucino-
gen? Garbo also reacted to light and water. Water! That's it. She
had lived near the water. I'm sure of it. She liked to swim and
sunbathe, alone. Gilbert once followed her, and watched her
staring at the ocean. Garbo didn't stay at Tower Road for very
long. Only months. It's all coming to me now.

After she left Gilbert, she lived in a hotel. Some crazy fan, a
girl, threw herself in front of Garbo's car. Horrified, the actress
realized that hotel living was dangerous for herself, and others.
She moved out of the Beverly Hills Hotel and into 1027 Chevy
Chase Drive. Less than a year later, that same girl reappeared at
Garbo's door, begging an audience with her idol. Garbo moved
again. In fact, she collected her mail in one place and lived in
another. But where?

I skim the *Photoplay* looking for a clue. The interview with
Gilbert portrays him as a gallant loser, taking Greta's brush on
the chin like a gentleman. His agent had advised him well. It
doesn't mention her residences.

The day is turning overcast with smog and chill winds, which
is how my brain is beginning to feel. I head back to Edmunds
Bookstore on Sunset Boulevard. Eddie will be getting home soon.
I want to beat him back, but I also have to make one more pit
stop. I need to know where Garbo moved after Chevy Chase
Drive?

This time I am waited on by an older, grizzly-looking man
who knows exactly what I'm after. Am I that transparent, or is
Garbomania a more common disease than I suspect? Yes, she
had moved many times. He knew of a house situated on the side
of a hill in the Santa Monica district, a few miles from the
Pacific, but he doesn't know the street address, and it will take
time to research it. But I'm all out of time.

Racing back to Eddie's, it strikes me that Garbo may have lived
within miles of where I'm now staying. All I have to go on is that
the house was part of an estate surrounded by towering spruce
trees overlooking the valley below, and was as impenetrable as an
old baronial castle. I had to find this house. What did the old

man mean when he said that I wouldn't find what I was looking for in Beverly Hills? Did he mean that I should look elsewhere? But where?

Getting stuck in traffic turns me into a road menace. I don't have the luxury of a tape deck. The radio doesn't work well either. One consoling thought is that Eddie might be stuck too.

Gilbert was nearly thirty when he'd proposed to Garbo for the last time. She was about twenty-four. Mauritz Stiller had died at age forty-five in Sweden, a broken man. A great Swedish director, he couldn't make the transition to American filmmaking. It was as though he'd been sacrificed on the altar of Garbo's fame. She had had nothing to do with his failure in this country, but she must have felt partially responsible. If it hadn't been for Stiller, she never would have come to America. He had discovered, molded and shaped her. She was his creation, until she began to create herself. To have succeeded, not only in the country where he had failed, but beyond his wildest dreams, must have riddled her with guilt.

Gilbert finally gave up on Garbo. Two months later he married actress Ina Clair in Las Vegas.

Eddie's car was not in its spot. I'd beaten him home by minutes.

CHAPTER FIVE

Eddie came home in a great mood. He'd landed the account, and wanted to celebrate, which we did in grand California style.

The California coastline is peppered with salt-air communities bearing lyrical Spanish names like Playa and Marina and Del Ray. As a present to himself, Eddie had bought a new, shiny, bright red motor scooter. We rode up and down the Pacific Palisades, going wherever the urge took us. We let our hair blow in the wind, and stopped at dives along the way for beers and seafood. We played Frisbee on the beach. Eddie taught me how to bodysurf. We rubbed one another down with sunscreen, and baked until neither of us could take it anymore. Grungy, still wearing our matching Hawaiian shirts, we stopped at a snobby restaurant where Eddie charmed the maître d' into lending him a tie and a jacket. He looked like a shoe salesman on holiday.

Except for the insufferable wine ceremony that Eddie has to go through every time he tries a new bottle—sniffing, swirling, studying, sipping, gargling and finally swallowing—the meal was fabulous. We returned home tired but happy, and soaked in the hot tub until our skin began to blanch and pucker. Afterward we made carefree love all over the apartment, like in the good old days of our relationship. I haven't indulged in such hedonism since I was a teenager. The whole time I kept wondering, "Would we do this if we were married?"

We had so much fun that Eddie took the rest of the week off. He treated me to golf lessons at a public club. He took me to see the Charles Eames house, built of stock industrial materials in 1949. He dragged me to an L.A. Dodgers game, where I yelled myself hoarse, but they lost anyway. I was hoping that he'd suggest an old movie, and give me a chance to ask him if he'd like to catch the Garbo flick on Sunset. Sensing that my bringing it up would spoil everything, I pushed it aside, and made him drive me around the Santa Monica hills, pretending to be fascinated with the architecture. One place could have been where Garbo had lived. I hallucinated traces of her ghostly presence everywhere.

We'd parked on a hilly cul-de-sac overlooking a sea of treetops. "Think you could get used to this?" Eddie asked.

I didn't have to answer him.

We went to Disneyworld, where he bought me a Minnie Mouse doll. Eddie tells me to grow up, then buys me dolls. I'd wanted the updated version, with Minnie in Reeboks, but he insisted on the one of her wearing a flowerpot hat. Everything was great until Eddie discovered my Garbo stuff. He found it while foraging around the house in search of a misplaced sweater.

"What's this shit?" he asked, waving the paraphernalia at me. Shades of the past: most of our arguments before he left centered on my "Garbo fetish."

I was in the living room flipping through his extensive country/ western compact disc collection.

"When did you get this stuff? I thought you were done with all that," he said, dumping it in my lap.

We had a huge fight. I can't stand being yelled at, it makes me hyperventilate, and then I can't yell back. But this time I managed.

"What business is it of yours? How dare you poke around my things. Do I explode over your adolescent fixation with baseball cards? If I even so much as breathe on those cards you have a fit."

"There's no comparison," he said, flinging up his arms and rolling his eyes.

"Yes there is, and I wish for once you'd realize it."

By now, I'm standing, and we've squared off, facing one another.

"Is this how you spent your days?" he spat. "In musty old bookstores with a bunch of fairies?"

"You're overreacting."

Staring at me in a squint, Eddie said, "Why are you so interested in that old dyke?"

I was so startled that I laughed. Was Eddie jealous of Garbo? Is that it? I couldn't stop laughing. My side hurt.

He slammed the door on the way out. This was where I came in. I vowed not to be there when he returned. I called the airlines. The next flight out was in a couple of hours.

By the time the plane landed at JFK, I'd worked myself up into a state of the Dire Dreads. There's something about returning to New York after being out of town that evokes feelings of doom and gloom under the best of circumstances. Traffic is stalled by an accident. As the taxi inches past the wreck, I see someone pinned behind the steering wheel. The front of the car is crushed, like an accordion. The cab driver crosses himself and mutters something in Spanish. Once we get past the tie-up, we sail up the West Side Highway and onto my street. The lights of Mrs. Wallace's apartment are thankfully out.

I wish I had a cat, a bird, a guppie; something alive to greet my return. The apartment smells of neglect. I open a window. The little red light of my answering machine is blinking madly. I cannot believe that Eddie hasn't called. Surely he must be wondering where I am by now? I didn't leave a farewell note. Maybe he thinks I took a long walk off the Santa Monica pier?

The next day, Sunday, I expect every ring of the phone to be from Eddie. On my way to Cara's I vow not to be the first to break down and call.

A man using a public telephone hangs up as I walk by. Interpreting this as a sign, I call Eddie, collect. He accepts the charges.

"Don't you care about what happened to me?"

"Okay, Rebeccah, what happened to you?"

"I mean, aren't you curious about where I am?"

"Okay, Rebeccah, where are you?"

I am so furious that I can't speak let alone come up with witty repartee. I hang up.

"I love Eddie, but I can't live with him," I tell Cara. She's baking oat-bran muffins. "He always wants to be on top."

"Talking dirty again?" Shel says, entering the kitchen. He's annoyed because I finished all the ice cream, even though it was bought especially for me.

"Where are you going?" Cara calls after him.

"To get some more."

"Pick me up a pack of Camels," she says. I hear the front door shut, then reopen. He returns, saying, "What?"

"You heard me," she says.

Shel leaves. The whole encounter is playful but serious at the same time. Cara has quit smoking. Shel has quit cholesterol. I am in complete suspense as to what he will do. In the meanwhile, the Grand Inquisition is underway.

Cara wants to know what my leaving in such a huff proved?

"You're such a hothead," she says.

"He's the one who slammed out the door. I'm tired of being bullied. What was I supposed to do, sit there and knit him a sweater until he decided to return?"

"Want some tea?" she asks.

"Regular or mud?"

"Regular."

"Okay."

Shel returns carrying a large brown paper bag. He places the bag on the table. Whatever is inside is sweating. Slowly, Shel upturns the bag and out spill two dozen low-cal frozen fruit pops.

He selects two coconuts, holds them up for Cara to inspect, mock-bows, then leaves to "catch up on my napping."

"You see," I say, as though the whole ice cream–cigarette

incident was enacted especially to prove my point. "With Eddie and me that would have turned into a knock-down, drag-out, door-slamming debacle."

Cara sighs. She's worried. She cares. She thinks we're just avoiding the unavoidable. She thinks Eddie and I are karmically mated. It's only a matter of time before we realize it and give in. In the meanwhile, a little interference, a little push, never hurt anybody. What would make me see that there is no one else for me but Eddie? Her face lights up. She has an idea. I've seen that let's-kill-two-birds-with-one-stone expression before.

"Oh, no," I say. "Not another blind date. I still have scars from battling Cyril, the horny accountant."

"This one's different. He's young, single, a lawyer. He looks like Mel Gibson, only taller."

My interest perks.

"Trust me," she says. "It's just what you need."

Stephen J. Beale, IV, is so good-looking that I gasp when I open the door to let him in. If Mel Gibson were slightly over six feet tall and had gone to an Ivy League college he might look like Stephen J. Beale, IV. I don't trust men who are prettier than I am; they're too conspicuous and tend to self-worship. I can't believe this guy needs to go out on blind dates to meet girls until he opens his mouth.

He talks as if his whole lower jaw has been shot full of no-vocaine. He reminds me of the girl in the original *Auntie Mame* movie who kept calling everything "top drawer." Stephen J. Beale, from Piping Rock, Long Island, attended Andover and Amherst. His sister schools horses on the family's front lawn. He lives in an Upper East Side apartment inherited from his maternal grandmother.

"Would you like a drink?" I ask.

"I made reservations for eight," he says, looking at his Rolex.

"I'll just get my purse." How, I wonder, am I going to get through the evening?

In the cab he says, "Hudson and Barrow," to the driver. The

address sounds familiar, and then I remember. "Omigod," I say, smacking my forehead.

"What's wrong?"

"Are we going to Holdesky's?"

Stephen nods.

"I was invited to the opening. I forgot all about it."

He's impressed. "I hear the food is *fab*-ulous," he says. "Everything on the menu is from famous restaurants and nightclubs from the past—the Stork Club, the Colony, Le Pavillon." I've never before seen anyone except for ventrilloquists speak without moving their lips. I expect his voice to be thrown, like on a dummy. Is this the kind of clientele Joel wants to attract? It throws him in a new light.

"How do you know the owner?" he asks.

"He picked me up on a street corner."

"Really," Stephen says, making it a statement of fact, not a question. He says it after almost everything I say, and frankly it makes for lousy conversation, but I don't have to worry about awkward silences. This guy makes better wallpaper conversation than my mother, who could engage a chair. Rattling downtown in the taxi, I learn the merits of skiing in Vale versus Aspen, shopping for shirts at Saks versus Brooks Brothers, and living on the East versus the West Side. While Stephen is entertaining himself, I run over a mental checklist of things to do tomorrow, deliberate over whether to tie one on tonight, and rehearse what I will tell Joel about not showing up for his big opening. The thought of seeing him again cheers me up.

The first impression of Holdesky's is one of understatement and retro-elegance. Two huge vases on either side of the reservation desk hold elaborate floral arrangements. Duke Ellington is piped in from the coat-check room. The bar is polished wood and brass with bevelled mirrors. The lighting fixtures are postmodern deco and cast a warm glow over the room. The linens and table settings remind me of luxury cruise liners. At any minute I expect to see Bette Davis and Paul Henreid appear hand-in-hand. The place is packed with well-dressed young couples and groups, who collect restaurant dining experiences like their parents do government bonds and rare coins. We're told by a leggy, crop-haired hostess in a little something from Soho that there will be a fifteen- to twenty-minute delay.

"We have reservations," Beale insists. "My secretary made them this morning."

"I'm sorry," she says, "but there's nothing I can do. We're backed up. Why don't you have a drink at the bar while you wait? It won't be long."

"Let me talk to the maître d'," demands Beale.

"Surely," she says, smiling like it's a stretch mark, "I'll get him."

"Stephen," I say, "I don't mind waiting at the bar."

"I do."

A large man wearing a tux that looks like it was borrowed from his brother-in-law looms our way.

It's the maître d'. Stephen does a double-take, but he keeps his cool. "My reservation is for 8:00 P.M.," he explains, as though he's talking to a foreigner. "I arrived promptly. It is now," he holds up his silver and gold Rolex for all to see. "8:15. We'd like to be seated."

"As the hostess already told you," says the maître d', "we're overbooked." He sounds like Sylvester Stallone in *Rocky*. "You'll have to wait at the bar."

"Let me talk to the owner," Stephen insists, but he sounds less sure of himself.

The maître d' grins. "He's busy."

"I'd appreciate it if you could get us a table now," says Beale, changing his tack. He palms a twenty into the hulk's hand.

"You'll still have to wait," he says, pocketing the money and turning on his heel. He mumbles something to the hostess, who laughs.

"We'll call you as soon as your table is ready," she tells Stephen, sweetly.

Beale is grinding his teeth and breathing through his nose. "Forget it," he says, in a loud, obstreperous voice. "I wouldn't eat here if you paid me."

"Does that mean you're cancelling your reservation, sir?"

"You don't know who you're fucking with," Beale yells at her. I want to dive under the bar. We are the center of attention.

"Let's go," I urge. "I know a great restaurant up the street." He doesn't hear me.

"Is he with you?" a familiar voice asks. It's Joel.

Turning twelve shades of red, I nod yes. He rolls his eyes.

"What seems to be the problem?" Joel asks. He looks different, and I realize that he's wearing a suit. His hair has grown out, and is brushed away from his face. It looks sexy.

"Who're you?" Stephen asks.

"The owner."

"You ought to do something about the rudeness of your staff," Beale exclaims.

Joel takes a deep breath. "We apologize for the inconvenience," he says, "but we just opened and aren't prepared for the crowds. Why don't you have a drink at the bar until your table is ready, on the house."

I admire his self-control. Semi-mollified, Beale, who recognizes real class even if he doesn't have any, agrees, and we follow Joel to the bar where Stephen makes a production of ordering a Bombay gin martini, straight up, very dry, shaken not stirred, with lots of olives. I order a glass of white wine.

"Put it on my tab," Joel tells the bartender. To Stephen he says, "It won't be long now."

To me, he says, "Nice tan. California? I missed you at the opening." Then he winks, says, "See you later," and disappears. There it is again, that incongruous scent of baby powder. While Beale discourses on the virtues of this gin versus that gin, and shaken versus stirred martinis, I wonder about the New Joel, and how well he adapts himself.

After a few minutes, the hostess escorts us to one of the best tables in the house. She's almost as tall as I am. Does Joel like amazons, or is it a coincidence?

Busboys and waiters attend to our every need. Customers stare at us with curiosity, like we're celebrities. An older woman wearing a lot of jewelry stage-whispers to her escort, "It's what's-her-name. The one who lived with the gorillas."

I identify instantly with Garbo's aversion to celebrity but secretly thrill to the attention.

If Joel wants to impress me it's working. All evening long he flits to and from our table, inquiring if we have everything we need, offering comments on the menu, the wine, the dessert. The suit, which I recognize as Armani, hangs on him with casual chic. Joel, I decide, is a walking bellwether of trendiness. I feel *beige* and want to ask the hostess where she shops. The cowboy boots add a few inches to his height, or is that short red-haired woman who never seems to be far from his side a midgit? She is vibrant, sexy, possessive; she is dressed in a bright red tube dress with matching lipstick and a wild, feathered black hat that hugs one side of her face. Out of the corner of my eye, I observe her pulling Joel aside, whispering to him. She seems to be looking in my direction. Joel frowns, shakes his head. She becomes insistent. Her hands fly as she speaks. She could be Italian, but that's not it either. He pulls away from her. She says something, and he stops, turns, says something back. She glares at him and strides away. Who is she?

Later, when I overhear her speaking to some people at a nearby table, I recognize the voice, the accent. She's the woman who answered the phone when I called him that Sunday.

By the end of the evening, I am replete—with food, wine, and Stephen J. Beale, IV, who typically presumes that our royal treatment stems from his aggression. I feel sorry for the next restaurant that deigns to keep him waiting.

A waiter appears with a bottle of *grappa*. "Compliments of the owner," he says, placing it on the table with two fluted champagne glasses.

Joel materializes. The redhead, of whom I've lost track, has vanished.

"This will put hair on your chest," Joel says, handing us each a glass.

"All success," Beale says, in his best Piping Rock.

"Thanks," from Joel. We all clink glasses and sip daintily.

"Great stuff," says Beale, then, "Will you excuse me?"

Joel and I are alone at last.

"Where'd you meet this joker?" he asks, sitting across from me.

"Blind date."

The corners of his eyes are crinkly. Why are laugh lines, like underarm hair, more attractive on men than women?

"You look great with a tan. What are you doing later?"

"Later?" It's nearly midnight. I have to get up for work tomorrow.

"Dump whitebread and have a nightcap with me."

"How?"

"Leave everything to me."

By the time Joel and I arrive at his apartment, we are both weak from laughter. The look on Stephen's face when we put him into the cab and he realized that I wasn't going with him was worth the effort. Launching himself into a monologue of the virtues of *grappa* versus *marc*, Beale didn't realize how much of the stuff he was consuming. Joel had the waiter serve him glass after glass of different brands of both until he couldn't distinguish coke from cognac. As he got drunker, he became surprisingly heartier, with a full-bellied laugh, the laughter of the fat man I could envision him becoming in a few years. He and Joel had a grand old time, and I was tempted to bow out when a waiter announced that Beale's taxi was waiting.

We are greeted at the door by a brown-and-white dachshund.

"Winthrop," Joel says, bending over to scratch his long, floppy ears, "I'd like you to meet Harriet Brown, alias Rebeccah Duffy."

He remembers! Harriet Brown, one of Garbo's many aliases, is the name I gave Joel when we first met.

"Rebeccah," he says, continuing the farcical introduction to his dog, "this is Adams Madison Oliveri Winthrop Sturken Montoya, Jr. But you can call him Winthrop."

I squat down and try to shake his tiny paw. Winthrop whines.

"He's named after all of my mother's ex-husbands," Joel says. "Next to my father, Winthrop was the best of the lot."

66

Joel's apartment is small, cluttered, messy. Filtering through my alcoholic haze is the thought, "Say Good Night, Gracie."

Winthrop follows me around, sniffing. Joel has an eye for modern painting, there's a very nice Jasper Johns and a Borofsky, but his taste in furniture and bibelots blares retro-Americana *kitsch*. I hate clutter.

"I hate clutter," I say.

A silver-framed photograph of a beautiful brunette catches my eye.

"Who's this?" I ask.

"My mother."

"She looks like a movie star."

"That was the problem."

Little by little I am beginning to piece Joel's psychology together.

"Where does she live?"

"In Mexico, with husband number seven, or is it eight? I've lost track."

"What a day," he says, taking off his jacket and tie. He drops the pocket watch he always wears on the cantilevered coffee table. "What can I get you? How about some decaf?"

"Go home, Duffy," I think.

"Decaf," I say, sitting down. The couch is heavily upholstered and covered in chintz. I sink into its cushiony folds. Lead weights have attached themselves to my eyelids, which flutter open in a struggle to stay awake.

The phone rings. I hear Joel speaking *sotto voce* from the kitchen, and envision the redhead on the other end of the line, urging, cajoling, threatening, controlling. Whoever it is has aroused Joel's temper.

"I'll call you tomorrow," he says, hanging up. The phone rings again, and again, and again. Finally, he picks it up. I can't make out the words, but his tone is more conciliatory.

"No, not tonight," he says, or I think he says it.

"Who was that?" I ask, or I think I ask it.

I remember closing my eyes for a second. I remember trying to unpeel my eyelids. I remember Joel saying, "Wake up, Duffy." I remember thinking, no saying, "I have to go," and then I remember nothing.

When I awaken it's nearly dawn. I am lying fully dressed on the couch. Joel had thrown an afghan over me. My head aches; the room is spinning. I hear the metronomic ticking of a clock, muffled sounds of traffic. I go to the bathroom, fumble for some aspirin, for some toothpaste, for some mouthwash. The water glass crashes to the floor.

Winthrop barks. Joel, in the baggiest boxer shorts I've seen, appears in the bathroom doorway. He hugs me. His body is warm.

"Don't go 'way," he says.

I am looking for my other shoe. Joel pulls me to my feet, leads me into the bedroom. He hugs me again. His excitement is evident. My excitement is building. I suppose the seduction has been a long time coming—back in the restaurant; on the Circle Line tour; when we first met on the street corner. A great deal of my attraction to Joel is narcissistic. He decodes something in me that I want to know more about. Joel also possesses a libidinous intensity that is as menacing as it is seductive. Last night I looked for tell-tale signs of a female presence in the household, but found none.

He kisses me. Our mouths become entangled like vines, and so do our bodies. Then I kiss him. It's like in a Garbo movie. The role of elegant and aggressive temptress feels both erotic and strange. Joel surrenders himself to sensuality, he's not afraid of making himself vulnerable. Eddie always holds back a little. Joel's lack of restraint both scares and arouses me. There's something ambiguous about his sexuality. He switches from passive and aggressive effortlessly.

I let him undress me. Why resist? Why pretend it isn't something I haven't already thought about and want?

As he undresses me, he nibbles, gnaws and kisses each revealed piece of my flesh. He slips out of his boxers. His slim body is taut, hairless, sculptured. Joel works out but he's not muscle-bound. The look on his face is one I've seen before, on Eddie. He crawls in beside me. His body heat merges with mine. The smell of baby powder becomes stronger.

Joel takes his time. I'm not used to it, and try to hurry him. He won't let me. He repeats my name, and the huskiness of his voice is like a caress. The words that Deirdre Holland and I had amassed to describe the differences between male and female sexuality, words like penetrate and enfold, begin with Joel to transform to words like fusion and infusion, blending and bliss.

I am aware of a pair of eyes watching us. Winthrop, with his two front paws on the bed and his tongue hanging out, is playing voyeur.

"Joel," I say.

He's too far gone to answer.

"Joel, the dog."

"Scram, Winthrop," he says, panting.

Winthrop issues a low growl, but doesn't move. The dog is spying on us, but it's too late to do anything about it now.

I oversleep, am late for work and spend the rest of the day in a torpor of disorientation. Every time I think of Joel I sink into a romantic swoon. Butterflies flutter inside my stomach at the thought of seeing him again, hopefully without Winthrop. For now I need a little time to figure out what's happening. Are we friends who happened to become lovers, or are we lovers who happen to be friends?

I thought the day would never end. Of course Eddie called when I was out last night, all night, and I bet half those hang-ups are his.

By 9:00 P.M., I am in bed, nearly asleep, clutching Minnie Mouse in one hand and a large, open, family-sized tin of baby powder in the other. I finally found out what Joel does with it.

The phone rings.

"Hello?"

It's Cara. All day long at work I meant to return her calls, but never got a chance.

"What did you do to Stephen J. Beale, IV?" she says. "He's barely speaking to Shel."

"Lucky Shel. Beale got drunk and we put him in a cab."

"We?"

"Joel and I."

"Tell," says Cara. She wants details.

"Um-Uhn," I manage. It isn't going to get any better.

"Call me tomorrow," Cara says. "First thing."

Yes, tomorrow, I'll think about it all tomorrow, like Scarlet O'Hara.

CHAPTER SIX

None of my obsessions command my total allegiance. Fickleness and I are well acquainted. Without taking a break, I have segued from Eddie to Garbo to Joel. My evening with Joel has taken on the patina of a dream, the texture of a fantasy, the persistence of a memory. I think about Joel, about Joel's body and the sum of its parts. I can still feel its heat, hardness, smoothness, and smell his powdery, musky scent. I can't help but compare him, neither favorably nor unfavorably, with Eddie. They're different: one is short and compact, the other tall and loose; one is intense, the other more playful. Once when I was performing oral sex on Eddie I threw up on his thigh, a brief, unmessy splat. Eddie laughed. Would Joel find that funny?

George Bernard Shaw said that people think about sex 75 percent of the time, but he's wrong. I think it's more like 90 or 95 percent. I should be paying attention to my work; I just got promoted, and am in the midst of negotiating a raise with the top brass.

The long and the short of it is that management won't give me a decent salary. I want the job. I know I can handle it, but I also know that I can't sell my skills for less than a fair increase.

Whenever the going got tough, Garbo, who thought argument beneath her, said, "I tank I go home now," and left. She negotiated with the leverage of her star power and box-office appeal. I have no such leverage. I'm a woman in a company whose senior members look askance at female engineers. They don't think I can cut it, and have done everything in their power to prove themselves right, including sending me to the Tennessee plant to troubleshoot for them—a little plan that backfired when the plant manager and I discovered that we had a lot in common, including a distant cousin on my mother's side.

When my boss left, and the department's Product and Development Manager position opened up, I asked for the job. The company tried to pull men from every function in the place, any male remotely related to the job, to fill in for Bob. But I am the most qualified, and everybody knows it. The men would say, "Go ask Rebeccah," when a problem came up.

Finally, the vice-president called me in and admitted that I was the best candidate. I asked about salary, and he tried to put me off. I persisted, and he came up with seven hundred fifty dollars more.

We're sitting in his beige office, sparring.

"This is my final offer," he says. "I can't pay you a penny more."

"I happen to know that Bob was making ten thousand on top of what you're offering me, even with the so-called increase."

Francis X. Magorian, Frank to his cronies, stares at me from beneath black, bushy eyebrows that make his dark eyes look satanic. Only the framed photographs of his wife, children and grandchildren give testimony to a more tender side of his personality.

Eddie and I used to commiserate with one another about the inequities of the system. He'd urge me to seek another line of work, one where women weren't so resented—like graphics or interior design—but something in me balked at the idea of quitting. My interest has always been in three-dimensional design.

Since I was a small girl I was fascinated not only by how things worked, and getting them to work better, but by the essence of a piece; the purity of inspired lines and shapes; stripping problems to essentials, and reworking the solutions aesthetically as well as technically.

Most of my idealism was drummed out of me by the time I finished college and had spent some time in the real world. No one seemed too interested in my design ideas, so I shoved my portfolio to the back of the closet and took a job as an assistant draftsman in a New York City–based company that manufactured everything from a variety of brushes to wallpaper kits. Quickly I learned that if I wanted to get anywhere in this business I had to master the language of marketing, manufacturing, packaging, and product development. Package design in particular interested me because, while it is hardly glamorous, it's the most challenging. From the beginning I involved myself on every level from blueprint filing to the redrafting of other people's usually bad renderings.

My big break came when I saved the company money by putting one of its products, a hairbrush, into a polybag. Previously, we had been using blister cards. For months I'd struggled with the conventional problems of construction and quality within the restriction of specific costs and materials. Finally, I came up with the polybag solution, and from there on in I became the polybag expert. I even won a package design award for which the purchasing agent took credit.

"Keep a low profile," I was told, and I have—until now. Now I am no longer content to let others take credit for my work, or not to be paid equally. Now I want my due, and I'm not sure why exactly. Cara says it's "Saturn Return," which I am supposedly entering.

"A time of great change," said seer Cara, "whether you like it or not."

My father has always taught me that going after a goal is not half as important as sticking with it no matter what. Magorian is making it clear that he isn't going to budge on the salary issue.

And I am mentally doing battle within myself; four different personalities claim ownership of me at this moment. One advises, "Give in, take it. Don't make waves." Another says, "Compromise: ask for less." Still another prompts, "Sue the bastards," and the last and loudest screams, "Stand your ground."

I could accuse Magorian of sexual discrimination, but I have neither the energy nor the inclination to fight City Hall. Garbo simply wouldn't budge from her position. Louis B. Mayer, the head of MGM, wouldn't budge from his. She called his bluff and eventually got her way.

"Your offer is unacceptable," I say.

"I'm sorry you feel that way," Magorian says, standing. He holds out his hand. This is a big man, with imposing bulk.

"Excuse me, Mr. Magorian, but what are we shaking on?"

His eyebrows rise like two circumflexes over his eyes. "Isn't it obvious, Miss Duffy? We like your work, but we can't pay you any more money."

"You mean you *won't* pay me any more money."

"Why don't you take a few days off to think about it?"

Now he's calling my bluff. Last summer I saw an osprey trapped in plastic rings from a six-pack. The image of the bird struggling to free itself has haunted me, and haunts me still. I wanted to help release it, and nearly had my hand pecked off. My mind is making connections I'm unable to decipher. Magorian's smug demeanor and the specter of the trapped osprey coalesce into a strange compound. Garbo could take or leave Hollywood. I can take or leave Magorian and his plastics waste factory and tell him so in no uncertain terms.

Our Human Resources department isn't sure whether I quit or was fired.

"I quit," I say.

"Magorian said he fired you."

"Just for the record, I want it made perfectly clear that I quit." (I sound like Richard Nixon.)

74

"Does that mean you won't be collecting unemployment?"
"I guess it does."

Cara says that I'm acting like a fool. At least if I say I'm fired, I
could go on the dole until I find other work, but she's missing the
point.
"What are you going to do?" she asks. We're eating tempeh-
burgers in her kitchen. She's smothering hers in ketchup.
"Isn't that defeating the purpose?"
"Are you short on funds? Because, if you are, Shel and I can
help you out until you get another job."
I'm touched by her offer and resist the impulse to hug her.
"Thanks," I say, between bites, "but I have some savings."
The tempeh-burger is making me gag. At least I hope it's the
food, and not what I fear it might be.
After throwing up in Cara's bathroom, I go home and call my
father at the office.
"Hi, Dad," I say, when I hear his voice.
"Rebeccah? How are you sweetheart?"
"I quit my job," I say, and then burst into tears.
My father has the most common sense of anybody I know. He
listens to my long, sad tale. I also tell him about Eddie, and the
California fiasco.
After I'm finished, there is silence.
"Dad? Are you there?"
"I'm here." He pauses. "Why don't you come home for a
while? Your mother and I would love to see you. We can talk
about your plans then."
Home. A line from an old Barbara Stanwyck movie comes to
mind: "Home is when you've got no place else to go," and in a
certain sense it's true. Cara tells me that we Cancers love our
homes. Queen Marie of Romania (a Scorpio) used to travel with
as many of her favorite possessions as possible, including dogs
and servants, to re-create a sense of home wherever she travelled.
I have mixed feelings about that. On one hand, objects bind and

anchor, and make me feel restless. On the other, being without them, the familiar and filial, makes me homesick. The things I love most also fill me with fear and loathing. For instance, this white porcelain egg, a gift from my father for winning the package design award. The egg is life-sized, pure, an inviolable object whose perfection is dual: as a piece of sculpture, and as a representation of nature's most flawless package design. Chinese emperors coveted porcelain's imperviousness to time and decay, the way I do Garbo's presence on celluloid, hoping some of the permanence will rub off. Still, a Freudian could read volumes into Dad's choice of present to his only daughter.

At the last minute, I stuff Minnie and her ridiculous hat into the suitcase. Eddie and I are speaking again, but it's like the Soviet Union and America at the summit table—détente. Every time I call him a woman answers the phone: either Maria, who must be making a fortune in overtime, or Sharon or Karen, or both.

"What are you running there?" I asked during our last telephone session, "A harem?"

I don't think either one of us knows what's going on anymore. Our relationship has reached a plateau. As far as I know, infidelity is a new item on the agenda. Eddie may not know about Joel, but I do, and even though he doesn't say so, I can't imagine that Eddie's proximity to Sharon and Karen, the porno queens, isn't netting some action. Also, what's the real story with him and Maid Maria? I hate confrontations, of any kind, but Eddie and I have to have one, soon. I dread it.

Joel never called, and my original wish to put a little distance between us is now turning into a giant anxiety that all I really was, was a one night stand. Cara bought me a do-it-yourself pregnancy kit, which I stick in the bottom of my shoulder bag. She also wants me to take the AIDS test. But it's not necessary, or is it? Sex with Eddie has always been safe. I'd brought my diaphragm along but, well, what a pain it is to insert during moments of careless abandon. Joel took precautions, or at least I think he did. Before leaving that morning, I recall seeing Winthrop chewing on something that he was holding between his tiny paws. On closer inspection it was a condom.

"Used or unused?" Cara asked.

"Cara! *Gross!*" I said, but the point had been made.

Mrs. Wallace agrees to collect my mail for the week.

"Going away again, so soon?" she says, in her booming voice.

"Yes, to see my folks, for a visit."

She peers up at me suspiciously.

"They give you a lot of vacation time there," she says.

"Three weeks," I lie. No need to tell her I'm out of work.

For a stupid woman Mrs. Wallace has an uncanny intelligence about hidden agendas.

"You need a rest," she says. "You've been working too hard. Oh, before I forget, someone left this for you."

It's a small box wrapped in plain brown paper. Something inside is ticking. Perhaps Magorian is sending me a token of his affection, like a minibomb? I unwrap it in the cab. It's from Joel, a pocket-watch, encased in black plastic. I recall admiring his collection in his apartment. He'd said that his father had left him his. "After Pop died, I began collecting pocket-watches, and my mother husbands."

Staring out at me from the dial is a tiny black-and-white reproduction of Garbo's face. I recognize the still; it's from *Mata Hari*. Her hair is slicked back and she is unsmiling, looking defiantly into the camera. Scribbled on the box are the words, "I vant to be alone . . . with you!" A simple telephone call from him would have done, but I am learning that Joel hates predictability.

Mom meets me at the Pittsburgh airport. It's so good to see her.

"You cut your hair and got it frosted," I blurt.

"It's called 'highlighting,' " she corrects. "Women in *my* mother's generation got their hair 'frosted.' "

"Sorry. How is Granny Peck?"

"Rebeccah, honey," Mom says, peering up at me, "you look awful. What is that city doing to you? Are you eating right? Getting enough sleep? On the way home I'll stop off at the market and pick up some vegetables."

It's good to have Mom take over, and to be home. The closer I get to the house, the further away my New York life seems. Nothing changes in Sewickly, and I find this comforting.

Along the way, Mom and I make chitchat. She tells me local gossip, asks about Deirdre, have I heard from her? I got a letter, which I have to answer. Deirdre is on one of her jaunts around the world. She's been to Africa on safari, and backpacking in the High Sierras. Now she's in Tibet, trekking in the Himalayas. Deirdre's father is so rich that she never has to work for a living, although between jaunts she takes temporary jobs—mostly working for art gallery owners, interior designers or congressmen. She owns a small townhouse in Georgetown which she calls home when she's not gallivanting around more exotic shores. A lot of people are put off by Deirdre because she tends to be snotty, but I know it's a cover-up for basically low self-esteem. That's why she runs around the world trying to prove herself.

My room beckons me. Mom had taken my collection of stuffed animals out of storage and crammed them together into one of the wicker chairs. I stick Minnie in their midst. How baleful they all look. The human need to reproduce the animal world strikes me as sad and curious. Poor Val. She'd like to recapture and preserve the innocence of my childhood for as long as possible. With me in New York and my brother away at college, she gets lonely.

After dinner Mom accused me of suffering from bulimia.

"You're too thin," she said. "I heard you in there throwing up."

"I'm sick with flu," I said.

I've been banished to bed.

"Rebeccah, what are you doin' with this huge container of baby powder?" she asks.

78

Over thirty years of living with my father in the North have not erased Val's Tennessee drawl.

"It's a long story," I say.

"You sure are actin' peculiar, honey," she says. I have to agree.

Dear Joel, I begin to write on some notepaper I found in my old desk. It's bright red with a light gray, art deco-ish border. He'll like it.

I quit my job, but it's a long story. I came home to visit my folks and get myself together. I love the watch! . . .

This is not altogether true. I'm too perplexed by it to love it. On closer inspection, I notice that it has no hands. Joel must have taken them off to glue the tiny picture on the dial. Why did he choose a still from *Mata Hari?* Why not something from *Flesh and the Devil,* or *Queen Christina?* Does Joel think I'm a spy in the house of love?

. . . although I have some questions about it . . . Like why it has no hands?

I'll be here for a week. Call me: 412–752–1960.

How do I sign off? *Best wishes? Love? Ciao, baby?*

I decide to risk *Love.*

Rebeccah.

P.S. Did you use a condom that night?

P.P.S. I may be pregnant.

Crumpling the paper, I throw it away. I'll try again when I'm less tired. Tomorrow Mom is dragging me to the doctor. She doesn't think that whatever's ailing me can be cured by steamed vegetables and fresh air alone.

CHAPTER SEVEN

Unwanted pregnancy is no longer a life-and-death issue for women like me. Many women I know, including Cara, have had abortions in about the time it takes to visit the dentist. But my mother is distraught. She hails from an era when girls who got pregnant wound up in loveless marriages growing old before their time, or were treated as outcasts from society and family alike. Born and raised in Bristol, Tennessee, which shares the Virginia border, Mom considers herself a sophisticated hick who slides from Deep South to Moderate and back again depending upon who she's with, and her whim.

After the doctor's, she takes me to downtown Pittsburgh. The old Pittsburgh has been described as "hell with the lid off." But that was in the days of the now defunct smokestack steel industry. Over the last five years Pittsburgh has been undergoing a renaissance of economic growth and architecture.

Acting like a couple of girls playing hooky, Mom and I try on dresses, shoes, jewelry in various downtown boutiques. She treats me to a new frock, and to lunch.

In many ways, my mother and I couldn't be more different. We don't look alike, but we're alike in other ways and have become, after a few trials and tribulations, friends. When I was about fifteen I used to come home from school to find her half-smashed. She'd flirt with my boyfriends. I called her a drunk, and seethed with anger toward her for disappointing and embarrassing me like that. As I got older I figured out that the afternoon binges were symptoms, not the cause, of her problems. Once I mentioned it to Dad and he got mad at me, so I never brought it up again. Maybe he said something to her though. By my senior year in high school she'd at least stopped drinking during the day.

Valerie Burgess Peck hails from a family whose roots and history read like a Southern Gothic novel. Her mother, Granny Peck, lives in a big house in Bristol, which she is constantly redecorating. My grandmother has the airs of a Rockefeller or Astor grand dame, but she's just a well-born Bristol lady who terrorizes the servants and spikes her coffee with sippin' bourbon (she claims it tames her arthritis). Granny Peck's youngest and favorite son had a nervous breakdown and gassed himself in the garage. Her oldest son is fat and lazy and can do no wrong. And then there's Val, stuck in the middle and picked on. Granny Peck is "as mean as a chicken and as dumb as a post," as my dad says.

Mom and Dad met in college, the University of Tennessee, where she studied drama, and he business. Dad's an Army brat. He travelled around the country a lot as a kid and fell in love with the South. He said that Tennessee had the friendliest people in the country, except for Granny Peck. She hates my father to this day, and thinks that Mom married beneath her, no matter that my father has turned a small hardware business into a chain-store empire. Duffy's Hardware Emporiums are sprinkled throughout the South and Southwest. There's even one in Bristol, but Granny Peck's not impressed. She could forgive Dad's Irish (and some Scotch and Welsh) descent, and even his being Catholic, albeit lapsed, but she can never forgive him for being a Yankee.

So far Mom and I have successfully avoided the issues of my visit home, but I can see that she wants to have a heart-to-heart with our health-food salads. We won't know for sure if the rabbit dies until sometime tomorrow, but in the meanwhile she wants to know what Eddie's and my plans for the future are.

"Don't you think it's about time you two settled down?" she says, spearing a tomato wedge with her fork.

"How's Granny Peck?" This subject usually distracts Val for hours.

"Rebeccah," she warns, "this is serious."

I hate the term "settle down." As far as I can tell Garbo never settled for anything, up or down, and I don't want to either.

"I'm not ready to *settle down*," I say. "Eddie thinks he is, but he isn't either. Neither one of us knows what we're doing or what we want, and that's the truth."

"For the first time in ten years, I want a cigarette," Mom says, looking around for someone to bum one from.

People are always on the verge of relapsing into self-destructive habits in my presence.

"Look, Mom," I begin, but she doesn't let me finish. She's pissed, and let's me have it.

"Your father and I went through a similar situation," she says, and the lecture begins. I hear about the vagaries of love, and the vicissitudes of sexual attraction; the differences between men and women, and how women are smarter, but they've got to let men think they're in charge; on the realities of marriage and having children, and on change. The word "commitment" comes up a lot, and "compromise."

I have an overwhelming desire to brush my teeth.

"Rebeccah," she says, "I don't think you've heard a word I've said."

"I hear you," and I do, but they're her words, not mine. We might as well be speaking in tongues.

"Women don't have to pretend anymore," I say.

She looks at me questioningly.

"To pretend to men that they're weak and submissive. It's unfair—to men and to women."

"Listen, honey," Mom says, softening. "If you're not ready to marry Eddie, there's nothing your father and I can do about that, although you know how much we like him. He's already a part of the family. But no one's going to force you into anything. When I was your age, you were considered an old maid if you didn't marry by twenty-two, but times are different, I know that. When I was your age, being pregnant out of wedlock was considered a worse sin than being a Democrat."

She laughs, I grimace.

Wedlock is an expression that makes me cringe, along with "getting hitched" and "tying the knot." Why are all the idioms of marriage synonymous with imprisonment, enslavement and bondage?

Mom means well, but she's depressing me, and now she's upset.

"What did your father and I do?" she asks. "Is our marriage so bad that you act like we're advising root canal every time the word is mentioned? Were we such bad role models? Why, half the girls you know have parents who are divorced while we're still together, and still in love."

I question what my mother means by "in love." My parents share a life predicated on affection, comfort and routine. Their good times come from the bottle; so do many of their bad times. When I was ten I saw my mother kissing a strange man in the gazebo. The full moon cast them in an eerie glow. As an adult I can understand, even sympathize with how these things happen. Look at the mess I've gotten myself into. But the child's memory seethes with darker phantoms of pain and shock and disillusionment.

"I'm not like you," I say, but both of us know this isn't altogether true.

Val is on the verge of collapsing into tears. I want to run and hide and comfort her all at once.

"It'll be okay," I say, touching her wrist.

She attempts a smile, and I admire her for her valiance.

The waitress slips the check between the real and artificial sugar containers.

Mom takes it. "Let's go," she says. "We're finished here."

One of the things my mother and I share in common is our ability to sweep things under the carpet. In the car going back, we resume gossiping.

"Did you get a Christmas card from M'Lou this year?" I ask.

I'd been wondering about our dotty neighbor, who'd moved to Philadelphia years ago, since I'd returned.

"I get one every year, like clockwork. This year she sent me one from a family by the name of Bartleberg, or Battleboro, who live in La Jolla, California. It had a picture of them all out by the swimming pool in their bathing suits, wearing Santa Claus hats and beards."

I laugh. It's so M'Lou. For years she's been recycling her Christmas cards. I'm not sure if it's out of an ecological conscience or perversity? With M'Lou you can never tell.

"I've been meaning to call her," I confess, rolling down the window. It's hard to breathe.

"She'd love to hear from you." I can tell she's still upset by the white of her knuckles as she grips the steering wheel. The next day, Dad invites me to lunch.

My father hates change. He has in his closet clothes twenty years old, including shoes. When something wears out, he replaces it with an exact replica. For the past five years Dad has been dining in the same restaurant, which resembles a stately men's club, with lots of leather chairs and creaky male waiters in white jackets. Everyone knows and respects him and he is accorded fine service along with his dry martini. The martini reminds me of Stephen J. Beale, IV, about whom I tell Dad, making him laugh at my bad imitation of Piping Rock lockjaw. But Brad, Sr., is more bemused than amused.

By the time our main course comes, we have zeroed into the crux of the luncheon: what am I going to do with the rest of my life? Dad isn't going to lecture me about love and marriage, that's Mom's department. He's more interested in what place I want to make for myself in the world, and how, barring the present crisis, I intend to get there. To be honest, I haven't been thinking about it, not consciously.

"I don't want another technical job in a big company," I say. "I don't want to stay in package design. It's a stalled art, and I don't seem to possess the fight necessary to change it."

"What *do* you want?" he asks, popping an olive into his mouth.

Dad's hair is thinning. He has a new pair of glasses whose thicker lens magnify his hazel eyes. Fact: my parents are aging.

"I want to do less engineering and more designing."

He nods, sips, encourages me to continue.

"Do you remember when I used to redesign stuff around the house? I've been looking over all my old sketchbooks, and some of it is pretty good."

We both order the fish of the day.

"Lately, my head has been full of ideas, images. Most people look at hub caps and see . . . hub caps. I look at them and see a lady's purse, or a lighting fixture, or a new kind of salad bowl. It's crazy."

Dad's reticence is not meant to intimidate. He's a man of few words. He'll speak when he's ready.

"I think I'd like to work for a small product design house," I continue. "There are a lot of them now."

The fish is salty, but I'm hesitant to send it back. My appetite is waxing and waning like the moon.

"I also want to learn more about other design disciplines: textiles, jewelry, graphics," I say, and confide my dream to return to school. This reminds me of Eddie.

"Dad, can I have another Perrier?"

He summons the waiter. "How's the fish?"

"Mine is salty. How's yours?"

"Fine. Do you want something else?"

"No, that's all right. I'm not that hungry."

"Try the soup," he says, motioning to the waiter. It too tastes salty.

Eddie's quitting architecture has me more upset than I'd realized.

"It's just not the same between us," I blurt. "I feel like he's sold out, and it's eating away at him deep down. He makes money hand over fist, and buys adult toys and gadgets, but it's not enough. I want him to go back to school, to take up where he left off, before it's too late. He doesn't even have to become an architect, but just finish what he started. I think it's important."

"Does he know this?" Dad asks, stirring his tea.

"He must. I mean, I haven't said it in so many words, but he's got to know it on some level."

"Why don't you tell him how you feel?"

So simple a solution, and so true, but isn't this exactly what I'm afraid of? Yesterday, during lunch with Mom, the operative words were commitment and compromise; today it's commitment and prioritize. Both my parents are trying to tell me something.

"But Dad," I say, "what takes more commitment and priority than a baby?"

There, it's out. My father stares at his plate. "Do you know that for sure?"

"No, I mean, the doctor's tests aren't in yet, but she's pretty sure I'm in the early stages."

My father is a Victorian with some Puritan mixed in. He detests waste, and scorns the frivolous. He's in the midst of lecturing me on the cowardice, dishonesty and irresponsibility of sacrificing my training and talent, my future, on an unwanted child, when I blurt, "Excuse me, Dad. Nature run," and flee the table.

I make a collect call from the powder-room pay telephone to Cara at work. Thank God she hasn't left for lunch.

"What's wrong?" she asks.

"Why haven't you ever had a baby?"

"Rebeccah, where are you? Are you drunk?"

"Worse, I'm pregnant."

"Are you sure? Did the swab turn blue?" Then, "Just a minute." I hear her say. "Tell them to call back." Then, "Rebeccah?"

"I'm still here. I'm in Pittsburgh, having lunch with my father, and I'm freaking out. I'm waiting for the results of the doctor's tests."

"What about the do-it-yourself thing?"

"I'm afraid to try it."

"How are your folks taking all this?"

"Better than I am. Cara . . . ? Do you want kids?"

"Shel and I have been trying for nearly a year. We're afraid we might become one of those infertile couple statistics. What are you going to do?"

"I don't know."

"Does Eddie know?"

"No. But it might not be Eddie's."

"What?" she says, but not to me. I can hear people clamoring for her attention in the background.

"Rebeccah, I have to go. Call me tonight . . . Rebeccah?"

"I'm here. Okay. Bye."

We hang up.

"Are you all right?" Dad asks when I return to the table.

"Yes, sorry. I'm fine. Where were we?"

But the moment is lost. My father is reluctant to pick up the thread, and so am I.

"Let's not count our chickens before they hatch," he says.

"Bad aphorism," I say, laughing. Dad, smiling, agrees. He summons the waiter. "Check, please."

"You have to learn . . . ," he begins.

". . . to take one step at a time," I say, finishing his imitation of Mom. Sometimes we collude against Val. I always feel a little guilty, but it passes.

"You know," he says, leaning his arms on the table, "you remind me a lot of your Aunt Becky. Not in terms of looks, but in terms of your ambivalence." He signs the credit card voucher, and we leave. "Your Aunt Becky never knew what she wanted. She wanted to get married, then she wanted to run away to Africa and be a missionary. She wanted children, then she didn't want them around. She wanted Don to work harder, then she wanted him to stay home more. She wanted to sell everything and move to the country, and she couldn't stop buying and had to buy a bigger house in the suburbs."

"I imagine she wanted to live, too."

"I imagine."

The car pulls up. We get in.

"I miss Aunt Becky."

"So do I."

"Someone by the name of Joel Halduski called," Mom announces. She's fluttering around the dining room table vase with sprigs of flowers and leaves in her hand creating a perfectly beautiful centerpiece.

"Holdesky," I correct, wondering how he tracked down my number. He must have gotten it from Mrs. Wallace. I feel a tremor of anticipation.

"Now who's this Joel?" Mom asks, curious, suspicious and interested all at once. It's just like old times.

"A friend."

"Is he someone you're seeing?"

"You could say that. I mean, we've been out on a couple of dates."

"What does he do?"

"He owns a restaurant."

Mom looks impressed. I feel nauseous. "Did Dr. Yale's office call?"

She nods.

"How pregnant am I?"

"About six weeks."

The reality of being pregnant, unwed and unemployed is hitting me by degree. I have an excruciating headache, but am fearful of taking anything for it.

"Why don't you go lie down, honey," Mom says. "Don't worry about a thing. Your father and I will handle it."

"Hi, kids," I call to the platoon of mute stuffed toys. My favorite was and still is a giraffe, a present from M'Lou. She got me over the shame of being tall and not petite like Val.

"Mom," I call as she whizzes by my room. She's checking up on me.

"Yes?"

"Do you have M'Lou's address and phone number?"

"Somewhere in the kitchen. How're you feeling? Do you want anything?"

I shake my head. In another minute I'll be sucking my thumb.

"I'll call you when dinner's ready," she says.

"Okay."

I can't stop thinking about Aunt Becky. She died of cancer the week before my college graduation. Going to the funeral meant driving over three hundred miles each way. I wanted to go, but I also wanted to celebrate four long, hard years with my friends. My mother exhorted me to do my duty, and come. My father told me that whatever I decided to do was fine with him, it was my choice, he'd honor it. I didn't go to the funeral and remember crying under the spray of hot water in the dormitory shower for hours.

Did Aunt Becky envy my father his natural assumption of place and position in the world? Maybe ambivalence is a female trait. I remember her as jolly, though, not torn between her choices.

Joel's present, like my life, is ticking away, handlessly. I stare at the tiny picture of Garbo's beautiful face.

Garbo never got pregnant, and except for *Anna Karenina* (a remake of the earlier *Love*, with John Gilbert) she never played a mother on-screen. The scenes with her film-son are tender. Her self-possession appears to be total, absolute, uncompromising, sacred. Yet I've read that the young Garbo borrowed a neighbor's children and passed them off as her own family. When I used to haunt her neighborhood hoping to get a glimpse of her, I'd mentally chart her day: early to bed, early to rise. Yoga before breakfast, then a walk. Lunch. Then more exercise, more walks. Dinner. Perhaps a shot or two of red vodka? A cigarette after dinner? Then bed. How her early fans grew to despise this Garbo, who denied them a happily-ever-after ending. She is the high priestess of her own temple, a sacrificial celibate. Do I project the restlessness, the rooting and searching in hidden places that I suspect her of ceaselessly doing? Do I also project her laughter (not tears) in the dark?

I hear Val talking to someone in the kitchen. Curious, I go to see who it is.

"Bunny!" I exclaim, rushing into her arms. We hug and squeeze each other.

"How are you, ReeBee?" she says. Her conciliatory manner tells me she knows about my plight.

"I can't complain. How are you? How's Leroy?" Leroy is her husband, who's been ill. Bunny seems weighted by family problems; a sick husband; one daughter who'd just left her husband and returned home to heal her wounds; a maverick son she hasn't heard from in over four years.

"He's fine, fine. Much better. Now what's this I hear about you quitting your job?"

When I was a kid I'd often come home from school to find Mom out volunteering. But Bunny was there, always, and she used to listen to me while she prepared dinner. The smells of fresh baking and Bunny's unending sympathy enveloped me in warmth and hearth. How I'd taken it all for granted, and now it's gone. Bunny, too, looks older, more worn. Her skin resembles the once-dark bark of an old ginkgo tree, blanched by time and the elements.

"Why don't you take your coat off? Have some tea? Stay awhile," I urge. Bunny has retired as our housekeeper, but she and Val still see a lot of one another.

"Much as I'd love to, I can't. I just stopped by to tell your mother something. When are you going back?"

"Friday."

"I thought you were staying through the weekend?" Mom pipes in.

"I want to stop off in Philadelphia and visit M'Lou."

"I'd better get going," Bunny says. Bunny never had any patience for the family's love of our eccentric ex-neighbor. "Leroy is waiting for me."

We hug again, making promises to spend more time with one another during my next visit. Holding my hand, Bunny looks up at me with her large, liquid eyes and says, "Little ReeBee. You're not so little anymore." This makes us laugh. "Whatever it is, it ain't so bad," she says and is gone.

The woman should have been a shrink. The humanity emanating from her is worth ten psychiatry degrees. She can diffuse fear and anxiety with a word, a look, a touch. It occurs to me that somehow Bunny was probably responsible for Mom's quitting daytime drinking, not Dad.

"It ain't so bad" becomes my mantra. For how long can I cling for comfort to this echo of Bunny's soft voice? I fall asleep chanting it, but awaken in a cold sweat in the middle of the night, a disbeliever.

CHAPTER EIGHT

M'Lou Henderson lives on a wide, leafy street filled with odd corners and superb Georgian and Federal row houses. The Norman Rockwell Museum is a stone's throw from her front door. This makes me laugh. M'Lou is the antithesis of everything that Rockwell represents—idealized, mittel-American schmaltz, she used to call it. She delighted in shocking people like my parents, but with such good humor that nobody minded her irreverence, and she gained the reputation amongst Sewickly's staid and sedate as "a character."

Rumors abounded about her and her husband Jake. Nobody knew for sure if they were legally married or common-law. Jake was a handsome Swede, a retired government scientist, whose nebulous past fired coffee-klatch gossip. Some thought that he'd worked for Germany until the Nazis came to power. He met M'Lou, an American vaudevillian acrobat travelling with a troupe, in Berlin. Val told me that M'Lou, after a few drinks at a bridge party, had bragged about dancing with Heinrich Himmler, who had had no idea that he was cradling in his arms a woman of Jewish blood. I don't know which shocked Val more— M'Lou's alleged Semitism, or her proximity to one of the world's most heinous criminals. I used to spend a lot of time over at the Hendersons browsing in their great library of books from all over the world. One day I asked M'Lou, Was it true she'd danced with Himmler?

She laughed uproariously. "I sure did, Pumpkin," she said. "And with von Ribbentrop, and a few of the others."

She had even devised a plan to have them all assassinated. "I would have done it, too, if it hadn't been for Jake, who sent me packing to Scandinavia. I might have saved a few lives," she added. You never knew when M'Lou was serious.

The Hendersons settled in Sewickly by accident. Jake's older brother, a lawyer, had established a practice in Pittsburgh and had urged Jake to leave war-torn Europe and follow. In those days Sewickly was little more than pasture for cows, and the Hendersons bought their house with cash. Jake died over ten years ago of a heart attack while puttering around his beloved garden; a few years before, their daughter was killed in a car crash while vacationing in Florida. Jake was never the same after Laura's death, and M'Lou never completely recovered from the loss of both husband and child.

At Jake's funeral, she looked small and frail and bereft.

"I'll never forgive you," she said, shaking her fist at the casket, and I'm still not sure what it is exactly that she refuses to forgive?

Soon after the funeral, M'Lou packed up the Sewickly house and moved to Philadelphia.

The door of M'Lou's residence is painted glossy black and possesses a large, brass eagle door-knocker. I knock a few times.

"I've been expecting you," she says, flinging open the door. Her appearance shocks me. She is wrinkled, shrivelled, puckered. Like much about her, M'Lou's age is a mystery. She could be seventy or even eighty. Her steel-blue eyes still possess their clarity and twinkle, though, and her warm gaze reassures me that I'm welcome. Barbara Stanwyck is wrong: Home is not when there's no place else to go, but when there's no place left to run.

We hug. She smells of glycerine and rosewater, homemade.

"Did my mother call? I left her a note."

"She sure did, Pumpkin. I told her that you'd call the minute you arrived. But that can wait. Let's have some breakfast together first."

Ravenous, I trail after her to the kitchen. M'Lou's silk caftan billows as she walks, her arm bracelets clank. She looks like a gypsy crone who is about to read my cards.

"Do you still do the Tarot?" I ask.

"The answer to your problems isn't there," she snaps, reminding me of the eccentric California artist who'd said that what I was looking for wasn't in the hills.

M'Lou's kitchen looks and smells like an old-fashioned apothecary. Cara would go ape-shit here. Everywhere you turn there are jars, vials, crocks and canisters filled with exotic herbs and mixtures. Twines of bulbous roots and ropes of odd-looking reeds and weeds hang from the ceiling. My father affectionately calls M'Lou "the old witch," and suspects her of dabbling in magic.

"Are you hungry?" she says. "As I remember you were always eating and never gained an ounce. Let's see, I have cereal here, somewhere. Or would you prefer an egg?"

The thought of eggs makes me gag. "No eggs."

She nods, like she understands, and places a large box of cereal and a pitcher of milk on the table. The brightly colored bandanna she wears barely contains her white frizzy hair. Turquoise drop-earrings dangle from her earlobes. To the shock and dismay of my mother, M'Lou had had her ears pierced before it became fashionable. I'm glad to see that she still favors lipstick and nail polish in colors she called "whore-y."

"I hear you got yourself knocked up," she says, her bright blue eyes twinkling.

"That's one way of putting it."

Her levity diffuses all sense of catastrophe; I begin to unwind. It's like Bunny placing her hand on my arm and saying, "It ain't so bad."

The tea M'Lou is brewing smells awfully close to Cara's brand—Old Sock.

"Drink it," M'Lou insists, "it's good for you."

Sitting down, she says, "So?" and inserts a cigarette into the perennial ivory holder.

"What's the point of drinking herb teas when you smoke?" I ask.

"I don't drink that stuff," she says, making a face.

"Now," she adds, "tell me what's going on."

I don't know what M'Lou put into my tea, but it knocked me out. After breakfast, and the great verbal disgorging of my soul, I was tucked into a large feather bed where I fell unconscious.

Sounds filter through, as if from very far away. I hear the ringing of bells, the murmur of voices. How long have I been sleeping? It's dark out. M'Lou calls my name.

"It's your father. I can't stall him anymore."

I never want to leave this womb of a bed, but I drag myself to the phone. My father is even-tempered. It takes a great deal to make him lose it. The last time he yelled at me like this was when I was in high school and had stayed out till dawn without calling. He's ranting about my amoral and profligate ways, my blatant irresponsibility, my total lack of consideration of his and Mom's feelings. Then Val gets on and starts to cry. Feeling helpless, I reassure her that everything is going to be fine.

"Eddie called," she manages.

"Did you tell him anything?"

"No."

"Mom, please don't say anything to Eddie. I want to handle it."

There are more muffled noises.

"Mom?"

"Here, your father wants to talk to you."

"I want you to take the 8:00 A.M. train tomorrow morning. Your mother will meet you at the station."

"But Dad . . ."

"8:00 A.M.!"

"How about a nice glass of Madeira?" M'Lou suggests after I hang up.

"Got anything stronger?"

"Now where did I put it?" she mutters, searching the kitchen. "It must be in the parlor."

M'Lou's livingroom is crammed with hundreds of books that spill out of bookshelves and are stacked in piles on spindly-legged tables and the floor. Between them the Hendersons spoke five or six different languages. International journals lie around in various stages of perusal. M'Lou is scavaging amongst them.

"Ah, here it is," she says, extracting the Madeira bottle from between a mass of papers.

She pours us a couple of glasses. I'm not really in the mood for it. The fight with my parents has shocked me out of my stupor.

"Drink up," she says. "It'll take the edge off."

"I don't know what to do," I say. "I'm so confused."

"I've been meaning to ask you," she says, inserting another cigarette into the holder, "where'd you get that funny-looking watch?"

"Joel gave it to me. I can't figure it out. I mean, I wonder why he chose a picture of Garbo from *Mata Hari* . . . ?"

"Maybe that's all he had lying around the house. Maybe that's *his* favorite picture. Are you going to tell him about the baby?"

"Do you think I should?"

"What I think doesn't matter. Here, have another shot."

Sometimes M'Lou exasperates me. She seems insensitive, flippant.

"Why is everybody giving me such a hard time?"

"Stop feeling sorry for yourself. You got yourself into this mess and you have to get yourself out of it."

M'Lou collects paperweights. They're strewn all over the house. I pick one up, a beautiful crystal with a white rosebud frozen in its center, and toss it from one hand to the other.

"I've always looked forward to having a baby, it's marriage that I object to."

M'Lou laugh is raucous.

"What's so funny?"

"Katharine Hepburn once said that men and women should live next door to one another and visit once in a while."

"That's not what you did."

"No, but I still think Hepburn has a point. Jake could be as big a pain in the ass as anyone. But then, so could I. It's getting late, Pumpkin. Are you hungry?"

"Sleepy."

"Let's continue this in the morning," she says, rising. "Sleep as long as you want. I'll call your parents and tell them you're staying a while longer."

The next day, while M'Lou and I are eating a late brunch, we hear a knock at the front door. She answers it and returns with an attractive woman who is holding a kitten in her arms. M'Lou introduces me to Kathy Bouchez who lives next door. Her cat has just had kittens. Does M'Lou want one? Much to my surprise, she says yes. Kathy hands the kitten to M'Lou, who hands it to me.

"Here," she says. "A gift. It will be a hell of a lot more use to you than that damn silly watch."

"What in God's name am I going to do with a kitten?" I say after Kathy has fled.

"What are you going to do with a baby?"

M'Lou's eyes are focused upon me like two beams of light. My father's right: she is a witch.

"I can't keep it. I don't know how to take care of it."

"Then you'd better learn."

Small, cuddly, furry things make me melt. I am a sucker for cute. Damn, M'Lou. She's interfering.

The kitten curls up in the crook of my shoulder with perfect faith that it has found a safe harbor. I am deluged by mixed feelings: protectiveness, tenderness, anxiety. If one tiny kitten can evoke such strong responses what would a baby do?

I want to take a walk and hand the kitten back to M'Lou, who's watching me closely.

"Oh, no, Pumpkin," she says, backing away. "I'm too busy."

"M'Lou!" Three syllables.

"Oh, all right," she says, taking the kitten, "but only for a little while."

The day is cloudy, overcast, but it feels good to stretch my legs and move about. I understand the solace Garbo gets from walking. The thought of someone or something being so totally dependent on me for its survival presses down upon me like a heavy weight. I pass a woman on the street pushing a baby carriage. In less than a year from now, that could be me. My mother used to stroll me in a similar carriage. She has a snapshot of herself standing behind the carriage pasted into a photograph album. She looks young in the picture, happy, fulfilled. There are other snapshots of Val holding me as an infant. In one she is gazing into the distance with a dreamy, wistful look on her face. This was the one I always came back to. Was she thinking of me, and the joyful years of maternity that lay ahead, or was she rueing the loss of her own youth? Later pictures of Mom and me reveal her as still pretty, and smiling, but the bloom is gone from her cheeks, the light in her eyes has dimmed. By the time my brother came along, there's a resurgence of the original joy, but serial photographs reveal it as diminished with time. I can recall seeing pictures of Granny Peck pushing a baby carriage containing Mom. It's generational, matrilineal, this legacy that women pass on to one another in a conspiratorial silence. Isn't that carriage wrapped in plastic and stored somewhere in the attic, waiting for my day to come? My day, it seems, is here.

First comes love, then comes marriage, then comes Rebeccah with the baby carriage.

The jump-rope jingle pops into my head like a slogan. Something is missing. Does the rhyme end there, or have parts been truncated? What comes after the baby carriage? Will I have reached my ultimate objective in life? A little ditty of my own, a modern update, surfaces:

Next come bills, from Macy's and Sears, while mommy and daddy pursue their careers.

When I was a kid my parents once dragged me and my brother to the Norman Rockwell Museum during a family outing. It hasn't changed much. The museum is small and practically empty. The large, luminous Maxwell Parrish mural still stands. About sixty of Rockwell's famous covers for the Saturday Evening Post line the walls of this divided, dusty room. Most of them depict scenes of conventional, everyday, small town life; their preciousness arouses in me alternating feelings of nausea and claustrophobia.

Back out on the street, the fresh, moist air heralds rain. I inhale deeply. Rockwell said that he painted life as he *wanted* it to be, not as it is. Isn't that what we all do?

A woman holding the hand of a little boy, wearing a beanie with a tiny propeller on top, passes by. For one dizzying instant I fear I have fallen into one of Norman Rockwell's paintings. Do kids still wear those things? The wind spins the beanie's propeller. Transfixed, I watch it whirl. Strange disparate images of spirals, springs and propellers flood my brain. I feel myself mentally spiralling in ascendant and descendant patterns, moving from a fixed center of myself while constantly receding from or going toward one central thought. The fetus inside me is forming, growing. Who is the father? Is it Eddie? Or Joel? Sperm lives for three days. Either man could have sired this baby. Does it matter? Certainly not to the fetus at this stage. Who of the two paternal candidates, Joel or Eddie, would make the better father? Who would share equally with me the responsibility of pushing the baby carriage? Why is there no family snapshot of Dad or Granpa Peck pushing a pram?

The fact of this pregnancy is forcing me to think hard. *First comes love. . . .* Do I love Eddie, or is he a habit? Could I love Joel? Or someone else? I feel like a neophyte in these matters. When Eddie slammed out the door to find himself in California, he left me in New York to my own devices. The loneliness I suffered was profound at first, and I found solace in going to the movies. Then I saw Garbo in *Queen Christina* and in some strange way it turned me around. The image of Garbo's face in the last frame as she stared out over the ship's railing still taunts me. Queen Christina wound up alone, without a man or a country, but somehow she made it seem heroic, not pathetic. I began to treasure my solitude. The hieroglyphics of autonomy are difficult to decode, but I feel like I'm on the verge of cracking it open and deeply resent all this interference.

As I walk along I hallucinate spirals in the shadows of trees on the pavement and in the formation of clouds in the sky. Doubled, spirals form twisting ladders that house DNA, the fount of all life. What holds them together? The romance between one helix and the other is a tango of chemical bonding and complementarity. Eddie and I are more like a pair of flamenco dancers, clicking our heels to different beats. The spiral is continuous in either direction, accelerating increase or decrease, ascendance or descendance, whirling to and fro in spheres ranging from the microscopic to the astronomic. It is the ascent, the spiral nebulae, not the descent, the DNA, that calls to me.

The urge to draw sends me spiralling back to M'Lou's. In a weird confection of mechanics and aesthetics, I mentally design and redesign the shapes I'm envisioning, selecting those that are the most pleasing to the eye. Forsaking function for pure form, I imagine creating pieces of jewelry that mimic unusual applications of the helix and helicoid: twisting bracelets of gold and silver; platinum and diamond spiral necklaces; pendants of hammered metal. Other shapes take hold: propeller pins; spring rings; ball-bearing earrings made from semiprecious stones.

I can't wait to share my ideas with M'Lou, but when I get home she's in a bad mood and greets me with, "What took you so long?" It seems the kitten awoke and knocked over a flower vase whose contents spilled all over one of M'Lou's favorite antimacassars.

She orders me to take the cloth to a laundromat to wash it before it's indelibly stained. Her washing machine, as it happens, is broken.

"And here, take her with you," she says, handing me the kitten. I know M'Lou is playing out this charade for my benefit. The lesson is being relentlessly driven home. I confront my ambivalence at every turn: protectiveness wars with vexation; I hold the kitten close, yet take umbrage at its intrusion.

"Don't you think you ought to give the cat a name?" M'Lou calls after us.

I am walking so fast the kitten is fearful. I can feel its tiny heart beating against my hand.

"It's okay," I repeat, as it stretches its neck to peer over my shoulder. "It's okay. We'll manage somehow."

My attachment to the animal is growing, and the idea of giving it up becomes increasingly painful. If I give it a name, I will claim it, but no name comes.

A young woman wearing a T-shirt with the logo IKAIA imprinted on it is unloading the dryer. Curious, I ask her what it means. Expecting to hear that it's the Eskimo word for mother goddess, or some kind of bizarre acronym, I'm slightly surprised when she says, "It's the place where I work."

Before I can ask her what or where this place is, she's out the door. I've heard of IKEA, a well-known import housewares store, but not IKAIA.

Another woman, unloading her wash from a dryer is wearing a T-shirt that blares, BABY ABOARD. What is this, a conspiracy? A gold wedding band graces the third finger of her left hand. Noticing me staring, she smiles. Seeing the kitten, she approaches, and pets it.

"It's adorable," she says, and as if on cue, it starts to purr.

"Do you want it?" I ask.

She looks at me like I'm mad. "Are you kidding?"

"No. I'm not. It's not really mine. I haven't given it a name."

"No, thanks," she says, backing away. "I can't use a kitten right now."

I feel something warm and liquid on my hand. Little Thing is peeing all over me.

"Oh, no," I say, holding the animal away from me. The woman laughs, sympathetically.

"It's like having a baby," she says, indicating her big belly.

"I'm beginning to realize that."

My feet have a will of their own. After I wash and dry the antimacassar I'm not surprised when I find myself knocking at the front of Kathy Bouchez's door.

I hear a crash. A baby cries. Female voices rise and fall, one of them in lilting Gallic accents. Someone is being bawled out. Footsteps approach from behind the door.

"Who is it?" Kathy asks.

"It's your neighbor," I say.

She unlatches the door.

"I'm sorry to disturb you," I begin, "but . . ."

"Oh, no," she says, "don't you want her?"

"I, um, er. . ." I feel idiotic.

"It's not that I wouldn't take her back. Don't get me wrong, but we still have two left, plus its mother."

She smiles at me appealingly. Fine lines crinkle the corners of her dark eyes. I guess her to be thirty-something.

A wide-eyed toddler, sucking hard on a plastic bottle of apple juice appears. She half-hides behind her mother's skirt.

"This is my little girl, Alexandra," Kathy says.

"Hello, Alexandra," I say, bending over.

"Kithkat," she says, excited. Then, "All the toys."

She's a bundle of cuteness. She tugs at my heart. I want one, I do, but . . . The urge to ask Kathy Bouchez if marriage and motherhood is all that it's cracked up to be hovers on the tip of my tongue.

I can't believe what I'm saying.

She stares past me, blinking rapidly, like she didn't hear right. I visualize her husband, the savvy French art dealer. They travel back and forth to Paris. Kathy dresses well, with an ersatz chic picked up from her Parisian sojourns. M'Lou said that she operates a small import clothing business from her home. I've seen the telltale weariness in her eyes in other working mothers. I remember women at work who practically lost their minds trying to juggle everything—arranging baby sitters, cooking dinner—and that was on average days. On days when things went wrong—the sitter was sick with flu—they had to interrupt their work schedules and deadlines to handle the domestic dilemmas. Most of these women had supportive husbands, and help, but the burden of responsibility still fell upon their overpadded shoulders.

"I'm sorry," Kathy finally says, "What did you ask me?"

The kitten meows.

"Kithkat," repeats the little girl in a tireless monotony.

Inside, the infant bursts into another round of squalling. I hear someone talking to it in lowered, foreign tones. Kathy looks oddly embarrassed, like I caught her at an awkward moment; like all this is an aberration of the usually perfect order of her day. Would I be like that? This woman makes lists, and follows them, checking off each item as it is accomplished. She works out, eats right, doesn't drink and is punctual. She is the way I should be but never will be, no matter how hard I try. I need things to be natural, spontaneous. If something is established, it sets up tyrannies, and all I want to do is kick them down. M'Lou once said I was like a goat, "fine until you try to tie you up." Kathy Bouchez is determined to have it all. The mere thought exhausts me on the spot.

"Well, I can see how busy you are," I say. "I just stopped by to ask . . . if you have any ideas for a name for the kitten?"

A tired expression blinks on and off Kathy's face, until she sees through the lie.

"Alexandra," she says, "what should the nice lady name her kitten?"

"KITHKAT!" shrieks the child, and we laugh.

"KITHKAT!" Alexandra is on a roll.

I thank Kathy Bouchez for her time and trouble.

"I'd invite you in for cup of coffee," she says, hurriedly, "but the baby isn't feeling well, and I'm late for an appointment."

I understand. There's no need to explain, but she seems intent on reaffirming perfection at all costs. Again, I wonder, would I be like that? Wandering back to M'Lou's I mentally switch places with Mme. Bouchez. It takes no quantum leap of imagination to envision me, with an infant in my arms, answering the door of Eddie's Mies-box by the sea. A messenger hands me a manila envelope full of work, which I've contracted as a freelance product design engineer for one of the Valley's numerous venture capital startups. Like Kathy, I would have help. Several nights a week I'd take courses at Stanford, working toward my Masters in design. Eddie is on the road a lot. We spend weekends together with the baby, and Kithcat here.

It's not a bad scenario, but something is wrong, and I can't put my finger on it. Something is either missing or doesn't fit. If I were to shoot Kathy Bouchez full of truth serum I'm certain that she'd never admit regret over having had children, but she might be driven to confess that there's a clear advantage to not having had a child and not knowing what it is you'd never regret. For the time being, this thought, as convoluted as it sounds, not only consoles, but grips me like epiphany.

After depositing the kitten in my room, I follow up a hunch I have about IKAIA, which turns out to be a Finnish-American product design company. The operator puts me through to their personnel office. I speak to a man named Camille who transfers me to a woman named Gary. I explain myself to Gary, who speaks with a southern drawl, How did I hear of them?

"I saw a girl wearing a T-shirt with your name on it in the laundromat."

She laughs. "That's Susan. She took the day off. Do you have a portfolio?"

"Yes, but not with me."

I'm informed that they look at portfolios every Thursday afternoon. No appointment is necessary. Since today is Thursday, and my stuff is scattered in Sewickly and New York, that makes it impossible to go there at the spur of the moment.

"We're always looking for good new designers," she says. "Drop in any Thursday with your work."

"Thanks, I'll do that."

I call Mom to tell her that I'm taking the 3:00 P.M. train home, and that I've decided what to do. She's acting peculiar.

"What's wrong?" I ask.

"Well, Eddie called and spoke to your father who told him that you're pregnant."

"Who told him to do that? He had no right!" I am so mad I shake. The blood is pounding in my ears.

"Rebeccah, as the father of your child Eddie has the right to know. And we thought it might help clear up matters. You've been acting so strange lately . . ."

"You have no right," I repeat, with the metronomic accuracy of the Bouchez toddler. I am quickly spiraling down, down, down.

"Eddie wants to fly East, to . . ."

"What if Eddie isn't the father?"

"What do you mean?"

"Just that. Oh, never mind. I'm furious with you and Daddy. I'm capable of making my own decisions, of living my own life. Forget my coming home. I'm going straight to New York from here."

"Rebeccah, I think you should speak with your father before you do anything rash."

"I'm not doing anything rash. I'm simply going home. I'll call you when I get there."

CHAPTER NINE

Kithkat and I take a train that looks like a giant stapler on wheels to Penn Station. I feel as though I've been away for a year; it's only been a week. Several homeless people accost me. One spits at me as I pass. Is it possible that Sewickly and New York City exist on the same planet? I feel like I'm emerging from hyperspace into a far more savage and brutal dimension.

The rift between me and my parents has unsettled me. I am terrified of losing their love, their approval; of having to stand by the emotional choices I've made alone. Quickly, I calculate how much money I have: savings, some stocks and bonds left in my name from Granpa Peck. For now, it's not a problem.

The walk from the train station to my apartment is like an obstacle course in confrontation. Everywhere I turn I see young mothers, and some fathers, out with their offspring. Some of the women look cheerful, others beleaguered, and a few downright depressed. I hear behind me the insistent voice of a little boy who wants his mother to race with him to the corner. She doesn't answer. He runs ahead without her. She doesn't call or chase after him. I'm afraid to turn around, to stare at whoever she might be.

I cut through the park and see nannies rolling baby carriages and strollers. Bunny used to do that with me when Mom was occupied. Val wasn't around much until my brother was born, and it was Bunny, not Mom, who saw me take my first steps, heard me utter my first sentence. I don't think I'd want to miss out on my baby's first anything, but I can't blame working mothers for hiring help either. And fathers seem to live without it.

Kithkat is lolling placidly inside my zippered jacket. M'Lou and I spiked its milk with a little whiskey, "an old trick," she said, winking at me.

It's starting to rain. The woman up ahead struggles to open an umbrella and negotiate a collapsible baby stroller simultaneously. The umbrella is a breeze: one push of the button, and zip, instant results. The baby stroller is another matter. One end is loaded down with plastic grocery bags and tips over when the toddler, reluctant to be strapped in, escapes. Taking pity on her, I offer to help. Between the two of us we finally unfold the stroller and strap in the child. The portability of these contraptions is one of their most salient points, but the design leaves a lot to be desired.

The woman thanks me profusely. I let the child pet the kitten.

"Kittykat," he says, repeatedly, and I am struck by the universality of children's innocence and trust.

Raindrops keep falling on my head, and so do ideas. Of course! I think. Why not a portable stroller that operates like a push-button umbrella? In fact, a woman or man could carry it like an umbrella and inflate it with one touch of a button, freeing another arm to grapple with baby and bundles—no muss, no fuss, no struggle.

"Not a bad idea, er, Kithy?" Poor little thing regards me with half-opened eyes. I hope I haven't turned it into a drunk.

The design ideas that had assaulted me on the Philadelphia streets are quickening. At some point I must buy cat food, kitty litter and all the other paraphernalia that goes with owning a cat; I must think about shots, and declawing and neutering. But for now, a small dish of water and some newspaper and rags in the tub will have to suffice.

"Sleep it off," I say, shutting the door.

The back of the closet looks like a junk shop. My New York portfolio contains a few disappointments and many surprises. I was into redesigning household tools in a big way. Some of the conceptual sketches and renderings are very good, some are not. It's been a long time since I sat at the draftsman's table, one of Eddie's and my first purchases but long ago relegated to a corner of the bedroom where it gradually fell into disuse.

It's time to get to work.

The double helix, when enlarged, looks like a twisting ladder. On paper lines take form, and form usually follows function. But all that matters now is the rendering, the doing, the expression. I feel a tingling sensation at the back of my spine and neck. This is better than drugs. Time zones in and out, from left lobe to right, in a spatial warp that erases everything but the exigency of the moment. I don't know what half the sketches mean, but does it matter?

When I'm finished, I'm spent, but content, and lie down on the bed to rest and stare at the Garbo and Barrymore still.

"Can't you two ever get it together?" I ask.

Sometimes I stare at it so hard I could swear there's movement. I'd have to see *Grand Hotel* again to see, Who lets go first? The thing about Garbo is that even in the movies, regardless of the part, she is unequivocally herself. Something always shines through, whether she is the lover or the beloved, and try as Barrymore will he can never possess her totally. No one can.

As far as I know, she never cared about what people thought, never betrayed her own convictions.

M'Lou had told me to listen to what's inside. Well, I'm listening, but all is quiet in there. I hear nothing but the gurgling of my stomach and the continual hum of my mind. She also said, "Choose life, Pumpkin. Always choose life." When I accused her of right-to-life rhetoric, she laughed, and said, "You take things too literally."

Now I realize that she was speaking qualitatively, alluding to the ramifications of my decision one way or the other.

I'd forgotten that I'd turned off the phone completely. In the midst of an impulsive clean-up campaign, as I'm throwing things away and feeling positively righteous, the doorbell rings.

"Cara! I was just thinking of you."

"I've been calling you for hours," she says, breathless from the stairs.

"I turned off the phone."

"Do you realize how frantic your parents are? What's the matter with you? They've been calling me at work."

"Oh, God," I said, smacking my forehead. "I got carried away with my work. I forgot all about them, about everyone. I've been drawing again. I'm really sorry they bothered you."

"What's going on, Babe?"

Kithkat mews.

"What's that?" Cara asks.

Awake, hungry, irritated, the kitten is attempting to crawl up the sides of the tub. Every attempt results in a backslide. Cara laughs. "How cute! Where'd you get it?"

"M'Lou."

"What's its name?"

"*It* is a she. I don't know. Nothing inspires."

Glancing at the trash bags, Cara asks "Are you moving in or out?"

"Neither," I say, curling up on the other end of the couch, spooning the kitten some warm milk. "It's my minimalist period."

Cara's studying me and the kitten. Grinning, she says, "Is this a practice run?"

I laugh, shrug, shake my head.

"What are you going to do, Babe?"

We stare at each other, her dark eyes are pulling at mine.

"I've been thinking it over for days. I . . ." This isn't easy.

Nothing about this is easy. "I've decided not to have the baby."

"Are you sure?"

"Positive. I have all I can do to take care of myself, and Kithy here."

Cara searches in her purse, like she's looking for cigarettes. She pulls out a pack of grape bubble gum. "Want some?" she asks, tossing two wads into her mouth.

"Sure."

"Why don't you wait?" she says, popping her gum.

"Wait for what?"

"Shouldn't you talk all this over with Eddie?"

"Eddie may not be the father."

"You can take a test to find out who the father is. It's called DNA fingerprinting. They use it for rape cases. All you need is a sample of the father's blood. They match that with the baby's. It's like amniocentesis. I can give you literature on it if you're interested."

Why is Cara doing this? I thought my decision not to have the baby would be received by her as a given choice.

"Even if I do as you suggest, what will it prove? It's a no-win situation."

I think Cara sees what I mean: if it's Joel's baby, Eddie and my parents will be pissed. And if it's Eddie's baby, everyone will want me to marry him when I don't want to. Cara cracks her gum, several times. I get a glimpse of her as a Long Island teenager, hanging out at the mall.

"You think I'm acting irresponsibly," I say in my own defense. "I'm not. Maybe for the first time in my life I'm not."

"You're such a purist," she says, shaking her head, and cracking her gum.

"How do you do that? I could never master it."

"What if you have this abortion and you can't get pregnant again?"

The question throws me. It's like asking, "What if when you cross the street you get hit by a Mack truck?"

"I never told you this," she begins, "but years ago, before I met

110

Shel, I was involved with a guy and I got pregnant. As it turned out I didn't love him, so I had an abortion. Now Shel and I are having trouble in that department . . ."

I don't know what to say. She's extrapolating.

"The opposite could be true, too. I could have this baby and never be able to have another."

Cara blows small bubbles which she pops. I remember when she smoked how she blew perfect smoke rings, usually in succession of threes. I've never seen her so dolorous and bemused. We are both chewing away like a couple of cheap tarts.

"I've been drawing again," I announced. "Come, let me show you what I've done."

I drag her to the draftsman's table. The helicoid and spherical shapes don't interest her, but the other renderings do.

"What are these?" she asks.

"Rough designs for push-button baby strollers. I saw a woman in the park struggling with one of those things, juggling packages and a toddler. It gave me an idea."

She looks at me with questions in her eyes. "What are you doing, overcompensating?"

"Maybe."

She glances at her wristwatch. "I've got to go," she says. "Are you sure you're all right? Want to spend the night?"

"Yes. No. Thank you." Then, "Cara, will you come with me?"

"When are you going?"

"As soon as they'll take me. I have a preliminary appointment on Tuesday. Just routine. I'm in the seventh week. I'm hoping to have the whole thing over with on Friday."

"I'd have to take off work." She's thinking out loud.

"It would only be in the morning . . ."

"Sure," she says. "No problem. I'll take the whole day."

Then, studying my face, she adds, "I just hope you know what you're doing."

The doorbell rings and startles us.

"You expecting anyone?" she asks. *Crack crack* goes the gum.

From that point on the evening unravelled like a French New Wave movie. I felt just like Jeanne Moreau in *Jules et Jim*. First Joel arrived, dripping wet from the rain. I introduced Joel to Cara whose instant distrust of him was as obvious as the pull of gravity. After she left, he offered to cook us dinner and ran out to buy groceries and wine. While he was gone, and I was thinking of slipping into something more comfortable, Eddie arrived looking like a drowned rat. While he was changing clothes in the bathroom, Joel, laden with grocery bags, returned. At first I tried to pass him off as the delivery boy, but neither one would have it. So I introduced them, then went into the bathroom to throw up. In the meanwhile, these two jokers discovered that they share a distinct and superior taste for fine red wine, and proceeded to sample Joel's selection. The groceries, forgotten, had been dumped on the floor. I offered to cook, but neither would hear of it. Rolling up their sleeves, each vied with the other for the Julia Child Impromptu Gourmet Feast Award. Joel did things to chicken I didn't know existed. Eddie whipped up a scrumptous lemon meringue pie. His spinach souffle didn't quite make it, but by then he was too blotto to care. Happy cooks deserve a happy eater. I did my best not to disappoint either one. Eddie's proprietary behavior towards me was not lost on Joel, who played footsy with me under the table. Joel's seductive manner towards me was not lost on Eddie, who made allusions to my "condition" which were either ignored by or lost on Joel. Early in the evening I excused myself to catch up on some reading. As they became drunker, they became noisier. Mr. Hennessy pounded on the ceiling. Joel and Eddie pounded back. Finally, they went out for some Armagnac and cigars.

I didn't hear Eddie return. He'd passed out next to me on the bed.

Neither one had bothered to clean up after himself and the kitchen was littered with debris from last night's revelry. Swearing to the kitten, who nearly drowned herself chasing after dishwater bubbles, I set about washing up, and seriously contemplated taking a vow of celibacy.

Eddie, apologetic, solicitous and hung over, shuffled into the kitchen.

"You drink too much," I said.

There is between Eddie and me a jealous and possessive lust that fuels our passion. Joel's presence in our lives has had a catalytic effect upon our hormones. We began making love in the kitchen and worked our way to the bedroom. It was like California, only more desperate.

Afterward, we lay in bed holding on to one another, not speaking. I felt like we'd been driving in circles for years and had reached a cul-de-sac. Neither of us was ready to tackle the question of what we were going to do with ourselves and each other on an empty stomach.

On the way out, we bump into Mrs. Wallace. Her face when she sees Eddie is that of someone gazing upon the countenance of God. Her eyes widen, and a smile of beatitude forms upon her mustachioed lips. I fear she is going to genuflect. She hugs and kisses him, saying how good it is to see him, asking how long he's going to be here, hoping it's for good, and inviting us in for apricot strudel, which she will make in an instant. Eddie kibitzes with her for a few minutes, exerting the old charm. He needs a shave and a haircut, and looks a bit downtrodden, but Mrs. Wallace sees only what she wants to see: the return of her penitent, surrogate son.

We escape to a Chinese-Cuban dive which has long been one of our favorite haunts. The waiter, recognizing us, ushers us to a booth in the back. Coupledom is like riding a bicycle; it all comes back to you. I know Eddie will order the *huevos rancheros*, and he knows I will order the French toast made out of challah, with extra syrup. He will consume enough caffeine to generate a small power plant. I will sip tea heavily laced with milk. He will hog the Sports, Business and Real Estate sections of the *Times*. I will devour the Arts & Leisure, Travel and Magazine sections. It's just like old times, with a few major differences. We have reached a stalemate.

Eddie taught me how to play chess. He bought me a wooden chess set in Mexico, where we went on a vacation. We played for hours on the beach. Gradually, I got better and soon beat him every other game. Then I beat him consistently. He'd knock all the pieces over and storm away. Later, we'd forget that it ever happened until the next time.

At the restaurant, after I tell him of my decision about the baby, Eddie doesn't raise his voice or lose his temper. He simply pays the check and leaves me sitting there. I feel like all the pieces have been knocked off the board again.

When the going gets tough, the tough get walking. This is my exercise, my solace, my salvation. The drizzle feels good against my skin and hair. The leaves of the trees are the color of steamed broccoli before it peaks. The air smells fecund, and hints of things primeval, ancient. I wonder if Garbo's love of water and rain stems from a yearning for a less complicated millennium? Paleontologist Stephen Jay Gould has said that the human race is here because an odd group of fishes had a peculiar fin anatomy that could transform into legs for crawling onto land. We're here because the earth never froze entirely during an ice age. We're here because a small and tenuous species arising in Africa a quarter of a million years ago has managed to survive. We're here because we're here—an old college drinking song.

The realization that we cannot read the meaning of life passively into the facts of nature takes hold. We must construct answers ourselves, from our own wisdom and ethical sense. There is no other way. Eddie said things that hurt, but what did I expect? Perhaps I was wrong to tell him about Joel? Perhaps I am still punishing him for moving away, and leaving me, or am I "triangulating"—a term M'Lou threw at me—bringing in a third person to avoid facing problems? I'm tired of picking up the pieces after Eddie.

I try four public phones before I find one that works.

"Hello," Eddie says.

"You're still there."

Silence.

"Meet me at Holdesky's."

"You must be out of your mind, Rebeccah."

"No, I'm in it, for the first time in ages."

"I have a plane to catch."

"Eddie, let's put this all out in the open."

"What do you want us to do, *duel* over you?"

"You and Joel both *cooked* over me, what's . . . ?"

He hung up. The problem with Eddie is that he's lost his sense of humor.

Joel is not at the restaurant, nor does anyone seem to know when he's due back. It occurs to me that life with this man would be a constant war with impatience. You'd never know where he was, what he was doing, or who he was doing it with. Uncertain about my next move, I wait at the bar, nursing a Poland Springs water with a twist, chuckling to myself over the irony. It's quiet, between shifts. A busboy is sweeping up. The bartender is desultorily wiping the inside of glasses with a white cloth.

The redhead appears, from out back.

She regards me steadily, approaches, says, "Are you waiting for Joel?"

"Yes."

"He won't be in for a while." She's neither friendly nor unfriendly, just curious. "Forgive me," she says, finding her manners, "my name is Lori Biro. I'm Joel's wife."

I choke on the mineral water, which is spritzed all over the bar. "Sorry," I say, coughing.

"I can see that he didn't tell you." She climbs up on the stool. "I'll have the same, Harry," she tells the bartender. "He never does. Joel is a dog-man. Do you know that expression? No? In the East Village, where I live, it means he sniffs every skirt."

I can't quite place her accent. Perhaps she's of Polish stock, like Joel? We are surveying one another boldly, and I'm shocked by my reaction. This is all new to me, this female rivalry for a man, this jealousy which is giving me heartburn. I didn't know

I cared this much. We are sizing up one another. She is European, older, self-possessed. A woman with the confidence to wear weird hats and dayglo lipstick colors must have a healthy ego. I feel like I'm something that washed ashore with the tide. My flyaway hair looks like a lion's mane after a bad perm. Makeup hasn't graced my face for days. My trenchcoat is soiled and soggy, and my jeans are beginning to smell in the crotch. Lori eyes me from head to toe, and the impulse is to back down.

"Look," I begin. "I have to talk to Joel. Please ask him to call Harriet Brown." I don't know why I'm using one of Garbo's aliases.

"Harriet?" she says, like it's ringing a bell. "Oh, yes. He told me about you. The Garbo girl."

"He never told me about you."

"No," she says, sadly, "it rarely works that way."

It's still pouring out. She interprets my hesitation as disdain for the inclement weather.

"Shall I have Harry call you a cab?"

"No, thanks. I want to walk some more."

This idea is as alien to her as I am. Even Garbo knew when to come in out of the rain.

I am tooling along Hudson Street when a cab pulls up. The door opens. "Get in," Joel says.

"I want to walk."

The cab follows me, slowly. The rain begins to fall in pelts.

"Where's the flaming flamingo?"

"If you're referring to Eddie, he's probably on a plane headed back to California by now."

"Will you get in?"

"I'm pregnant."

"What?"

I stop, turn, and yell, "I'm pregnant!"

Two gay guys pass. One of them says, "Congratulations, honey."

Joel leaps out of the cab. The driver halts, and begins to curse. Joel, grabbing my arm, pulls me inside the taxi.

"Sixteenth and Sixth," he tells the driver.

"Now," he says, once inside, "run that by me one more time."

"I'm pregnant."

For the first time I am appreciative of those horrendous plastic partitions between driver and passenger.

"Whose is it?"

"It could be yours, or Eddie's. At least I think it could. Did we, I mean, did you take any precautions that night?"

"No, I thought you did." He lights up a cigarette. "Does Eddie know about me?"

I nod. "He's pissed, but I had to tell him the truth. Then I realized that I had to tell you, too. Even though it doesn't matter. I'm not going to have it."

Joel gnaws at a fingernail.

"He wants to get married," I ramble, "but not before I take a test to see who the father is. There's this test, DNA fingerprinting it's called. Cara told me about it. I'd need a sample of either your blood or Eddie's. Then they stick a needle in me and get something of the baby's. It's like matching parts of a zipper. It's 99.9 percent sure."

The driver swerves suddenly, throwing Joel and I against one another.

"I'd elope with you," he says, "but you'd bolt like Garbo."

"You're already married."

"So," he says, slipping the driver a five. "She told you. Keep the change."

"Thanks, buddy."

I'm a delayed-reactor. The full impact of what a little bastard Joel is doesn't hit me until we're halfway through stuffing our faces with pierogies. I had learned by then how Joel and Lori had met—when he was studying film at NYU; that she's seven years older than him; that Joel thought she was a knockout, and still cares for her. She'd wanted to live in America, and as a favor, he married her. In the beginning, they tried living together, but it didn't work. They fought all the time, threw things, which is what I want to do now, throw things.

After I dump the plate of pierogies in Joel's lap, I leave. It's dark out, and still pouring. There isn't a cab in sight. By some small miracle, one turns the corner, and I practically throw myself under it. Joel emerges from the restaurant, and gives chase. He's shouting something at me, but I can't make it out, can't tell if it's homicidal or suicidal, don't want to know. Mother never told me there'd be days like this.

CHAPTER TEN

The apartment looks like it's been ransacked.

Kithkat is playing with a small, white object. On closer inspection I see it's the Ping-Pong ball I'd given Eddie in college. The red lacquered I LOVE YOU rolls in and out of sight. I wonder how the cat got hold of it? Eddie must have taken it from the fornicating-octopus cup. I walk around the apartment retracing what I think are his steps, looking for clues as to his movements.

All I want to do is clean up the mess—of my living quarters and my life. When I turn on the vacuum, the kitten runs and hides. Curious, she reappears and makes tentative advances toward the machine. How monstrous it must appear. In a lightening gestalt I visualize what it would be like to have a baby in the house. Suddenly home appliances, electrical wires, wall sockets, high places, and kitchen utensils become menacing, unsafe. The entire complexion of life would shift and change. I would watch television with a censoring mind, and become shocked by rock lyrics, like my mother did, and her mother before her, wondering "what this generation is coming to." I wouldn't want my daughter to emulate Madonna, whose sexual self-parody is too subtle for prepubescent fans who take her seriously.

While carting the trash bags down the stairs, I bump into Mr. Hennessy, who tips his hat and makes way for me on the stairs. Mrs. Wallace and B. B. Ottermeyer are talking in a huddle. B. B. is wearing her usual dark glasses and bloodless smile.

When she sees me, she grins, then floats out the front door.

"I didn't mean to chase her away," I say.

"She's a little meshuggah," Mrs. Wallace says, shrugging.

"Spring cleaning?" she comments, eyeing the trashbags. The landlady interprets the clean-up campaign as a sign that Eddie is moving back. I don't have the heart to tell her that he's gone, probably for good. She'll figure it out by herself eventually.

Feeling faint, I collapse on the stairs.

"Aren't you feeling well?" Mrs. Wallace says.

"My knees just gave out."

Her beady eyes scope me from head to toe. Bruce, smelling the kitten on me, sniffs and growls. "You're too thin," Mrs. Wallace concludes. "You gotta eat more."

"Mrs. Wallace, if I ate any more they'd put me in the Guinness Book of World Records."

She doesn't get it.

Eddie used to quote Lennie Bruce when referring to our landlady. "All I can think of to say to her is 'Thank you,' and 'I've had enough to eat.' "

I hear the phone ringing, a good excuse to escape.

"Bye, Mrs. Wallace," I say, taking the stairs two at a time.

"The Feldstone-Kleins were broken into," she yells, after me. "Lock your door at night."

"Hello?"

"Rebeccah, it's Cara. Eddie's here. He's upset. Why don't you come over. Shel and I will disappear if you want to talk. Later, we can all go out for Chinese."

Before I head over to the Shelstein's and my appointment with destiny, I review my drawings from yesterday. This morning, a thousand years ago, Eddie had said that he liked them. I was surprised to discover how much his opinion of my work still matters to me. He gave me some good criticism for revisions.

The rain has let up. The city is shrouded in mist. Out of the darkness and fog I imagine Garbo, dressed in a mackintosh and rubber boots, trekking toward me. But it is the Garbo of yesteryear, the one that Cecil Beaton took photographs of eight years after she'd left Hollywood. Her face, while still beautiful, is beginning to age. The eyebrows are plucked, the mascara is heavy, the look is wan, pensive, still sphinx-like.

"Is that you, Rebeccah?" the fantasy-Garbo says. Her voice is low, coated with years of cigarette smoke and world-weariness.

"Yes, it's me."

We walk together along deserted streets. The streetlamps glow like freaky one-eyed guardians watching over us. Everything is black-and-white, and comes out of memory, mine. We are safe, enveloped by fog and an invisible, impenetrable boundary.

"What would you do?" I ask as we walk together side by side, comrades-in-arms against a prying, interfering world.

"Oh, what a dangerous responsibility it is." Her basso-profundo voice resonates compassion.

"What do you mean?"

She laughs, then says, "I am a misfit in life. Don't follow me. I follow the Fleet." She laughs some more, and says, "I have no belongings."

She quickens her pace.

"But people must belong to someone, to something," I say, straining to keep up with her.

"It's dangerous, dangerous," she repeats.

"But where are you going?" I call after her.

"To buy fertilizer."

Since this is my fantasy, I'm rather annoyed with how it turns out. Reluctant to go indoors, I encircle the block, trying to re-conjure the apparition of Garbo, but it won't come. It's gone. She will not be captured, not even by imagination. I want to ask her how she can value personal freedom and liberty to the exclusion of all else? I want to ask her if it's been worth it?

The Shelstein's living room, like their kitchen, is an eclectic mix of high-tech and retro. Cara re-upholstered the plush Queen

Anne couch inherited from her grandmother in a brightly patterned chintz. Eddie, Shel and Cara are sitting around the glass-
topped coffee table playing chess.

"Hi," they all say, as though I'd just returned from a beer run.
Unobtrusively, the Shelsteins leave Eddie and me alone.

"How's your hangover?" I ask.

"Better," he says. "What did you do today?"

I hesitate. He looks skyward, mumbles. "Oh, right." He takes
a deep breath, then says, "So? What was *his* reaction?"

"He took me out for pierogies."

For some reason this makes Eddie and me laugh. Joel is the
stranger, the foreigner, the outsider. Momentarily, he protects us
from ourselves and each other.

"When are you going back?" I ask.

"That depends."

Eddie is meticulously realigning the chess pieces on the board.

"Look, Rebeccah," he says, "I've been thinking it over, and
while I don't agree with you about our getting married, I think
we're both ready, but you just don't want to accept that fact for
some reason. No. Please. Let me finish. Forget marriage. If it's
marriage you object to, the hell with it. We don't need a license.
We have plenty of time for that. But I want this baby."

"Even if it's Joel's?"

He doesn't say anything. I don't say anything. I can hear Cara
and Shel, in the bedroom, not saying anything.

Looking for something, Eddie rifles under a stack of newspa-
pers and magazines. "Where is it? Ah, here it is."

He hands me a pamphlet about DNA fingerprinting.

"I know all about this."

"It's no big deal. I'm prepared to go with you tomorrow. We
can call the Runt tonight and ask him to accompany us, or give
us a blood sample."

"Don't call him the runt. And answer my question, Eddie.
What if I agree to do all this? What if it's Joel's baby? Then I can
get rid of it, right?"

"What the hell do you expect of me?"

"A lot less than you expect of me."

"You're so damn selfish. You won't compromise."

"I won't play dice with an unborn child's life."

"But you're willing to kill it?"

"Answer me this, Eddie. If the baby is not yours, do you care? Would you give it your love, and support? Because I would. If I had it I wouldn't care who the father is. This isn't some damn ego trip."

He glowers at me, and turns away.

"Would you be willing to stay home and take care of it?"

"Who'd pay the bills? You don't even have a job."

The missing pieces fall into place. Even when I was working full-time Eddie made more money than I did. The bottom line is inarguable, and so is the rage I feel over the whole lousy setup.

He's watching me, reading my mind.

"We're not a couple of penguins, Rebel," he says, alluding to our past fascination with the mating habits of penguins. Androgynous, both the male and female share equally in the care and feeding of their chicks. I pick up the phone.

"Who are you calling?"

"You'll see. May I please speak to Joel. No, it's important. Tell him Rebeccah is calling."

"Hang up the phone," Eddie barks just as Joel gets on.

"Duffy," he says, "this is a bad time."

"It's as good as any. I'm with Eddie. I have a question. What if this baby is yours?"

"I can't marry you."

"I know that."

"What is the little son of a bitch saying?" Eddie demands.

"Joel, answer me. What if it's yours?"

"Get Lori," he tells someone. "You picked some time for this," he says to me. Then, "Here, Lori wants to speak to you."

"Joel!?"

" 'Allo," she says, "Harriet?"

"Rebeccah," I correct.

"Pardon?"

123

"My name is Rebeccah."

"Oh." Then, "Joel and I have been discussing it, and we'd like very much to talk to you."

"We *are* talking."

"This is something more serious, not for the telephone. Can you come to my loft tomorrow, for dinner."

Eddie grabs the phone. "Hello," he barks. "Who's this? Who?" He can't believe his ears.

" 'Allo, 'allo?" Lori says.

"What do you want to talk about?" I ask.

"It is sensitive. Please. Tomorrow, for dinner."

"I don't know . . ."

"You think about it. Here, take the address, and my phone number."

I write it down.

"Let me know. Call me. I will wait."

We hang up.

Eddie, looking triumphant, says, "She said she's Joel's *wife?*"

"They want to talk to me."

"Rebeccah, wake up and smell the coffee."

"Eddie, I'm exhausted. I have to go. Can we continue this tomorrow. By the way, my parents are coming up. They'll be here at 10:00 A.M."

"I'll be on a plane."

"Where are you going?" Cara asks, emerging from the bedroom.

"Let her go," Eddie says. "She's running away. It's what she knows how to do best."

He should talk! His remark rankles. The more I think about it, the angrier I become. For the first time in my life I am making my own decisions, my own choices, following the dictates of my own conscience, and nobody, with the exception of M'Lou, wants to hear it. Both my parents think I've cracked up, Cara reserves judgment but I sense her disapproval, and Eddie calls it running away. He's the one who ran, not me. He put three thousand miles between us allegedly to get his head straight.

Before he left I was so immersed in our life together that I didn't know any better. I had a nine-to-five job with raises and promotions, a live-in boyfriend, and a future I thought I could depend upon.

Now I have Kithkat, who jumps up on my lap, purring, and a major headache. "Do you know who your parents are?" I ask it. In my next life, I want to be a cat. Cats are very Zen. They sleep when they're tired, eat when they're hungry, and plug in and out of your affection according to their immediate need.

"I'll be right back," I tell the kitten. "I have one more mile to go before I sleep tonight."

There's an all-night Korean deli on Columbus which sells just what I'm looking for.

A sleepy Cara, in a fuzzy pink bathrobe with matching slippers in the shape of bunny rabbits, lets me in.

"He's not doing too well," she says, alluding to Eddie. "We went out to dinner and he got drunk on plum wine."

Eddie's on the couch, with an arm flung over his face. His breathing is heavy, regular, but he's not snoring.

"How can he sleep at a time like this?" I ask.

"I think you two should seriously consider therapy," Cara suggests before disappearing into the sanctuary of her bedroom.

"Eddie," I say.

No answer. I can't tell if he's sleeping or playing possum.

"Eddie," I whisper close to his head, "only the camel knows the hundredth name of Allah."

Still nothing.

"I love you." The words, blurted, ring in my ears.

Still no response.

"I haven't told you that since we first came to New York. That's a long time ago. I love you, Eddie, but that's not enough. I know you won't believe this, but I look forward to the day when I'm a mother, and settle down, and go the whole nine yards. But I'm not ready to live on Sesame Street yet. And neither are you."

He still doesn't respond.

"There isn't anyone else. Joel is . . . an accident." He's also a lot of fun in an erratic, madcap kind of way, and an all-time prick, but I edit this out.

"Eddie, just because we're older doesn't mean that we're grown up."

Maybe he really is asleep?

"Okay, I made a mistake . . . several mistakes."

I want to pounce on him, rouse him, shake him.

"Eddie, I'm only, *we're* only, twenty-something. We're too young to turn into our parents. Remember how we vowed we'd never do that?"

Cara's apartment echoes the sounds of the city. I've learned to tell the difference between ambulance, police and fire engine sirens.

"You were a fool to drop out of architecture. I was a bigger fool to let you. We lost something, and neither one of us can get it back. Remember the great houses you were going to build for the masses? Remember the good designs I was going to create for the people who lived inside those houses? Remember how we were going to make a contribution? There's still time for us, Eddie, but we've got to work at it."

The lack of response is getting to me. It's like talking to the dead.

"When it comes down to it, Eddie, which do you care more about—me, the real me, or the me that you want me to be?"

I feel like a part of me is dying. It's strange.

"Octaman," I whisper and suddenly feel so sorry for him that tears well in my eyes. I sympathize with his rage, his frustration, his pain. How selfish he sees me as being, not to mention cowardly. I don't know how to explain that the opposite is true, or that at this point in our lives I'm not sure which is scarier: life with him or without him? This is the hardest decision I've ever had to make, and the urge to yield is so strong that I marvel at my ability to withstand it. It's like when I stood up to Magorian. The trapped osprey, its feet entangled by six-pack rings, still struggles to free itself, and haunts me at the most inopportune moments. I envision it flapping its wings, and hear it cry out. How I want to liberate this bird that has taken possession of me—or have I of it? Possessing the osprey in mind and memory, I can either grant it eternal victimization or eternal freedom. The power of this thought intoxicates. I want to pounce on Eddie, to wake him up and tell him the good news—that we're both free, free to choose or not to choose, but free! If only he'd release me from his memory. I am as constricted by his denial of, and resistance to, change as he is by my stubborn refusal to stay the same.

I dump the contents of the grocery bag on the floor. One by one I open the plastic bags and empty them over Eddie's long supine body, covering every inch of him with a blanket of dried garbanzo beans.

I've got to hand it to him, he still hasn't budged.

"Meditate on these," I say, when the last bean is in place, and leave.

BOOK
TWO

The Secret Place is hardly a secret anymore. I've been calling it that since I was a kid, and in a way that name still fits because few people know about the Henderson's mountain cabin retreat. I've spent happy summers here, and some sadder times, too—after my dog Murphy got hit by a truck, and Granpa Duffy died, and the summer before college, after I broke up with Jay in high school. Every Christmas I seem to bump into Jay at home. Once he was with his wife and baby daughter. The wife had a department store–cosmetic counter prettiness, and, Jay, once a star athlete, looked out of shape and bilious.

He introduced her to me.

We smiled at one another. She had tiny teeth, nice skin.

"Hello," I said.

"Hi," she said.

We've become nodding acquaintances in supermarkets. Every time I see her, I think, "That could have been me." It's always followed by a flood of relief.

Sometimes when I think about the past year it all seems like a weird movie, starring somebody else. Other times I'm so caught up in it that I can't function. Things got pretty bad in New York after Joel and I broke up. I'd get drunk and call M'Lou in the wee hours. One night she suggested that I come to the Secret Place, "to recover from your New York life."

I can see the snow-capped peak of Mount Davis from the cabin's front window. A brook-trout stream, a tributary of the Youghiogheny River, runs below the ridge where Jake and I used to go fishing. My old rod, fishing vest and waders still hang in the garage, alongside Jake's, and the sight of his gear makes me miss the big, lumbering Swede terribly.

The water by the house is knee-high but becomes treacherously deep as it heads north. Jake had taught me how to walk cautiously in the water, looking out for unsteady rocks and sudden falls. He taught me what brook trout like to eat, and how to tie dry flies, and about loop control and the different kinds of casting. He taught me how to use heavy leaders, and how to fish upstream, and to watch for mucky banks that are clustered with deadfalls.

The warmer weather melts the winter's accumulated snow cover, making the streams flow high and muddy. In mountainous country the runoff can be severe, and most fishermen tend to ignore the stream during runoff, preferring to wait for the more or less ideal conditions of midsummer and fall. But some good trout fishing can be had during the runoff, and not just on bait either. Even fly fishermen—those notorious "gin clear water" fanatics—can do well.

Spring thaw in the Secret Place begins gradually, and picks up speed. By mid-May, the streams have become muddy and start to swell toward their high-water marks, when the water looks "too thick to drink and too thin to plow." One of the best ways to approach a stream in runoff is to fish it deep with nymphs.

The resinous mountain air distills ozone, and like Emily Dickinson, I am inebriate of it, taking deep inhalations. The water is cold, almost too cold to enter, but I feel determined. Bucking the rushing water is rough at first, but the longer I stand my ground, the better I feel. It's better than bucking the rushing back-currents of my mind.

My parents blame me for Eddie, and our breakup. Their sympathies reside with him. That hurts, because the least I'd expected from them is complete understanding, *un*conditional love, the works. I read somewhere that the first condition of motherhood (which includes fatherhood) is of *not* murdering the baby. When I read that, I thought, *Whaaat?* But apparently this murderous impulse to stifle forever the squalling cries of a demanding infant is more common than most people would care to admit. Once you get over that hump, then you bring up the baby, nurture and guide it as best you can.

I think all three desires—to kill, comfort, and tell me what to do—were operative the day I met my folks for breakfast in their hotel suite, a dreary Monday morning.

"Where's Eddie?" dad asked.

"He left," I said.

"What do you mean he left?"

When I was little I loved to hunt for the monograms on my father's shirts. He had discovered ingenius places to put them— on the cuffs, the collar, different parts of the shirttail. How I wanted to play hunt-the-monograms that morning, and forget all the other stuff.

"I mean, he went back to California. I told him you were coming, but he left anyway. He said he had to get back . . ."

"Don't talk to me in that tone of voice."

There was a knock on the door. Saved by Room Service. The attendant set up. The smell of coffee and bacon started me salivating.

"Hmmn, that smells good," I said, spearing a piece of melon with my fork.

After the attendant left, all hell broke loose. Dad wanted a detailed explanation of Eddie's absence. My mother commiserated with my father, and I got indigestion. Was it my imagination, or were we all taking out our frustration on the hotel china? Someone listening at the door would have sworn from the mad clinking sounds that we were dueling with knives and forks.

"Rebeccah," my mother said, slipping into her haute-Virginia mode, "there's no point in owah being heah without Eddie."

"I know that, Mom, but I couldn't make him stay. Can I have your bacon?" She always orders it then eats less than half.

"We'll order more bacon if you want it," Dad said.

He was pissed, and I couldn't blame him. I felt more sorry for them than for myself—for the futility and pathos of their visit. Mom's hair needed refrosting. She was beginning to look root-y. Dad's dry look wasn't holding up. Hair, usually mine, has always been a focus of my mother's. If it's long she wants me to cut it, if it's short, she wants me to grow it long. Once she brought home stuff that guaranteed to straighten it. This time she criticized my hair for being "out of control." Even I had to admit that it looked like an unruly mane of knots.

"You need to do something about your hair," she said, more than once that morning.

"So do you," I thought, and bit my tongue.

I can't remember my mother without a lace, perfumed handkerchief, and couldn't tell at one point if she was crying over the state of my life or my locks.

"Where did we go wrong?" she asked repeatedly, burying her face in the hanky.

My father began to yell at me. He called me selfish and inconsiderate and obstreperous. His words stung. After he got it all out, he busied himself with idle pursuits: counting the change in his pocket, rearranging the cufflinks in his shirt cuff, paring his nails with a pocket knife.

Gargantuan and contrite, I hovered over Val, saying, "Please don't cry" and "It's not as bad as it seems" in a vain attempt to mollify her. Gradually, she got a grip on herself.

My parents' visit didn't accomplish much except to prove that they cared. They each viewed my reluctance to make a commitment to Eddie as symptomatic of deeper problems—shadowy realms of self they were reluctant to exhume. They wondered why I, like so many of my generation, couldn't embrace both love and work, career and motherhood. Most people know and accept the fact that life is compromise. What was wrong with me?

"Look, I can't do it all," I said. "I don't even want it all, at least not all at once. I value sleep too much, and privacy."

"You have resources, Rebeccah," Dad said.

"You could have help," Mom said.

"I'm just not ready."

They lapsed into an aggrieved silence.

"This whole thing is a mistake," I said.

"We thought we could help, honey," Mom said.

"I don't mean you, or your coming, the pregnancy."

"What exactly did Eddie say?" Dad asked.

"Eddie is part of the problem, not the solution. Look," I began, in earnest, "it's not Eddie I'm rejecting, it's the whole deal. Weddings are so humorless. Did you know that the only reason brides wear white is because Queen Victoria did. So it became the fashion. Why women continue to emulate that dowdy old queen I'll never know. If I ever marry it will be in living color."

"I swear I don't know where she gets her ideas from," Mom said. Then, "Were your father and I such bad examples?"

"Even if I wanted to marry Eddie now, it wouldn't work. We don't seem to get along anymore. He's changed."

"So have you."

"We all change. Isn't that what life is about? Change? I need time to work things out."

"Your father and I have been talking, and we'd be willing to pay for a good psychotherapist."

"I don't need a shrink, I need an abortionist."

"I always knew your stubbornness would get you into trouble one day."

It was useless, hopeless. We were talking to one another across a generational abyss. I'd never be able to alter their opinion that my refusal to embrace their traditional values was anything more than some mule-headed trait I'd inherited from their combined gene pool. I tried to explain that you can't expect someone who feels untoward relief when she returns rental videocassettes and library books to commit overnight to marriage and babies. I tried to share with them my design ideas, and my desire to return to school to learn more about graphics, and interior and jewelry design. I spoke to them of my need to travel, to expand my knowledge of myself and the world. There are more important things than biological imperatives, reproduction, and convention—at least to me. While I dreaded my parents' disapproval, it felt good at last to speak my mind.

Thinking it would cheer them up, I recounted all the synchronicitous events that had led me to IKAIA, and the impending job interview.

"Will you have to move to Philadelphia?" Mom asked.

"I don't know. I've been so busy getting a portfolio together I haven't given it much thought."

"It's about time you stopped living in the clouds," my father said.

Seeing red, I said, "What if I decided to have this baby on my own?"

My mother gasped.

"You're pushing it," he warned.

This was an old argument. He thought that people like Jessica Lang and Susan Sarandon who had babies out of wedlock were acting irresponsibly, creating bad role models for poor black girls. I pointed out that poor black girls don't usually emulate rich white movie stars. It was girls like me that he had to worry about.

We locked eyes, like horns. Originally, Dad was the one who'd noticed and encouraged my mechanical ability. Mom always thought it was something I'd outgrow, like climbing trees. Against her wishes, he bought me an erector set. I am in large part his creation. Neither of us thought we'd see the day when the pluck he'd ingrained in me would turn against him.

I saw his pride in me clash with his growing disapproval, and something else, something rueful and plaintive.

The first to back down, I said, "Don't worry. It'll never happen."

"It wouldn't be the first time in the family," Mom quipped, recovering. Cousin Aileen's thirty-year-old illegitimate son, who'd tracked her down, was now causing the family grief.

"None of that would matter if I was ready," I said.

"You keep talking about this being 'ready.' What's that mean exactly?" Mom asked.

"I'd want to give any child of mine *more*, not less, of myself. Right now I only have less—less in terms of a self, and of time. I need more experience, to live more."

"Honey, don't you think you're a little too old to be sowing wild oats?"

"I'd rather be single and unfaithful than married and unfaithful."

My father looked up from his study of the hotel rug pattern. Val's mouth opened, forming a perfect little "O." I regretted my outburst instantly. I could never be bad like my brother Brad; I can't stand the idea of deliberately hurting either of my parents. It kills me. Their vulnerability is too obvious. Now, I thought, is the time to tell them about Joel. But what would be the point? I feared exacerbating my father's temper and my mother's distress. Besides, Joel was history. I never wanted to see him again.

There was a knock on the door. The waiter came to collect the dirty dishes. My father stood, stretching his long legs.

"Let's get some fresh air," he said. "Nothing we can say will amount to a hill of beans anyway."

It was good to escape the hotel room. Dad steered us to Fifth Avenue where we joined the throng of busy shoppers and workers on their lunch hour. He said that he'd honor my decisions whether he agreed with them or not, and he made it clear that he did not. I felt panic snake its way through my gut. Wedged between them, I grabbed each parent by an arm, hanging on.

"I'm so glad you came."

"I can think of more fun times we've had," Mom said.

We wound up walking aimlessly around the gaudy pink marble lobby of the Trump Tower. I felt worse and worse. I chastised myself for being selfish, and considered relenting, surrendering to their will, anything to be back in their good graces. Switching gears, I rationalized by telling myself I'd been on my own for years. I didn't need their support, either emotionally or financially.

My parents were chatting about taking in a Broadway play. I'd forgotten that I'd already made plans for the evening. Without thinking, I blurted that I was busy. Before I could recant, it was too late. My mother's face collapsed into a pool of injured feelings. My father shook his head and said that he never thought he'd live to see the degree of disrespect that I was displaying that day. I started to cry, to blubber like a baby. I apologized for the mess I'd made of my life, and theirs, for disappointing them, for the hurt I'd caused them, for living. But I didn't back down, not even during the worst of it.

Mortified by this public display, my parents each grabbed an elbow and steered me back to the Wyndham Hotel. We talked some more. They tried to comfort me. I tried to comfort them. We were all pretty uncomfortable. The paradox of being a parent is that you have to maintain a balance between two compelling but opposing drives: egotism and altruism. There's a fine line between guidance and governance, and in the end I admired their self-control.

They decided to return home that evening. Dad rented a car to take them to the airport and I went along. I could sense their relief, duty done, to be going home. Mom insisted that she fly up to be with me for the abortion, but I could tell that it was the last thing in the world that she wanted to do.

"The whole thing takes about ten minutes," I said. "Let's talk about it tomorrow. I'll call you."

I hugged each one tightly. They looked a handsome, if oddly matched, pair. Next to Mom, his little gem, Dad is a giant.

We waved goodbye madly. I learned a lot that day—more about parenting than any of us had bargained on. My mother's last words were, "Be sure to get a haircut, honey. It looks like a rat's nest."

I don't know why I decided to accept Lori Biro's dinner invitation. Even as I gave the driver her address, I equivocated. I almost called out my own street number, but something stopped me. Curiosity was not the least of what I felt. I was buoyed by a self-confidence that bordered on the glandular. I was on my own now, captain of my fate, master of my destiny. What harm was there in spending a few hours with this woman? What could she possibly say or do to fracture further my already fractured world? Whatever it was, I was hellbent on finding out.

Lori lived in a huge, renovated loft in a delapidated Lower East Side neighborhood that made me fear for my life just scanning the building numbers. A toothless old man, who couldn't or wouldn't speak English, pointed to a building which turned out to be hers.

Lori buzzed me in. I climbed stairs in need of repair, and full of debris, expecting the worst. The door opened, and I gasped in pleasant surprise. Huge, the place resembled a small modern art museum. Paintings lined the walls, and sculpture was placed strategically along the floor. Sections of the loft had been partitioned by clever arrangements of furniture, bookcases, and sculpture, including a beautiful lacquered Chinese screen. The floors had been scraped, sanded and polished with polyurethane into a high gloss, the walls painted stark white. Natural light filtered through cathedral windows. Custom-made window bars adorned the outside. Pale pink shades made out of cloth sat at half-mast and cast a warm glow over the room. A complicated network of track lighting, regulated with a dimmer, traversed the length of the loft. Above the lights a grid of pipes and tubes had been painted in gleaming silver and red.

One piece, a triptych, caught my eye.

"Do you like that?" she asked.

"I don't know. It's . . ."

"I know. Everyone reacts to it in one way or another. Do you know Hieronymus Bosch? His 'Garden of Earthly Delights?' "

I nodded.

"This is a modern version."

"Did you do it?"

She looked wistful. "No, a friend."

The painting overflowed with meticulously oil-painted scenes of sexual and psychic depravity. The participants looked like they derived no pleasure from their actions, no delight whatsoever, just pure mechanical lust, obsessive probing and delving. Depressing, I thought, looking away, but during the course of the evening I'd return to the painting, as if to memorize it. Many of the pieces in the loft bore sexual themes, some erotic, others pornographic, but none as disturbing as the updated Bosch.

By the end of the evening I'd begun to feel like one of those creatures in the painting. A woman of tremendous will and energy, Lori had set out to seduce me into accepting the offer she was about to make, but first the calf had to be fattened. I was plied with delicious food—Hungarian appetizers whose names I couldn't pronounce—attention, and good conversation. She's an accomplished artist with a vast range of knowledge about her craft. She works in steel, and huge pieces with weird shapes and configurations cut out of them hung on the walls. There were also sculptures that looked like the missing pieces from the wall hangings. She cut them out with a blowtorch, "like cutting paper dolls," she said.

"Why steel?"

She shrugged, as if to say, why not? "I've worked with wood, plastic, acrylics, oil, bronze, clay, marble, stone. I like steel best because it is . . . friendly to me."

I asked her to explain further. She hesitated. "It is pliant yet indestructible. I like that."

"Come," she said, "I'll give you a tour."

She showed me some new acquisitions, large, abstract watercolors awash in wild colors expressive of what looked like male and female genitals. I began to have that queasy feeling I get when I'm in situations that I know are way over my head, and wondered for the umpteenth time what the hell I was doing there.

I've seen several movies about women who are in love with the same man who attempt to befriend one another. I realize now that my curiosity stemmed from insecurity. I compared myself to her, measuring, weighing, judging. She was more Joel's body type than I was. They were both slight, wiry, kinetic while I was long and lanky. As the evening progressed, I found myself studying her more and more from Joel's point of view. Lori exuded sensuality and magnetism. She had the kind of face easy to imagine in the throes of sexual passion. I saw what Joel saw in her, but what, I wondered, does she want from me? His conspicuous absence reminded me constantly of his presence. While helping her to set the table I asked as casually as possible whether or not he was coming?

She made a Mittel-European sound, like "Ach," as if to say, "Who knows?"

"Doesn't that bother you?"

"He may come, he may not. It makes it more interesting, no?"

"No, I mean, it would drive me mad."

"He's very good at that," she agreed.

Was she so sure of him, of their love, that she could afford to share him with other women? She should be poisoning my food, and tearing out her hair, or mine, not serving me dinner.

"People don't live this way," I thought, "except on the Oprah Winfrey show."

Lori's personality and lifestyle both attracted and repelled me. Like a tightly wound spring, I found myself coiling and recoiling all evening long, spiraling in and out of like and dislike, acceptance and disdain. If she noticed, she never showed it. Over dinner we kept the conversation light, chatting about everything from cooking to zits. While I had little to share on the former, I shone expertly on the latter. The way she overcomplimented my complexion made me nervous. Perhaps I'd imagined it, but there was a sexual overtone, and I thought instantly of the Bosch-like painting with its incriminating weirdness.

"American women are spoiled," Lori decreed. "You have everything, so you want more. Everything must be perfection. This is not possible, no?"

"Yes. I mean no, I guess not."

"Please, don't misunderstand. I love this country, and I am the first to try a new hair color."

We both laughed. Hennaed to the hilt was how I described her coif to Cara.

After dinner, we sipped decaf cappuccino on the plush leather couch, whose soft folds enveloped me. I felt inundated, and yet there was more. I think I knew what was coming before she said it. She'd been hinting at it all night long by small acts of omission. Not offering me alcohol was the biggest tip-off. Why would she be so solicitous of my condition if she didn't have some kind of vested interest? But first there was the prelude. In far more detail than I cared to hear, I learned of how she and Joel had first met. They were standing in the registration line at New York University.

"It was love at first sight," she said, her eyes glassy with remembrance. "He looked like a young James Dean, sexy, moody, vulnerable. I had to know him, to speak to him. I asked to borrow a pencil, which he didn't have, so we looked for one together."

That was over ten years ago. The fact that she was seven years older than he was of no consequence to either of them.

"He was, how do you say, a diamond in the buff."

"You mean 'rough,' " I corrected, laughing.

"Yes."

Thinking himself the next Martin Scorsese, Joel was studying filmmaking, and Lori, who'd earned herself a scholarship, was working on final credits toward a Ph.D. in fine arts. She could barely speak English then, and he got a kick out of her malapropisms which he jotted down in a little book: "He treated me as a leopard," "I had to sleep in a yamulke," "She is very bush."

"I entertained him," she said, and it was a source of pride.

When her visa was up, she returned to Paris. He visited her. She wanted to live in America but couldn't get a work permit. As a favor, Joel married her, I guess for the entertainment value as much as anything else. That they are still married has become a small miracle in their eyes. Each cherishes his and her autonomy, but is still committed to the other.

She began to speak in tautologies. "We are committed without being totally committed. The best of both worlds, no? We are a married couple and still independent."

She made it all sound so simple, so natural. I felt like a hick from the hills.

Throughout her tale, Lori poured me cup after cup of decaffeinated coffee, but my brain crackled and sizzled like it was full of loose wires. She spoke, I listened. I wanted to scream, "Enough," but instead sat quietly, skewered with curiosity. I heard about Joel's brief stint as a filmmaker. When he despaired of being the next boy-wonder director, she suggested that he make good use of his waitering experience and open up a restaurant. A co-partner, she put a lot of her own money into the business, which was beginning to net a profit.

My eyelids began to feel heavy, and flutter. Under Lori's true grit lurked a lot of darker passions—possessiveness, acquisitiveness, control. I felt myself becoming entangled in her web and wished she'd get to the point. When she did, I wished she hadn't.

"I cannot have children," she said. "It is my one regret."

She viewed my pregnancy as a good omen, a godsend. She wanted to become the adoptive mother of Joel's baby which she presumed I was carrying. Cara said that I may have imagined the ménage à trois allusion, but I don't think so.

When I studied chemistry in college I learned about how certain cements are mixed with argillaceous and calcareous substances that are cooked and fused, then ground to a fine, powdery dust. That's how I felt after I'd left Lori, like a pile of fine, powdery dust. Emotionally, I had been ground into a powder so fine that it would have floated if sprinkled on hot, humid air. The least little wind would disperse it forever. I arose to go. The staccato pitter-patter of her high heels followed.

"I don't mean to insult you," she said. "It is something to think about, no? There are stranger things in this world."

I couldn't answer, except to thank her for the dinner.

Earlier, I'd written down the recipe for chicken paprika and stuffed it into my shoulder bag.

The sun is a bright white dot punched out of a hazy, marbleized sky.

Realigning the visor over my eyes, I recast the line, flipping the weighted nymph rig far enough upstream from the run that it has time to sink to the bottom. Jake taught me to fish on a line tight enough to indicate strikes, but slack enough so that the nymph drifts naturally.

"Woolly buggers," he used to call the best nymphs for off-color waters, or "woolly worms."

I've known a few woolly buggers and worms in my life.

Some birds are flying up above—I can't tell if they're ospreys, mergansers, herons or eagles, all predators of the trout. The birds here fly high and free. One, an osprey, swoops down and snatches at the water and comes up with a large trout in its claw. Must be fish down there. I reel in the line and flip the woolly worm anew, my thoughts returning to Joel.

He was waiting for me after I'd left Lori's. Chain-smoking cigarettes in the doorway of her building, wearing dark glasses, acting *louche*.

"*You*," I spat when I saw him.

"I had nothing to do with it," he said, falling into step alongside me. "I told her that her offer to turn you into a Mary Beth Whitehead would be futile, that you'd never go for it. I couldn't talk her out of it. You saw how she is."

He grabbed my arm.

I jerked it away and quickened my pace.

"Listen, Duffy. Stop. Just give me a few minutes. I care about you. I care what happens. Gimme a break."

Why did I do it? Why did I stop? Is this weakness that women have for men, this tendency to yield, atavistic? Does it spring from some primitive reflex of self-preservation? Or is it a socialized reaction?

"How about a cup of coffee?" he asked.

I shook my head no.

"Okay, let's walk. Let's go to our special place."

We trekked up York Avenue to Garbo's neighborhood. It was the first that I'd known that Joel considered it "special." He talked the entire way up, filling in the spaces that Lori had left blank. He explained how uprooted her life had been. Her parents were landed gentry, some minor Hungarian nobility. From the way he spoke, I could tell how impressed he was with her blue blood. When the Nazis came in, Lori's father was forced to give up their home and land.

"Ah," I thought, "that explains the love of steel."

The Biros returned to Hungary just in time for the Communist takeover. Heartbroken, her father died. She, her ailing mother, and two younger sisters moved to Paris permanently. Lori worked in a textiles factory, waitressed in restaurants, did secretarial work, you name it, to help support them all. She went to night school to study art, and finally achieved a doctorate in fine arts. He painted the picture of a woman of indefatigible energy and determination. He bragged about her talent as an artist, her shrewdness as a businesswoman. But I'd had enough of Lori for one lifetime, and of Joel, too.

"Look," I said, "I'm tired."

Why was I always searching for nonexistent taxis in Joel's presence?

"Listen, you've got to hear me out."

"I want to go home."

He grabbed my arm and propelled me toward a park bench. Every now and then he'd glance around, as if he thought someone was following us. His illicit behavior, the danger implicit in it, gave me a curious rush. The back of my neck and scalp tingled.

Still talking, Joel lit up another cigarette. He wanted me to believe that his marriage to Lori was nothing more than a convenient arrangement, a social, not a love, contract.

"Stop bullshitting me. She means more to you than that."

"Of course she does, and so do you, but she's European."

"What's that suppose to mean?"

"She understands men."

"She *what?* Are you serious? I can't believe this. For the past couple of days I've been besieged by people staking a claim to my life, and I've had just about enough. Eddie wants me pregnant and barefoot in the kitchen. My parents want me to marry and become respectable. Your wife has just made me an offer of surrogate motherhood. Don't talk to me about *understanding men.* Frankly, I don't give a damn about understanding you right now."

"Lori can't have kids. Maybe it's her age, but it's making her nuts."

I made a sound, a cross between a scream and a sob, and rose to go. He pulled me back, and held onto me tightly.

"I'm sorry, Duffy," he murmured against my hair and shoulder and the crook of my neck. "I'm really sorry." Then, "I missed you. You're the greatest thing that ever happened to me. I need you."

His words snaked through me like one of those bullets that are supposed to keep going once inside, ripping through your organs. I breathed in his soft, talcum-powder smell. His breath was warm against my cheek. I wanted to believe him. We kissed, a sweet, lingering kiss, using our mouths as antennas to sense one another's receptivity. I was the first to pull away. There were too many loose ends, too many unanswered questions.

"Why didn't you tell her about Eddie?"

"Is he still here?"

But I didn't want to talk about Eddie, not with him.

"Give me one of those," I said.

"You don't smoke."

"I do now."

Before he could light my cigarette, I lipped it first, then placed it in his mouth.

"Oh, yeah," Joel said, remembering—Garbo and Gilbert in *Flesh and the Devil*.

I cupped my hand sensually over his as he lit the cigarette. He took a long, seductive drag than placed it between my lips.

"Do you think she's home?" I asked.

"Who?"

"Garbo."

He laughed, and shook his head, as if to say, "What a strange bird you are, Duffy."

His eyes probed mine like he was searching for something deep and special. Joel always acted confident in his evaluation of me, like he saw things nobody else did, like he *understood*, and I found this irresistible. How many people find others who reflect their narcissism so perfectly?

"Answer me something," he said. "From the first day we met I've wondered why Garbo? Why not Monroe or Vivien Leigh? I asked myself, 'Why does she identify with someone who walks such a singular path, whose life is so mournful?' "

"Monroe and Leigh were victims, Garbo isn't."

"Isn't she?"

I thought about this. I'm still thinking about it. But I memorized every word that Joel uttered that night. He said he thought my obsession with Garbo masked a die-hard romantic who prefers fantasy to reality. He saw my admiration of the Swedish actress as more than a little melancholy.

"You got any Scandinavian blood?"

"Not a drop. Some American Indian, on my father's side."

"That might explain some things, not others. It's an ego thing," he said.

"What is?"

"The need to deify other human beings. Did you ever wonder about it? I used to, a lot. First we worshipped animated spirits, and these turned into gods and goddesses who lived on a mountain top and mirrored our behavior. We're still doing it. Hollywood has become Olympus. Don't you see it? Your crush on Garbo is an ego trip with something extra."

"What's the extra?"

This launched him. As far as I could tell from what he said, the "extra" was the reciprocal relationship between the fan's admiration of and identification with the star. It's all a projection. Whatever it was that I loved about Garbo, I possessed within myself. My adulation was a weird kind of self-love. Joel said he wanted to encourage it, but he also wanted to destroy it because it was threatening to him, to men.

He accused me of being ambitious, desirous of the extraordinary, but I was hampered by my bourgeois upbringing. That's probably the most honest thing he said that night. What a smooth talker—glib, articulate, eloquent in the vernacular. I could have listened to him forever. He said I had a need to create my own myths, my own mystery, and I believed him, but he was talking about his need more than mine. I'd had no idea then how far into his personal life his entrepreneurial drive extended. Every man chooses the woman whose ideal he secretly covets. Transvestites and female impersonators act this out literally. Other than sexual, I'd never been the object of a man's fantasy before, his feminine ideal, except that I wasn't Joel's, not yet. Pygmalion had only just begun to shape his Galatea. He continued to feed my engorging ego by comparing me with a young Garbo. Then he started talking about virgins, and I questioned his sanity.

"I'm no virgin!"

"Oh, but you are. Not the wimpy, passive, hysterical virgin of today, but the one of ancient times. She was strong, powerful, self-possessed. Like Garbo. Don't you get the feeling that no matter how many people she fucks, she's always virginal?"

"I've never thought about it."

To conquer the virgin of Joel's imagination was both the seduction and the destruction of that which made her compelling, and the ultimate challenge. If I'd listened with my head instead of my heart I would have foreseen the entire blueprint of our relationship, but I was too distracted, too seduced. Everything else receded—my parents' visit, Lori's proposition, Eddie's rage, even my dilemma. All that existed was Joel, and his hypnotic voice, which penetrated inside me, deeper than sex. Without skipping a beat, he switched the subject to himself, and talked confessionally, sharing his feelings, his fears, his dreams. These reached out like invisible tendrils to embrace me.

There are no shortcuts to true intimacy, but I didn't know that then. No sensors had alarmed me to the incursion of Joel into my soul. I sat spellbound, in a state of delayed excitation, feeling more sexually aroused than I had ever remembered. In Tantric yoga the delay of orgasm is said to inversely increase its pleasure. I restrained myself from touching him, because even the slightest touch would set me off.

My body tensed, my breath quickened. I'd forgotten the cigarette, which had burned itself out between my fingers. I watched the last of its languorous smoke drift over the sound of his voice, toward the opaque, starless sky. I felt that I was free-falling through space, and had begun orbiting a black hole, a massive star which has collapsed inward at the speed of light. If it's true that the center of the universe is a black hole, and that the universe is contracting, not expanding, then we are all falling inexorably towards its vortex. The gravity of a black hole is so powerful that nothing which has crossed a certain point can return once it has entered. I had already passed the point of no return. It was too late to pull back. The last of my resistance dissolved in his embrace. His lips brushed mine, and became like suction. I remember wondering, "Who kissed the first kiss and tasted not of flesh but infinity?" I no longer cared about what we were doing, or where we were doing it, or who might have been watching.

"Hush," he said, "hush," when my cries became too loud.

I often think of that night with both fear and longing. Instead of stars, the sky became embedded with thousands of staring eyes looking down on us, but these only heightened the pleasure of my abandonment. I learned a lot about myself with Joel, not all of it good, or pleasant, but now that it's over I have no regrets. It was like the first time I tried a hallucinogenic drug, or backpacking in the mountains. After it was all over, I was glad I'd done it.

CHAPTER THIRTEEN

There's a tug on the line. I reel it in, bracing the fishing-rod against my gut. This is a big one. Excited, I strain to keep the line tight, then it goes slack. Every angler has a saga about the One That Got Away. This is mine.

In retrospect, I'm surprised that Joel and I weren't arrested for lewd behavior. We wound up in his apartment. I couldn't get enough of him. Winthrop barked and dogged us in every room, but this time I didn't care. Joel said that he hadn't had this much gonadal capacity since puberty. It lasted throughout the night and well into the next day, and the next. Between appointments he'd rush home to make love, change his clothes, and run out again. Watching him select what to wear became a highlight of my day. He had various costumes for various parts he liked to play. There was the arty entrepreneur who dressed in T-shirts and Giorgio Armani suits; the cowboy in fringed suede jacket and Tony Lama lizard boots; and his favorite, the punk rebel in a motorcycle jacket and jeans. I was content to let him go because I knew he'd come back to me, often several times a day. (I felt like Ann-Margaret lusting after Jack Nicholson in *Carnal Knowledge*.) Instead of a slip, I hung around the house in my underwear and one of his shirts. I was overcome by a lassitude born of sensuality and heat. A few weeks, a month, a year of this and I would become as fleshbound and indolent as an odalisque.

The third night he suggested that we go out, and I was crestfallen. Why wasn't his abandonment as total as mine? Why wasn't he as ready as I to forsake everything and everyone in deference to our ardor? It was Joel who awakened me from my supineness, reminding me that I had more pressing concerns. He offered to come with me to the abortion clinic, and I couldn't figure out his motive. Was it out of sympathy and guilt, or to taunt Lori? He assured me that she'd taken my rejection of her proposal with the fatalism of a Shiite Moslem. But she didn't strike me as someone who would take no graciously. He assured me that with regard to our affair, she closed one eye and turned the other way.

Cara said that I'd fallen in with a pair of sadomasochists.

"Then what does that make me?"

The question hung in the air, where, presumably, it's still flapping in the breeze. Joel drew out a part of me that I'd suspected existed, but had submerged. The sybarite and the puritan live in eternal conflict. Sinner and saint each demand a sacrifice of the other. Who said "the road of excess leads to the palace of wisdom"? Was it William Blake? Doing anything in excess undermines health and sanity, but if you can survive you come out ahead. Joel became my drug, my opiate. Addiction eats you up, and steals energy for other pursuits, people, responsibilities. I want to say that Joel threw me off balance, but he only helped. I did all the rest.

I don't know what I would have done without Cara who, despite her exasperation with me, never flagged in her concern. She reassured Val that the abortion took about eighty-five seconds, and the worse I'd feel physically was cramps. There was no reason for her to fly up unless she really felt it was necessary. Mom worried that I'd be attacked by fanatical right-to-lifers or that the clinic would be razed in the midst of the procedure.

"Don't worry, Mrs. Duffy," Cara said, "this is New York City."

That was her stock answer for every contingency. Val and I stayed in telephone contact, which was best because emotionally I couldn't have handled her being around. Afterward, so many mixed feelings came into play: relief that it was over accompanied by futile regret that it had to happen in the first place. The people at the clinic couldn't have been nicer, or more compassionate. I wondered why I felt so badly? Cara, whose grasp of sexual politics is far greater than mine, explained it all to me as we plowed through a couple of quarts of Heavenly Hash ice cream back at my apartment.

"How can something so personal and private arouse such a public outcry?" I asked.

"It depends on who you talk to, but it has a lot to do with power and control."

We delved into the irony of our situations. Cara wanted desperately to have a baby. She'd given up caffeine and nicotine because she'd read that each affects the chances of getting pregnant. She confided that she and Shel had gone for tests, and it was discovered that his sperm was malformed.

"How awful," I said. "Poor Shel."

"It's not as bad as immobile sperm, or too few. There's this procedure, it's still in the experimental stage. The doctor removes the eggs from my uterus and creates a tiny opening. This gives the sperm bigger odds of breaking through. It's all done in a laboratory. The fertilized eggs are returned to the womb till term."

"Are you going to do it?"

"It's not 100 percent sure, but then nothing is. Shel and I want to go for it."

My eyes welled with tears. "Oh, Cara," I said.

"Yeah, I know. Life's a bitch."

The doorbell rang. It was Joel bearing flowers, two dozen roses. Although he'd tried his damnedest to charm her, Joel's attempts produced only borderline civility. He insisted on arranging the bouquet in a vase himself, and his knack intrigued me. I watched, fascinated, as he carefully selected each stem, which he then examined and trimmed, all with an incongruous delicacy of movement. I'd seen this quiet grace before. It was usually reserved for more intimate moments, and always held me in thrall. While he worked, he talked amiably about the zealousness for flowers possessed by all Polish people.

"In Poland, people would rather go without food than flowers. My father loved them. Give him a paper cup and some dirt and he'd create a garden. He taught me the language of flowers. Everybody knows that roses stand for love, but there are over a hundred varieties of rose, and each has its own nuance of meaning. There's even a rose that symbolizes war. These are red and white cabbage roses. The cabbage rose is an emissary, an ambassador. Deep red ones represent the blush of first love, and white stands for worthiness."

"They're beautiful," I said.

"I'm allergic," Cara said, sneezing.

None of his winsomeness worked on her. She mistrusted him, and that made him try harder. She warned me repeatedly that he was bad news and to dump him. To me it seemed like I was always in the process of dumping Joel, but he was undumpable.

"I can see what you see in him," she said, after he'd left, "but what do you see in him?"

"Sex."

She thought about that for a minute. "I used to date a guy. It was pure sex. I saw him, I melted. My knees weakened, you know, the whole schmear. He married someone else. I married someone else. I saw him recently. Not with his wife, with some young girl. He was obviously putting all his moves on her. My knees still weakened when I looked at him, but I'm sure glad I didn't marry him."

Cara holds men the way Louis Armstrong held music: there's good and there's bad. She thinks you marry the good ones, and you get rid of the bad ones before they get rid of you. When I was around Joel I didn't know whether to reform, mother, or fuck him. He had that kind of effect on me. Obviously, Cara was immune, but then she was five years older and happily married—

154

although she didn't see what one had to do with the other. She chastized me for dumping Eddie for Joel.

"That's not true," I said. "I didn't dump Eddie for Joel. It just seemed to happen that way."

She grunted. We were still lounging on the couch in a state of insulin overload from the ice cream.

"Do you think people are capable of loving more than one person at a time?" I asked.

"No."

"I'm not so sure. I love Eddie, and I want Joel, and maybe that could turn into something deeper. I saw my mother making it with a strange man once, like she really meant it. I'll never forget it. She never acted that way with my father."

"At least not that you ever saw."

"Do you believe in monogamy?"

"What is this?" Cara said, rolling her eyes.

"I don't know if I do."

"Free love isn't practical," she said, scraping the sides of the carton with her finger and licking it.

"I think Moses figured that out. That's why he came up with the Ten Commandments, to keep everybody in line while crossing the desert."

"You've been reading too much D. H. Lawrence. You sound like some kind of dipshit hippie."

Sounding like one and acting like one were two different things, and I know that my affair with Joel became reprehensible in Cara's eyes. His intrusion into my life began to interfere with our friendship. She didn't approve, and I hadn't realized how much I had relied on her approval until she withdrew it. To my knowledge alienation is not integral to autonomy, but that's how I felt; and misunderstood. Like Garbo, I didn't want to *be* alone, but to be *left* alone, to my own devices. I sure got my wish. I was as azygous as an amoeba. Cara stopped calling, and my parents escaped with their cronies on a long cruise to the Florida Keys, where they made an occasional ship-to-shore phone call.

Every student of science knows that nature abhors a vacuum.

So apparently did Joel, who'd rushed me in those early, halcyon days of our affair. In the beginning, I naively worried about how Lori was taking his infidelity. They had an arrangement, he said. But he didn't want to discuss it further, and neither did I. After a while the refuse of our repressed conversations began to seep from its container like hazardous waste. But we had a while to go yet before toxicity set in.

I never could have kept up with Joel if I'd had a nine-to-five job. He stayed up late, and rose late. He ran around all day and half the night chasing ventures like a good little capitalist. My life became subsumed by his, and I found myself rearranging my schedule for his convenience. Joel talked about opening up a second restaurant, the first was doing so well. He wanted me to come up with some interior design sketches for the space, a large rectangular room in the East Eighties, near the river. His request excited me, and I set about the task enthusiastically, not realizing how much time it would take away from my own work. Shared ideas and creativity would add a new dimension to our relationship, or so I imagined.

Joel didn't need more than four or five hours sleep a night. After a late dinner, I lunged for the couch and the remote control switch. He wanted to go out. Club and restaurant owners all over town knew him by name. We spent part of our time snorting the drug of the moment in V.I.P. rooms with the celebrity of the moment, and the rest catching spinners, rotating D.J.s, who ranged in both music and clothing style from far-out freaky to merely outrageous. I felt positively decrepit at most of these places, populated with unemployed teenagers in Halloween costumes. Joel loved to dance, and to schmooze. I'm no good at either, but I learned that after a few shots of vodka and lines of coke, I could boogie and wiseass with the best of them. I picked up voguing from a beautiful Puerto Rican boy by the name of Rafael who moved like a cross between a runaway model and a ballet dancer. He and his friends adopted me, and Joel observed me dancing with them from the sidelines like he was playing a hunch.

I guess he'd started reinventing me on the park bench, and the rest all fell into place. He started coming by with gifts, shopping bags full of goodies: oversized Gap T-shirts, faux-pearl and crystal beads, tight mini-dresses ("to show off your legs"), hats, a long, black cape. The hats and cape perplexed me.

"These are things that Garbo would wear," I said.

"Yeah," he said, grinning, "that's the ticket."

I don't know if Joel's powers of persuasion were great, or my willpower deserted me when in his presence. I suspect it was the latter. Gradually, I overcame the reluctance to costume myself in the androgynous garb of my idol. One evening, dressed in the fedora (which also looked like something out of an *Indiana Jones* movie), dark glasses, and the cape, some paparazzo mistook me for a celebutante and snapped my picture. Cara called the next day to tell me that it had appeared in WWD's *Eye* with the caption, "Mystery Amazon."

"I don't think I'll send that to Mom," I said, although I bought several issues of the newspaper. I cut out the photo and taped it to the bedroom mirror as a testament to my fifteen minutes of fame. Attention of this sort is heady, intoxicating. I got a taste, and it was both sweet and sour. On a large scale, like Garbo's, your fame turns you into a public utility and everyone claims a common share of the stock. It's a powerful aphrodisiac. Men came on to me, women, couples. Half the time I missed their messages because I wasn't looking for it, or used to it, or interested. My sexual myopia tickled Joel, and aroused in him a latent prurience. He'd tease me about my new "star" status, and my "fans." Wasn't I interested in any of them? Garbo was a switch-hitter. How about a ménage à trois? He'd badger me, watching for a reaction. If I became too offended, he'd back off, and tell me to lighten up, not to take sex so seriously. I never did with Eddie. And more than half the time I'd question my right to feel the way I did, which was the worst part of all.

Before the WWD photo, I'd more or less accompanied Joel everywhere like an extra appendage. In public he had a kind of macho act that I grew to hate. He loved the limelight, and deflected any attention I got to himself by taking credit for it. In private, he'd polish furniture or meditate on arranging one flower so that the light hit it just right, but he kept this side of himself concealed and his reluctance to reveal it became the source of most of our arguments.

For a while I was content to go along, amazed by how little it took to create a new persona. While Joel wheeled and dealed, I got down. My gay male dancing partners fussed over me and became like girlfriends. I made up a name to go with my night-time self, Leta Velveta. Every morning I'd stare in the mirror looking for a sign of recognition from my myriad selves, all contesting for dominance. Leta Velveta and her crowd had a swell time, but her lifestyle was taking a terrible toll on Rebeccah and her more prudent acolytes. Sober, I'd feel demoralized from the past night's wretched excess. Dark circles waxed like half-moons beneath bleary, red-shot eyes. I rarely rose before 3:00 P.M. The Graduate School Admissions applications I'd sent away for piled up on the living room floor. I didn't draw, I didn't think; I procrastinated. I'd ask Joel repeatedly what he thought of my interior space renderings, and he put me off. After awhile, I wearied of asking him, trying to convince myself that I didn't care. But his reticence about my work affected me like a slow, insidious poison. I began to notice other things. How he'd shut down, for instance, whenever I presumed closeness. I missed the intimacy that we'd shared in the beginning. I worried about the lack of honest disclosures that usually evolve from daily contact with someone. He shrouded his activities in secrecy. He'd barrage me with questions about my day, then lose interest in my answers. Something alien and distasteful was being demanded of me. Joel's elusiveness became like a fin encircling me in the water.

A photographer friend of Joel's was having an opening exhibition at The Museum of Modern Art. I was to meet Joel there, and took a cab over. On the way I ruminated about how pivotal the

Museum had been in my life: the first time as a kid discovering "good design"; seeing my first Garbo movie with Eddie; my first date with Joel. It all seemed like it had happened in another millennium, to someone else.

I overtipped the cab driver and got out. A homeless black woman, who had parked herself outside the Museum's bookstore, was being chased away by a porter who threw buckets of disinfectant over the grates where she'd been. The unmistakable odor of urine permeated the entrance to the lobby. All evening long I imagined inhaling whiffs of the stench that had seeped like a stain into the texture of evening.

I hadn't really wanted to go. I was tired of Leta Velveta and her mock-Garbo act. I hadn't reached the point of dissatisfaction where I could resist temptation, but there were small acts of rebellion. Forsaking the fedora and T-shirt, I dressed in one of my old silk dresses from Lord & Taylor's, a relic of a shopping spree with Mom.

One of the best things about the museum is the Sculpture Garden. Deirdre Holland once said that she didn't see what all the fuss was about a lot of stone and metal objects surrounding a big, droopy tree. But then, Deirdre had never lived in New York City, where you grow to appreciate places other than your apartment that afford you quiet in the midst of bedlam. The longer I stayed in New York City, the more it struck me as medieval in its cruel divisons between rich and poor, fed and unfed, clean and unclean. The street beggars and homeless echoed the luckless vagabonds and vagrants of the Middle Ages, victims of the wars, who used to parade their ill-fortune and disease before the more fortunate as some kind of punishment.

That night the Sculpture Garden had been dressed as for a garden party. Elaborate floral arrangements decorated tiny cocktail tables draped in pastel summer shades of pink, violet and blue. Waiters held silver trays of champagne-filled tulip glasses. I grabbed one, quickly downed it, then another.

I looked for Joel and saw him talking to Lori and her escort, a man who resembled a younger version of himself. She was often in places where Joel took me, and I never got used to her false friendliness. She'd gush over my outfits, usually selected by her husband, and compliment me to the point of puking. They both acted like nothing was *wrong*, and that *I* was deranged for thinking that there was. The part of the self-denying vamp who preys on betrayal and another woman's man didn't suit me. Somehow Garbo had always carried off the role on-screen, but off-screen she was another person. In reel life, Garbo dressed like a mistress; in real life, like a bachelor. Her fans had resented it. This schism, this inability to merge her screen persona with her true self has hounded her her entire life. But even when she's performing "bad womens" she's intrinsically good. She brought to her roles an integrity that I admire. She has been quoted as saying that she wished she was two people—one for celluloid, and one for life. Standing in the Sculpture Garden watching Joel interact with his wife and her boyfriend, I began to wish not for division but for quantified unity.

He waved me over. I waved back.

"What's the matter with you?" he asked, pulling me aside. "Why are you acting so strangely?"

He eyed my silk dress.

"What's that you're wearing?"

"Like it?"

He didn't, but fortunately we had no time to discuss it.

The star of the show, a tall, striking man in a tux and a small ponytail at the nape of his neck, had arrived. We were introduced, and Joel left us alone to hustle someone else. I congratulated the photographer on the exhibition, and asked him how he'd gotten the mental patients to pose for their portraits? Over time, he'd said, and with painstaking effort. He possessed a degree in clinical psychology, and had worked with many of them professionally for a number of years.

"It's like your camera got inside of them," I said. "They look like ordinary people, only more so."

He smiled, and darted his eyes around the garden.

Beyond his right shoulder I saw Joel talking alone with Lori, their heads bent in conversation. What were they discussing? Business? Me? I'd ask Joel if he was still sleeping with her, and he'd say, "Who has the time?" But seeing them together I suspected that he made the time. The photographer watched me watch them. Voyeurism feeds on itself. The irises of his eyes shuttered open and closed, like he was taking mental photographs.

"Lori and Joel have been together for a long time," he said. "I was curious to meet this new girl of Joel's I've been hearing so much about."

Just then the curator of the show approached and corraled the photographer, who excused himself. The words *new girl of Joel's* bounced off the walls of my brain. I looked over to see Lori cup Joel's face in her hands and drink from it like she'd just crawled out of the Sahara. She must have seen me watching. She must have done this before. I saw myself standing in a long line of *new girls of Joel's* while Lori, secure in her seniority as first concubine, lorded it over us. I grabbed another glass of champagne from a passing waiter and strode to the north side of the garden. The fountains gushed frothy, geyser-like streams of water. Eddie liked fountains. Every architectural rendering of his included a fountain somewhere. I had a keen and sudden desire to see him, to lean my head against his shoulder and sigh audibly.

There were three women at the party with their babies in tow. Since the abortion, I've become supersensitive to children and if one is within a hundred-square-foot radius, my sensors go on alert. One woman, holding a dark-eyed little girl over her shoulder, stood to my right. The child looked straight at me with an open, innocent gaze. I melted on the spot. Not all babies by virtue of being small and cuddly affect me this way, but this child was a heart-wrencher, and I wanted more than just to hold her, I wanted *her*. I could have had a baby like that. But this kind of thinking is dangerous, and I felt myself spiraling downward.

Needing to get a better grip on myself, I stooped and dipped my hand into the fountain's cool water. Some loose change laid at the bottom; idle dreams, forgotten wishes. Looking up, I saw a woman wearing large, dark glasses watching me from across the way. She was half-hidden by the hanging branches of the weeping birch tree.

It looked like . . . ? But it couldn't be. She was dressed in slacks and a baggy top. Her fading blond hair fell to her shoulders. Who was she? I couldn't see her eyes but I sensed their reproachful gaze. I moved towards her, stumbling on the step of the small concrete bridge leading to the other side. When I looked up she was gone. There was no one behind the tree. I peeled back the branches in search of her.

"You can't go in there, Miss," snarled a security guard.

I walked away. The party swirled around me.

"There you are," Joel said.

He peered at me. "What's wrong? You look strange."

"I . . . nothing. Nothing's wrong."

"You okay?"

I nodded.

"There's someone I want you to meet."

"You won't believe who I just saw, or who I think I just saw."

"Who?"

"*Her.*"

"How many glasses of champagne have you had? Maybe you'd better lay off for a while."

"But I saw her, or someone who looked just like her," I insisted. "She was standing behind that tree, watching me."

Joel wasn't in the mood to humor me. I met a lot of people whose names and faces I'd forget within minutes of meeting them. All evening long I looked for her everywhere—over my shoulder, in corners and shadows, along peripheries. I knew I was losing it. Too many lines were blurring: day into night, wrong into right, reel into unreal. I needed a break from Joel, and desperately missed Cara who was ready to forgive me, but not without a few "I-told-you-so's." She let me back in with the condition that I purge myself of my past transgressions. I began to spend more time at her place and less at home. I'd given Joel keys to my apartment and considered having the locks changed. No-

ticing my change of heart, he'd ask me what was wrong, become
solicitous, make amends. He was good at that. He knew what to
do, what to say. He knew what buttons to push, how to play me.
We'd stay home, cocooned, and cook. I learned the myriad uses
of shiitake mushrooms, the significance of virginity in olive oil,
how to season with balsamic vinegar and emblazon salads with
sliced kiwi. He'd ask to see my design drafts, and make intelligent
comments, but he didn't have Eddie's eye. Joel mistook style for
substance. He embraced trends, and revered overwrought Art
Deco and kitsch; my designs were too aesthetically pure for him,
too subtle. Perhaps he didn't know how to tell me? Eddie's criticism always inspired me to try harder, to extend my reach. I use
to mistake it for dominance, and in a way it was, but it was never
intended to put me down, or keep me embalmed. I realize that
now.

CHAPTER FOURTEEN

It's the dead spots I'm looking for, the "pockets" with almost no current at all, which can sometimes be found just above the rubble of rocks on the streambed. Trout like to hide out in side channels and secondary current tongues where the currents flow slower. The osprey's catch indicates that the waters have been stocked, but I don't really care if I hook any fish. More than half the fun is just being in the water with them. Many times, Jake and I'd spend the day throwing back our catch, and wind up eating the fresh tomato and mayonnaise sandwiches that M'Lou had fixed for us.

Joel used to talk endlessly about a blues singer who made rare appearances. The mythic proportions he ascribed to her reminded me of my brother Brad when he talked about the Grateful Dead. What the blues singer and the Dead have in common is the devotion of their fans and their unavailability. This is also true of Garbo devotees, although I hadn't thought of it then.

There was a blues bar Joel and I used to frequent on the Lower East Side. The place looked like a holdover from the Depression, and was filled with characters who might have leapt from out of the pages of a cheap detective paperback, intermixed with preppies swigging beer from bottles and acting hip. Rumor had it that the infamous singer was appearing there one particular night. Joel and I squeezed ourselves around a tiny, smoky table with a lot of other hopefuls on the chance she'd show.

For nearly three hours we had to endure a rockabilly band composed of middle-aged men with potbellies hanging over their belts, fifties and sixties throwbacks. I was about to suggest our leaving during the band's break, when the piano player, a large black man dressed in a tux, arrived first. The crowd tittered. Then the singer came out. Everyone, including Joel, went wild. He'd first seen her with his mother when he was a boy. Those were the days when, between husbands, she'd drag him everywhere, including on dates with potential candidates. My childhood memories of outings with Mom and Dad are of trips to the circus, amusement parks, zoos. Joel's is of an albino drag-queen torch singer performing in toilets. Dressed in slinky red sequins and satin, she preened and pranced, trilled and warbled, in imitation of Barbra Streisand doing Liza Minnelli doing her mother. For the finale, which everyone anticipated with giddy delirium, she pulled up her gown to reveal a gigantic, fleshlike priapus.

I wanted to brush my teeth, and excused myself to run to the john.

Later, Joel blew up. He accused me of acting like a stuck-up prissy bitch.

"You're missing the point," I said. "The dildo doesn't offend me, her reliance on it as a cheap gimmick does. She has no talent as far as I can see except as a pathetic freak."

He started yelling. He criticized me for things that I didn't know had bothered him. He issued a string of four-letter epithets—some in Polish, I think—and called me a self-righteous bigot and a hopeless snob. He accused me of looking down my nose at him, his friends, his lifestyle. Unwittingly, I had sullied one of the treasured childhood experiences that had shaped Joel. I'd stomped on a sacred family ritual, perhaps the equivalent of Christmas tree-trimming and birthday parties.

We were standing on a street corner. I remember hearing the

metronomic click of the streetlight's metallic heart as the light switched from red to green to red. Each tick brought us closer to the end. The tableau recalled the Bosch-like painting in Lori's loft, where I imagined a small space had opened up to fit us in.

I didn't see Joel for a while. He stayed away. I spent a lot of time sitting on park benches with geriatrics and weirdos, hiding behind dark glasses and paranoia. I thought people were whispering about me, and imagined scenarios of private despair and personal disaster. Joel was right, I thought, I'm as square as a cube. It had been so easy for me to embrace his lifestyle rather than forge one for myself, but I was faking most of it, and badly. I missed Eddie, and our simple, normal life together, and thought about him often. Had he been the buffer between me and my self-destructive ways? Without him, I seemed to succumb to the extremes of either reclusivity or debauchery. Had he anchored me that much? Alone, I was swimming in dangerous waters and kept seeing the fin in the distance getting closer and closer. Was it Joel, or some abstraction of myself? Every so often I caught a glimpse of something, desire transformed from self-absorption to self-transcendence, but I couldn't hold on to it. Weary of the present state of my life, with its self-indulgence, manipulation and lack of precision, I yearned for a change, for release.

Joel reappeared without notice or warning, and announced that he was going to California to wrap up some deals, then to visit his mother in Mexico.

He held a bouquet of forget-me-nots in his hand.

Did he think I was that easy?

Catching my mood, but misreading it, he said that the separation would only be for a little while, a few weeks at the most. He thought it would do us some good.

Since I agreed with him, I didn't suspect him of lying. After we said goodbye, I ran to Cara's to tell her the news. Of all the voids I'd courted, Joel's absence promised to be the worst. There weren't too many places left to hide inside the concave walls of a giant Ping-Pong ball. Sometimes I imagined Eddie's giant eye peering in at me.

Recognizing me, the Shelstein's doorman said hello and let me pass without calling up.

Cara, rubbing her hands on a dish towel, opened her apartment door.

"What's up, Babe?" she asked, hardly concealing her annoyance. She was in the midst of cooking for a dinner party.

"I should have called," I said. "I'll come back later."

"Don't be silly. You just caught me at a bad moment. What's wrong? You look sick."

"It's over, but I don't know how to end it."

She looked skeptical, but said, "Come in," and stepped aside to let me pass.

It grieved me that the ticket of total re-entry into Cara's life was contingent upon the expurgation of Joel from mine. On the other hand, no one could fault her on her patience. She was always there for me in a pinch.

"Cara," I began, "if you ever need a lung, a kidney, an ovary, a hundred ovaries, you can have mine."

She stared at me like I'd finally gone over the edge, then smiled.

"Here," she said, handing me an onion, "dice."

The onion stung my eyes and made them tear, but we both knew it was from more than the fumes.

"Why don't you stay for dinner," she said. "We're just having a few friends. It's informal. I can always set another place."

She didn't have to twist my arm. I ran home to change and arrived at the Shelstein's door at the same time as Stephen J. Beale, IV. I could have killed Cara for not telling me that he was coming.

Tanned, and dressed casually in jeans, he looked more beautiful than I remembered him. Didn't this guy date? He always seemed to go solo. I pulled Cara aside and asked her if Beale was gay?

"You've been in New York too long," she said, laughing. "In fact, he's just broken up with someone, an on-again/off-again relationship he's had for years. Sound familiar?"

Beale had either forgotten or forgiven our last encounter. He spoke with that same ridiculous, patrician lockjaw, but appeared less pompous. I didn't recall the dark satirical streak, but I remembered the boisterous sense of humor. After dinner, he cornered me and confided that he'd wanted to impress me the night of our blind date, which was why he'd acted like such an asshole.

"You weren't the only asshole," I said.

He asked if he could walk me home, and I accepted. After life with Joel, the innocence of the act felt normal, refreshing, renewing. Cara was right. The first time out I hadn't dated enough shits to appreciate a basically nice guy like Beale. I felt as though I'd aged a lifetime in the space of months.

En route, I noticed the lascivious looks that both men and women gave him. Beale seemed oblivious, but I think it was his way of coping. One day he'd be a jolly fat man, but for now I felt I was being escorted by a movie idol in his prime. We lingered at the vestibule door. Beale's sexual restraint intrigued me. Was it because, similar to a beautiful woman, he felt that you had to earn his favors? Or because he was still being true to whatshername? Or because he found me unattractive? Or because he didn't kiss on the almost second date? It was a sultry night, indicative of sweaty sex. I wanted to invite him in for a drink, for further conversation, to get to know him better. I was on the brink of it when who should appear, as usual out of thin air, but Joel.

Beale and Holdesky remembered one another only too well. Stephen made no move to leave, which pleased me.

"I was just about to invite Stephen up for a nightcap," I said to Joel. "Would you like to join us?"

Joel's eyes flared. I thought he'd slap my face.

Beale glanced at his wristwatch. "It's late," he said. "If it's all right with you, I'll take a raincheck."

"*I was just about to invite Stephen up for a nightcap*" Joe mocked, after Stephen had left. "How long as this been going on?"

"Why aren't you in California?"

"Answer me."

"Jealous?"

"Over *him*?"

"Answer *me*. Why aren't you in California?"

"The trip was delayed."

"Joel, we have to talk seriously."

"Okay. Let's talk seriously."

Kithy run up to me, mewing, as I came in the door.

"Hungry?" I said, stooping to pet her.

"How many WASPS does it take to screw in a lightbulb?" Joel asked.

"*Don't!*" He reached for me. I pulled away.

"I have to feed the cat."

"What's bugging you?"

"A lot's bugging me. It's after 1:00 A.M. You say you're going away, and then don't, and then appear from out of nowhere expecting me to drop everything . . ."

It came out all wrong. I hated the whine, the reproach, and shut my mouth.

"Calm down, Duffy," he said. "You've had too much to drink."

"I have not!"

"Listen," he said, "I've been thinking. We need to go away, together. I was wrong. I thought the separation would be good for us, but it's not. We're growing farther and farther apart. I think about you all the time. I want you to come to California with me. No, listen. Let me finish. I've been thinking this over carefully. I have some boring stuff to do, some deals to close in L.A., but it shouldn't take more than three days, four at the most. You could sightsee, sunbathe, gaze at the movie stars, whatever you want. Then we'll go to Mexico, to visit my mother. I've told her all about you. She wants to meet you. You'll love her. She can tell you a lot of Garbo stories. She met her once. No kidding. Whaddayou say?"

He looked like the first day I'd met him, like the way he must have looked when Lori Biro first saw and fell in love with him, a tough but lost little boy in jeans and leather, full of bravado and shit. I felt myself emotionally spiral out of control. Would I spend the rest of my life endlessly sliding around a Möbius strip, a continuous one-sided surface? I didn't believe a word he said, but faltered. I'd recently read that people who sleep together adopt the same sleep patterns, which is why they suffer from separation anxiety when apart.

"C'mon, Duffy. Let's give it another chance."

His voice was moist with affection, his blue eyes limpid with lust. All I could focus on were his full lips, which I wanted to bruise with my own. I don't know how I could still want him, but I did. I felt a proprietary interest in his penis, like it belonged to me and me alone. At my command, it came alive, straining for the release that only I could give it. The sultry evening, Stephen's attention, Joel's jealousy—all combined to re-seduce me into the void that our relationship had become. Once it had filled it. We wound up on the living-room rug, as sensitive to one another's touch as a heliotrope is to sunlight. I never believed that what Joel and I shared was true love, but some facsimile of it, a compound of loneliness, Garbomania, sexual attraction and conquest. As much as I couldn't bear the failure of another relationship, I wanted to let go but held on at the same time.

Afterwards, we lay there, slippery and sated, searching for a reaffirmation of our identities in one another's gaze.

"Yeah," he said, sighing, lighting up his usual postcoital cigarette.

The sex was still good between us, but when it was over, I felt alone, bereft, empty. Whatever it was, it wasn't enough—but it was something.

It never occurred to me *not* to go to California with Joel. I'd made up my mind to go and to call Eddie once I got there. I hadn't heard from him since that night at Cara's. Every time I called, Maria answered and I hung up. Judging from the number of hang-up calls that I got, maybe Eddie did the same. And it never occurred to me that the reason for my trip would alienate him further.

The day before the trip, Lori paid me a surprise visit, catching me totally unaware. She looked like hell—disheveled, in need of sleep. It was the first time I'd seen her in pants—tight, black, capri numbers with red flats—and lipstickless. She had to talk to me, she said. She had to tell me what was going on, she said. Our eye contact was mutually minimal. I found myself listening to her as though from very far away, zooming in and out of focus.

"This is very difficult," she began.

For whom, I thought, you or me? Heart pounding, I waited for her to continue. I think I knew what was coming.

"When I heard that you were going with Joel to L.A., I knew I had to tell you."

"Tell me what?"

"About the others." She dug into her purse for a small hand mirror at which she quickly glanced.

"What others? Please, just get to the point."

"Joel is seeing someone else," she said, refocusing on me. She returned the mirror to her bag. "She's a dancer. She's, how do you say, a 'gypsy,' a chorus girl. Very young, very beautiful. He wants to put her in his Hollywood musical and asked her to go to L.A. with him. But she sprained her ankle and can't go. So he asked you."

"Why are you telling me this? Why should I believe you?"

Unable to sit still, I began pacing in small circles around the living room. Her eyes tracked me.

"I like you. You are different from the others, more open, and honest. I don't want to see you get hurt . . ."

She started to cry, and this pissed me off. In the midst of my pain and rage I had to take care of hers. I jumped up to look for a box of Kleenex, which I knew I didn't have, and wound up handing her a roll of toilet paper.

"Thanks," she said, blowing her nose with a loud honk.

I wanted her to go, but she was far from finished. Sniffing, and patting her eyes dry with wads of toilet paper, she regaled me with tales of Joel's indiscretions. Before me, he had the ex-nun, and before her the Italian princess. The princess gushed over him, calling him *"amore"* in public places. I could see that out of all of us, she had bothered Lori the most. Before her there was the physical therapist, and the magazine editor, and the runway model. I lost track. At some point I made us instant coffee. We could have been old pals gossiping about the love follies of a mutual friend—not me, anybody but me.

"Did the ex-nun leave the order because of him?" I asked. Lori nodded. "She was his madonna."

"And what are we, his whores?"

She laughed, but I didn't think it was funny. Throughout her story, I'd tried to sift fact from fancy. It occurred to me that she was lying, trying to interfere with Joel and me, but she could have done this before, why now? Puzzling aspects of Joel's behavior over the past few weeks began to make sense—why he was always later than usual, or forgot to call, and stopped speaking to me in the language of flowers.

"Why do you put up with him?" I asked.

"Why do you?"

She had me there.

"I love him," she said, blowing her nose again. I almost said, What's love got to do with it? I almost said, You can have him. But she already had him. We both knew that.

I began straightening up around her, anxious to throw away the visit with the trash.

After she'd gone I unpacked my suitcase, and madly flung garments, and products that professed to keep me eternally young, trim and beautiful crashing against the bedroom wall. I called Joel and left a message on his machine. Then I called a locksmith, and at great expense had new locks installed.

Frightened by the noise, Mr. Hennessey poked his head out the door. He feared someone was trying to break in. Does he always wear his hat indoors? I calmed him down, then Mrs. Wallace appeared. She practically made the anti-hex sign whenever she saw me now.

"What's going on?" she said. Bruce, wheezing, waddled behind her.

"I'm sorry, Mrs. Wallace, but it's an emergency. I just broke up with my boyfriend, and it's to keep him out."

Her small, crafty eyes settled on me.

"Don't say 'I told you so.' Treating that nice Mr. Geary so badly for that . . . that *gonif*. I hope you've learned your lesson," she said, wagging her finger at me.

Assuring her that I had, I went inside and wept in the shower.

Patience is not one of Joel's virtues. Early that evening he nearly broke the door down trying to get in. Afraid that Mrs. Wallace would call the police, I had to let him in.

"I told you Lori is crazy," he yelled. "Why do you believe her and not me?"

"I don't know what I believe anymore. I don't care. It's over, Joel. Finished."

"It's not over," he said quietly, implying, "until I say it's over."

I got out the dustbuster. The place was crawling with sleaze.

"What the hell are you doing?"

"What does it look like?"

"Shut that damn thing off."

Joel hates quiet. We stood there listening to the machine's dying hum. I knew what he'd do next. He turned on the television. A man and woman were fighting in a nighttime soap. Does life imitate trash, or does trash imitate life? I sat on the couch and stared at the tube. I had absolutely nothing more to say. I wanted him to leave. He started humming.

I can't pinpoint exactly the first time I'd noticed that Joel was a hummer. In the early days I had thought it endearing and cute, but it grew for me into his least cosseted imperfection. People who hum when there's a silence make me nervous. It tells me they're uneasy. This time I stonewalled him.

Finally, he said, "Look. I've got to do something. I'll come back later. We'll talk this out. You've got to hear my side. Will you do that for me?"

I didn't say a word.

"I'll be back," he said.

I couldn't sit still and took a long walk. Without realizing how, I wound up on the corner of Forty-second Street and Sixth, staring at the National Debt clock. Hypnotically, I watched the numbers rack up and up and up, ceaselessly, in rapid succession. Infinity comes in all forms. Science insists that the universe is not run by magic, that randomness and chaos play a larger part than we'd care to accept. Quantum mechanics posits that atoms and molecules must be defined in terms of stable particles. Does this apply to thought forms? The instability of my emotions generated a lot of conflict and confusion. Yet through it all there remained a constancy, because one of the physical laws of the universe dictates that atoms and molecules maintain their identities, shapes and patterns in spite of collisions and turmoil. This is why jade is not onyx, and trees bear leaves every spring, and flowers bloom, and birds fly, and Garbo hides, and Joel lies, and Rebeccah runs. The truth hurtled along a trajectory that I couldn't see; I sure felt it.

I ran home and put all of Joel's personal things, including his gift of the pocketwatch with Garbo's face on it, in a box, then awaited his arrival. His power of denial is much greater than mine. He acted like I was overreacting. I felt intimidated by his self-confidence and poise. He talked as if I were still going to L.A. with him the next day, despite the fact that I insisted that I wasn't. Lori had explained that Joel hated to visit his mother alone. He adored her, but he hated her. She was on a pedestal, but also had feet of clay. They always fought, and he needed a buffer, someone to neutralize the tension between them. Lori had stopped going years ago. The dancer had sprained her ankle. That left me. *He's lying to me.* That's all I could think, all I knew: *He lied to me,* and *He's always lied,* and *I wasn't first choice!*

The center of hell is ice, not fire. I felt frozen from the inside out. Joel pulled all of his tricks out of the bag. He said that Lori was threatened by me, because I was different from the others. She was afraid he'd file for a divorce, leave her for me. He said he was seriously thinking about it.

I studied an old wine stain on the living-room rug, looking for pictures in it as if it was a Rorschach test.

"I don't know what I'd do without you," he went on. "You protect me from myself. This girl I met, the dancer, she's just someone I want to put in the movie. That's all."

I wanted to scream.

Restless, he said, "Let's go for a drink."

"No."

"One lousy drink. Is that too much to ask for?"

"Yes!"

I didn't want another tense restaurant breakup scene. I didn't want to get too close to him, to give him the opportunity to suck the resolve out of me.

He began humming.

"Joel," I said. *"Please. Please leave."*

He looked at me like he couldn't believe I meant it, but I did. I gave him the dogsbane.

"What's this?" he said.

"They were out of Venus flytraps."

He dropped the flowers-of-deceit on top of the box full of his belongings. The fedora he'd given me, and the faux-pearl beads, were draped over the top of the hall mirror. He put the hat on. I knew what was coming, but I didn't want to play. I also knew that if he walked out this time, that would be the end of it.

"You're the cream of the crop, Duffy. I mean that."

Was this a movie line? I didn't recognize it. We exchanged looks. He signaled me with his eyes. It was the look of love, of sex, that we used to play across crowded rooms, at parties, and the clubs, colluding in the image of ourselves as the perfect couple.

"I dig chicks. Chicks dig me digging them. Dig it?"

I couldn't remember the name of the movie. Something with "beach" in the title. When he didn't get a response, he tried a different tack.

"You know, I have great plans for you. You're very talented."

"It won't work, Joel, not this time."

"You need me, Duffy. Garbo needed male mentors. So do you. You can't make it alone."

My anger imploded. I began to shake.

He repositioned the fedora at a jauntier angle, and dropping his voice an octave, said, "I hate men, every mother's son of them." *(Anna Christie.)*

"*I'M NOT GARBO!*"

He sailed the hat in my direction. By the time I caught it, he was gone.

CHAPTER FIFTEEN

Inadvertently, I've wandered up-stream. I'm chest-high in choppy water. The sun is almost blinding, even with sunglasses. Squinting, I see something coming towards me in the far distance. Is it a canoe, a raft, a log? Whatever it is, it's gaining on me and I don't want to know. Anyway it's time to get out of the water.

I hear mewing. Kithkat is calling to me from the stream bank. "Sorry," I said, "they're not biting."

Her true colors have emerged in the mountains. I had to tie a tiny bell around her neck to warn off the small birds and animals she stalks. Up here she's not much company, but I like having her around, and listen for the sound of her tinkling bell in the silence.

The mountain laurel grows freely here. I pick some for the dinner table wondering what the language of the laurel is. Joel would know. He used to leave messages scripted in flower bouquets for me: bluebells meant I'd see him that night; one red carnation meant he'd see me the following night; two, the night after, and so on. Yellow chrysanthemums signified hurt feelings, white forgiveness. Jasmine meant sex. He gave me a little book on flowers. I left it behind. Thoughts about him still pierce like arrows through my flesh.

When I first arrived at the Secret Place I was shocked by the cabin's deterioration. M'Lou hardly uses the place anymore, and it smelled of mildew and mold. I spent the first few days cleaning out the cobwebs and scouring away the stink. One of the cabin's greatest attributes is its lack of a telephone and a television. Jake refused all links to the outside world, which suits me fine. The nearest neighbor is over a mile away.

Sometimes I awake in the middle of the night from the quiet. The snap of a twig, the flapping of a bird's wing, the rustle of fallen leaves—all hint of bogey-creatures scudding about outside. My old childhood fears of the dark return, and I think of Garbo who supposedly never sleeps without a nightlight. I deliberated about buying one, then cancelled the thought. There are other things I need more—food supplies, fishing tackle, materials to complete my design models, gas for the car.

Every other day I make forays from one place to another, often just for the hell of it. It's good to be able to drive places again, and not have to rely on subways and taxis. For the most part the roads are deserted, but after Memorial Day all that will change when the summer season officially begins. Eddie's parents live in Somerset, less than thirty minutes away. I'm tempted to pay them a surprise visit, but I procrastinate. I also want to visit Fallingwater, and think about it every time I pass a road sign. How easy it would be now to take a left turn.

Just one small turn of the wheel and life becomes a Disney movie with me tripping down memory lane; skipping along the yellow brick road; singing in the rain.

Fallingwater is the world's most famous private residence. Built in the midst of the Great Depression by Frank Lloyd Wright, it sprang up at a time when most people couldn't afford to eat. Eddie and I used to marvel over that, and the fact that when Wright was commissioned to design and build the house he was approaching seventy, and his career was flagging. The success of Fallingwater rejuvenated him, giving him over twenty more productive years.

The parking lot is cradled by shade trees and situated a good distance from the house. Sometimes it's hard to tell the difference between remembering something you did and remembering something you dreamed you did. That's how Fallingwater occupies my mind, the hybrid progeny of reality and fantasy, cognition and imagination. Before he quit architecture, Eddie and I came here every chance we got. I used to dream about the place—strange dreams of the two of us chasing one another through the light, spacious rooms, sometimes in frolic, often in fear—either running from each other, or something menacing that sought the two of us. Sometimes the dreams were mystical, and filled with magical white creatures, in particular an albino buffalo who communicated in mental images. Sometimes the dreams were sexy, primitive, outdoors. Eddie didn't dream of the place as much as I did, and when he did it was in black and white, not in color.

We gravitated to Fallingwater for all sorts of reasons. We had cloaked so many of our private dreams and ambitions around the place that the structure came to symbolize for us a grand illusion. Taking possession of it intellectually and emotionally, we thought we could recreate it, or some equivalent of it, by sheer design and will. Youthful dreams and ambitions roam freely, like wild animals. Now I realize that to imagine re-creating Fallingwater is fatuous, but I miss the collaboration, the underlying drive and passion that had once united Eddie and me in a common cause.

It's all coming back to me. We used to picnic on a huge, flat-topped boulder, situated diagonally across the stream from the house, hidden by some trees, and talk Fallingwater for hours. Eddie would rhapsodize, comparing it to a poem, a prosody of stonework exploding from a central concrete heart. He used to tell me how, as a boy, he'd come here and pretend he was an explorer discovering Fallingwater before everybody else. The house had inspired him to study architecture and not to follow his father's footsteps and study law. Eddie bragged about how he was going to borrow Frank Lloyd Wright's paean to romanticism and modernism and build his own Fallingwaters, on a smaller scale, for the less privileged. In place of a real waterfall he'd build fountains; barring a forest, he'd plant trees and shrubs, both inside and outside the houses. Eddie wanted people to experience Fallingwater's harmonious bonding of nature and technology, to realize that one needn't be sacrificed upon the altar of the other. He wholeheartedly embraced Wright's belief that life was a continuum of aesthetic choices. If you live in a beige box you're going to become—think—like a beige box. If you live in something radical and innovative, you're going to adopt those principles and extrapolate. The problem with Eddie was that he talked a great game, but he didn't do his homework. From words to paper, from ideas to renderings, something was lost in the translation. I'd encourage him to dig deeper, work harder, push himself, and he resented it. I used to think it was laziness, now I see it as cowardice.

I don't remember the distance from the parking lot to the Visitor's Pavillion as being this long. Little of the area's natural beauty has changed, and I feel heartened by that. Years ago Fallingwater's heir turned the house over to the Western Pennsylvania Conservancy for safekeeping. I'm tempted to say hello to the dramatic rock formations and poplars that line the path and seem like old friends.

A tour has just left. Hurrying, I catch up with the docent. He is talking nonstop, but his words jumble in my mind. Fallingwater's architectural history doesn't interest me as much as the enchantment of my own memories; the oneiric quality of being there. The fantasies Eddie and I had cherished for ourselves and our futures had once seemed as immutable and real as this great, concrete house.

"What happened to us?" I mutter to myself.

"I beg your pardon?" asks the old woman standing beside me.

"Sorry, it's nothing."

She nods and inches sideways like a small, feisty crab; as if whatever I have is contagious.

The sonorous sounds of the falls are all-pervasive. We trail behind the docent who is reciting the catechism of Fallingwater to his eager flock: ". . . an engineering feat of genius . . . three kinds of cantilevering . . . appears to float at different horizontal levels . . . interior space extends to exterior . . . a marriage of nature and technology."

We used to bring sleeping bags and spend the night here, hiding out in the surrounding woods. At night the house was lit up from inside and became magical, like something out of a Grimm's fairytale, haunting and alluring, the way a favorite story read to you in childhood is.

Inside the house is as impressive as outside. The stone walls, floor levels, low ceilings, narrow hallways, and flat eaves all maintain their allegiance to nature, and to natural light. We use to imagine what it'd be like to wake up in the morning here and do such banal things like pee, brush your teeth, dress and read the paper while thundering water flowed beneath you on its inexorable plunge.

The group is standing on the living-room balcony, which juts out over the rumbling falls. Everyone "ohhs" and "ahhs" as we look down. Squinting, I peer across the stream to look at Eddie's and my sandstone boulder. Unchanged, it sits and endures while Eddie and I age, growing older and apart. We had great sex in these woods, great talks, great dreams. Yearning besets me. I want to recapture what's been lost. I want eternity in a moment with no thought to yesterday or tomorrow. There are more security guards now, watchful and suspicious, otherwise I'd sneak across. The tour turns back inside.

I've had enough, and leave.

A line from T. S. Eliot about "mixing memory with desire" and "stirring dull roots with spring rain" about sums up my mood as I head back home. I'd expected the visit to be apochryphal, but discovered instead that there is nothing left here for me but remembrance made painful by time, and recollection strained from longing.

Jake's tool shed is equipped with strange instruments that look like they were designed for the set of *Aliens*. We never could figure out what he used them for, and were afraid to ask. I am putting the finishing touches on the lingerie washboard when I hear a sound outside, like the crunch of gravel beneath the wheels of a car. I peer out the cellar window. I can't see the driveway from here, but there are no lights, no sounds, nothing unnatural.

The washboard has both vertical and horizontal glass insertions, cut into triangular shapes. Tinted orange, the glass is corrugated for scrubbing. The frame is composed of a light, moldable plastic, colored bright red. I had a handgrip carved out of the top for gripping with one hand while scrubbing with the other. I'm going to paint and glaze the rest of it in bright neon colors.

The woman's valet needs work. I am sculpting it out of wood and wire, but don't feel in the mood now, and return habitually to the automatic baby stroller, which poses a challenging engineering problem. When I worked for Magorian I was often called upon not so much to solve problems as to create new ones; to find temporary solutions that conformed to cost controls regardless of the new dissatisfactions and future disasters we may have been creating for people and the environment. After I quit, I vowed, "Never again!"

The trick here is not only to make the stroller unfold with a push of a button, but to be able to refold it without any hassle, with one arm in fact. This means the utilization of various body parts for bracing: hand, arm, hip, leg, foot. The wheel placements are a problem. They get in the way of the spring-action, which I'm pretty sure would work best laterally, not vertically. I spent time playing with $3.00 push-button umbrellas to get a feel for the spring-lever dynamic. But $3.00 umbrellas have no integrity; and are built for obsolescence, not endurance. I'm deep in thought when I hear noises coming from the garage. Cara had told me to get a dog up here, and how I wish I'd heeded her advice.

There's no doubt about it, someone is prowling around outside.

Picking up a crowbar and a flashlight, I sneak out back, and encircle the house toward the garage. Whoever it is, isn't being at all discreet. Perhaps it's a raccoon or a stray dog?

"Who's there?" I say, trying to sound brave, flashing the light.

"Where the hell is the goddam light switch? Did you move it?"

"*Eddie? Shit!* You scared the life out of me. What are you doing here?"

"Hi, Rebeccah. How are you? I wanted to do a little night fishing."

I flick the switch. We blink at one another beneath the garage light's glare.

"You could have knocked on the front door."

"I did. There wasn't any answer. I saw the light in the cellar, figured you were puttering around and didn't want to disturb you."

"Thanks for the courtesy."

"You've been fishing, I see. Catch anything?"

"No."

"You always were a lousy fisher."

He takes what he needs, then whistling tunelessly, trudges down the path to the stream following the beam of his flashlight. And I, as if caught in its tractor, dumbly follow.

"Eddie, isn't it a little late to go fishing?"

"Night fishing is the best kind. More challenging. You ought to know that. Remember how we used to do it? I got a yen for some fresh brook trout cooked over an open fire. Now if I'm not mistaken there should be a stone fireplace right along here somewhere."

"That was years ago. It's gone. I looked."

"We thought it'd last forever. We thought everything would last forever. Oh, well, we'll build another one."

I shivered as much from the chill night air as from the sudden apparition of Eddie. It was like I had conjured him.

He took off his Top-Siders, rolled up his Chinos to just above the knee and waded in the water.

"Brrrr," he says. "Colder than a witch's tit."

"Eddie, what are you doing here?"

"The same thing you're doing here."

"I mean, why are you in Pennsylvania?"

He's a better angler than I am, good wrist-action, and lobs the line farther than I can.

"You're looking good, Rebeccah. A little thin, but fit."

"I can't believe this is happening. It's like a dream."

"A bad dream," he says. "My father had a heart attack. He needed bypass surgery."

"Oh! God. I'm sorry. How's he doing?"

"He's fine. Mad as hell. Driving the nurses and doctors crazy with demands and threats. He gets out in a day or two. They move you in and out fast. Whoa. I think I got something."

"How's Myra taking it?"

"Like a maniac. Oops. Lost it."

Myra the Gyre, Eddie calls his mother. She's a bit of a flake, an obsessive-compulsive who gift-wraps the garbage, and will only walk on certain paths of the rug.

"She's ritualized the hospital visits," Eddie says. "She takes a particular route, and if it's upset in any way, she begins all over again. It took us three hours to go two hundred yards. She brings dad food in Ziplocs, only he can't tell if its fresh food or garbage."

This makes me laugh. Myra the Gyre puts everything from garbage to the family silver in Ziplocs. Her fetish for tidiness is boundless. She'd put her husband and children in Ziplocs if she could, carefully labeling, cataloging, and filing them away in a drawer scented with cedar and neatly lined with contact paper.

Eddie is reeling in his line. "Damn, lost it again," he says.

"Slacken it a little," I advise.

He grunts.

"I went to Fallingwater today."

"See anything interesting?"

"What's that suppose to mean?"

"You're living in the past, Rebeccah. It took me the longest time to figure that out about you, to figure out that not so deep down you were still the eager-beaver engineering major, and I the promising, boy-genius architecture major, dreaming dreams about us like we were two characters out of an Ayn Rand novel. I couldn't believe what you did. I couldn't believe it. I went back to California, thinking, 'This is a joke, right? She's getting back at me for leaving her. Any minute now she'll call to tell me it's a sick joke.'

But you never did. I wanted to kill you. I even thought about ways of doing it. I still think about ways of doing it."

He recasts. The bugs are biting. I stand there slapping my face, neck and ankles. Why is he here? To tell me all this? A surge of anger grips me, but I have the sense to control it. The moon is only half-full. I can't see Eddie's face. He's like a giant nightshade, arisen from the bottom of the stream that gurgles around him. The creepy thing is that he's saying all this like he's talking about what he had for breakfast.

"Man," he says, "are these the wiliest fish around, or what?"

"I went through the same thing today. They tease, but don't bite."

"Sounds like someone I know."

"Can it, Eddie."

The bugs are getting worse. I think about going in.

"Here," he says, tossing me what looks like a beeper.

"It's a supersonic bug-zapper. Keeps the little buggers at bay."

"Thanks," I say, strapping it onto my belt, wondering if perhaps it's not a small detonator? Eddie's gadget-lust is increasing, not dwindling, with age.

"All the girls I meet want to get married and raise families," he goes on, like he's thinking out loud, "every single one of them, but not you. Why not? That's what I kept asking myself. The more women I dated, the more I thought about you. I tried to figure you out through them. Where was I suppose to file you? Whoa! That's one. C'mom, baby, come to Papa."

Eddie struggles with the line, reels it in some, lets it go some. He does this until he can net it, then deposits the big, flopping trout at my feet.

"How do you like that wrist-action, eh? The Pittsburgh Pirates will never know their loss. That's a pitching arm. What a beauty. Let's cook this little mother."

He insists on eating alfresco. Together we build a small stone fireplace, and gather kindling and sticks for a fire—like we're kids at summer camp and there's nothing unusual about what we're doing.

185

Ouch, I think when he guts the fish. That's me he's doing it to. While I get more stuff from the house, he lights the fire. I've already eaten dinner, but the thought of freshly caught, sizzling pan trout makes me hungry.

The fish is already frying. I hand him a small plastic bag.

"Here," I say.

"What's this stuff?"

"Shiitake mushrooms. I thought we could . . ."

Too late I realize my mistake. Eddie glowers at me. He sees Joel, Joel's influence, and he loses it.

"How the fuck do you know what the fuck to do with shii-fucking-take mushrooms? You never even knew how to boil water!"

The question is rhetorical. He grabs the handle of the cast-iron frying pan, which has got to be hot. At first I think he's going to hit me over the head with it, but he spins himself around, like an Olympic discus-thrower, and hurls the pan, fish and all, across the run. It crashes against a tree.

"You've spoiled everything," he accuses.

"*Me?*"

He lurches toward me, hesitates, swears, punching the sides of his thighs, and jumps into the stream, either to cool off or to cross over, or both. I hear him cursing, and muttering to himself. Then a *thwack, thwack, thwack* as some poor tree trunk is the recipient of Eddie's rage. Obviously, he's found the pan. I use to think the amount of jealousy a person felt acted as a gauge of love. But having witnessed Eddie's reaction, I see it differently now. Jealousy, possessiveness, control—these are corruptions of love, perversions of emotion that, like the mythological Worm Oruborus, endlessly consumes itself. I'm no longer sure what love is, just what it isn't, and it isn't this.

After a few minutes, he returns, sopping wet up to his crotch, with both pan and fish intact, although the trout looks a bit worse for wear.

Throwing another log on the fire, he jabs it with the long-handled fork, then plops the frying pan on top. He pulls a bottle of white wine from the stream, uncorks it and pours nearly half over the fish, which sputters, hisses, and smokes.

Eddie gulps from the bottle, wipes his mouth with his shirt sleeve and crouches down to survey the meal. He takes another swig of wine, and says, "Now, where were we?"

"Feel better?"

"Damn," he says, "I knew I should have brought more wine. Got any in the house?"

"Just beer."

By the time the fish is done I've lost my appetite, but Eddie is ravenous. While I pick at the charred, white flesh, he tears into it like a caveman back from the hunt. Eating has a calming effect on him, and I remember how we use to act out our aggressions and repressions with food. We'd spend whole evenings after work gorging on junk food until we were too bloated and sated to talk.

I get some beers for us, and what's left of a store-bought cake for dessert.

We make small talk. He tells me that a California winery has offered him a job, but it entails going through an intensive, eight-week advanced management program at Stanford University. The winery would pay.

"It's tempting," he says, "more money, and prestige, but also more responsibility. I love the life of the road, of calling my own shots, being my own boss."

"So do I." He acts like he doesn't hear me.

"Those programs are like boot camp. Now I've got flexibility, and a lot of people I've worked hard to win over. They were hesitant at the beginning, difficult to know, to pin down. I had to break down their surliness. Now they tell other customers about me, call people with recommendations. 'Talk to Geary,' they say. 'He knows his stuff.' "

He pauses, sifting through his thoughts. It's like old times, except it isn't.

"Can you see me in an office? All that political backstabbing. I'd probably go to the bathroom every fifteen minutes, or go for a drink of water, or coffee. Everybody's watching, monitoring.

'Jesus,' they'd say, 'that's the third time he's gone to the john' or 'the fifth cup of coffee he's drinking. Doesn't he know that coffee isn't good for him?' This way, on the road, nobody's watching me. Nobody knows what I do. All that matters are the sales, and the sales come hard and fast now. I don't even have to try."

"Don't you miss the challenge?"

He scowls, as if to say, "What do you know?"

"Sometimes I have to drive four hours each way. The trips to San Diego or Palm Springs are grueling. I could live without that. Getting snarled in traffic, asphyxiating from gas fumes, up against a dissatisfied customer, or chasing down one who doesn't pay. Days like that make a desk job seem easy, welcome."

"I'm thinking about going back to school," I say.

"Is that right?" But he's not interested.

He won't let me in. It's like brushing up against sharp angles and corners. If he's still so pissed at me, why did he come, and why is he telling me all this? I want to talk about us, about what's happened, to try to salvage the relationship before gangrene sets in, but there's no opening, and I'm afraid of re-triggering another violent outburst.

"I knew you were up here," he says, poking the fire with a stick. "Cara told me. I'd visit Dad in the hospital, and daydream about trout. Some of my best memories are of this place. Crazy ole M'Lou, and weird Jake, the mad scientist. I almost didn't come. I didn't want to see you."

I have an eerie feeling of *déjà vu*. This has happened before, but where, and in what lifetime?

Staring into the fire, Eddie is lost in his own world. I realize now that I'd never really let go of him. The entire time with Joel, through the thick and the thin of it, I held on to the conviction that no matter how far apart Eddie and I strayed, we'd get back together. Does he feel that way too? Deep inside of me there burns a dense cinder of affection for him, one fused by time, tempered by memory, compressed by shared experience. I notice flecks of grey in his dark, curly hair. His father's heart attack must have scared him. If Mr. Geary dies, Eddie becomes the head of the family, inheriting the responsibility of Myra the Gyre and his two younger brothers. For all his faults, I've never known him to shirk responsibility, never known him to slough it off on someone else. I am besieged by his virtues, and my mood is melting faster than a displaced polar ice cap.

He looks over at me, at last.

"So," he says, "what brings you to this part of the woods?"

"Didn't Cara tell you?"

"Your turn."

Carefully editing myself, making no allusions to the abortion, or Joel, I tell him that I came here to escape the summer city heat, and to work on design projects.

"You just don't quit, do you?"

I don't know how to answer. I'm not sure whether he's denigrating or complimenting me.

We have so much to say to one another, and yet we are encroached by silence. Eddie believes that every effect must have a clear-cut cause, every act a reason. I think behavior is more random than that. Events conspire, and things just happen. You often make the wrong choices, and mistakes, but so what? You can learn from them and move on.

A noise startles me. I jump. "What was that?"

"Probably something's dinner. Get a grip, Rebeccah, you've been acting spooked all evening."

Now I wonder if I'm dealing with a schizophrenic? It's like the enraged Eddie has been swallowed whole by this more complacent one.

"How are things in California, overall?" I ask.

"Overall? Fine. The apartment is shaping up. I've bought some land further south, to build on one day. And I'm a genuine oenologist now, among other things."

"Sounds naughty."

"Why can't you take it seriously?" The hatred in his voice makes me wince.

"I'm sorry, Eddie. I was just trying to be light. Isn't that what you want?"

"I don't know what the fuck I want as far as you're concerned."

He helps me carry the cooking utensils back to the house.

"Place smells musty," he says.

"I know. I can't scrub it out."

"Well," he says, "I've got to go home. Myra the Gyre will worry. See you around."

See you around?

That's what you say to mere acquaintances. It's a parting shot at people you don't care about.

"Eddie!"

He turns on the path. What is it I read in his eyes? Revenge? There has been something retributive about the whole visit.

"I . . . Would you like a cup of coffee?"

"I wanted to see what it would be like to be with you again."

"Don't go."

"Keep the bug-zapper. The damn thing doesn't really work that well."

He's inside the car.

"What hospital is your father in?"

"Mercy."

I nod. I know it.

"He'd love to see you, they both would."

I watch the taillights recede as the car rolls out of sight.

I can't sleep, and lie in bed staring out the window at the stars. Back home I have a postcard with a picture of the Milky Way on it. An arrow points to a tiny white dot that announces, YOU ARE HERE. The dot is located at the farthest arm of the spiral nebulae, far away from its center. Astronomers predict that there are one hundred billion galaxies, each with one hundred billion stars. Is there a duplicate universe with a duplicate Eddie and me throwing temper tantrums across continents? No one knows how the universe began. Or what came before it. Or whether it is expanding or contracting into nonexistence. When science falters, philosophers and priests pick up the reins. Aldous Huxley wrote that God is a gaseous vertebrate. God may also be a giant, glowing cosmic disk, an accretion of stars, and gas, and photon dust, rotating at unimaginable speeds in radiating circles. This cosmic, godlike stuff, carried by solar winds, rains down upon us and infuses our daily bread. But what do we make of it?

Every time you gaze at the stars you stare into the past, which seems inescapable. Some of those stars were born millions of light years ago and we're just now receiving the birth announcement. Eddie accused me of living in the past, then waxed sentimental about the great times we used to have together here. He said he didn't want to come, he didn't want to see me, but came anyway. It's evident that he'd like to kill me, yet he shared his catch with me, became confidential. His contradictions are as confusing as mine.

All day long, especially at Fallingwater, I had this strong feeling that I would see him. This has happened to us before. Bats, penguins and dolphins possess the uncanny power to echolocate their mates. A penguin can seek out its spouse and chick from amongst thousands of its own kind just from their voices. In college Eddie and I decided to split up and date other people for a while. This was before we'd moved in together. I'd go to a frat party and pick out the sound of his laughter from all the others. He'd go to a football game and hear me hooting and hollering above the roar of the crowd. We'd echolocate one another at the commons, the local coffee shop, the roadhouse hangout. This ability amazed us, and we became obnoxious about it, carrying on so much that our respective dates would leave, usually with each other.

His visit here tonight wasn't coincidental, but deliberate. What was the point? To tell me of his father's illness? To break into a jealous rage? It occurs to me that Eddie is just as scared of commitment as I am, only he plays it differently, making me the heavy. If I were to chase him, I bet he'd run. Where did I get the idea that marriage would spoil our imperfect love? Garbo used to say to her suitors, "Are we married yet?" as though commitment to spending time together were enough. If that's the case, Eddie and I have been married and divorced several times by now.

"You're like Taylor and Burton," Cara had once joked.

Serial monogamy makes more sense to me that the standard kind which puts unrealistic expectations on two people. Eddie and I are confused by our interchangeable roles of mentor and lover, friend and adversary, possessor and possessed. Where do we fit in?

I've tried love without lust, and lust without love, and have found both lacking. Maybe what I want isn't realistic; I've been accused of that, too. But why can't two people commit to one another without all the interference run by church and state? Holy wedlock, indeed. Locks are for bank vaults, not relationships. And holy is what you truly feel in your soul. What I feel for Eddie is enough to base a lifetime partnership on, I know that now, but we have to redesign the package, and neither of us knows how yet. Our relationship has become mixed up with survival and control and need, so it's not off to a good start, but it's better than most because at least one of us is aware of the problem.

A tiny film projector in my head runs the tape loop of Eddie's night call over and over again. I feel like I've spent the evening with a cross between Sylvester Stallone and Alan Alda. Or was he doing Rhett Butler?

CHAPTER SIXTEEN

The next morning I awaken to a flood of design ideas. I haven't felt this inspired since the visit before last to M'Lou. Why didn't I get the connection between the double helix and the spiral nebulae before? The linkage of amino acids forms a spiral called the alpha helix. From the microcosmic to the macrocosmic, the spiral constitutes the stuff of life, nature's grand design for the universe from the tiniest to the largest, from quarks to globular star clusters. Every single cell contains within it a small universe analogous to the cosmos. As within, so without. My head is aspin with moving images that defy depiction. I envision Vincent Van Gogh's "Starry Night" with its serpentine spiral nebula whirling through the sky as if on a desperate mission of its own making. Elongated, spirals resemble curls and curlicues; contracted, they become springs and coils; flattened, they're like pinwheels, disks, or circular pathways. Eddie told me that there was even a spiral ball in baseball, a screwball. Doubled, with bars, spirals form ladders, or winding railroad tracks. The lines once drawn seek form, and form usually seeks function. But what function do these sketches call for? Is it jewelry, or sculpture, or consumer product? Always I come up against this same block. I need to know more, to learn more. The tendency to pick up the phone and call my father for advice overwhelms. Not to have that recourse makes me feel cut off, but it was the choice I made and he'd expect me to stick to it.

Where do I begin? The grad-school applications are here somewhere, turning yellow at the edges. I dust them off and read through them. My first choice is Cranford Academy in Michigan, which offers a two-year program in multidisciplinary design, but without my parents help, the costs are prohibitive. Selection becomes a process of elimination. The best program for all my needs seems to be at Stanford University, which offers a one-year course combining mechanical engineering with art and product design. The program seems almost custom-tailored to meet my qualifications. If I do well on the Graduate Record Examinations and can get a fellowship, then maybe, just maybe, I can swing it.

There are a few hitches. I'd have to move to California to become a legal resident in order to apply for the fellowship. What would Eddie say? How would he take this, especially after he confided that he may be going to Stanford himself? He'd think that I was competing with him, pulling a fast one.

I have to get out of the habit of caring what Eddie, or anyone else for that matter, thinks. I have to get organized. There's so much to do that I feel overwrought. The next time I can take the GREs is in October. I have to get a job between now and then. Beyond this point I find it impossible to plan; I iron a skirt to wear to the hospital.

Tim Geary, Eddie's father, has a booming, oracular speaking voice which echoes through the hospital corridors. From the sound of it, he must be feeling much better. Eddie got his sense of humor from his dad, who sounds like he's kibitzing with some of the nurses. Here goes nothing, I think, entering the room.

"Rebeccah," Myra Geary says, rising to greet me. "It's so good to see you."

She's tall, stout, matronly, with fluffy white hair like Barbara Bush.

"It's good to see you, too," I say, kissing the air beside her cheek. "It's been a while."

"Yes," she says, sadly, holding my hands in hers, "it has. Too long."

Her hazel eyes are warm. When I look into them I imagine seeing the eyes of another woman living imprisoned inside of her, signalling an S.O.S. through a semaphore of blinking.

"You didn't happen to bring me a bottle of cold ale and some cigarettes?" Mr. Geary says.

"No such luck." I lean over to kiss the top of his shiny bald pate. "But I did bring you some jelly beans, a box of pick-up-sticks, and two airline bottles of scotch."

"I'll take that," Myra says, grabbing the bottles.

"Spoilsport," he says.

"You don't know what's good for you."

She's aggrieved, angry with his illness, and its ramifications for the family.

I almost didn't notice Billy, who looks like he wants to disappear behind the window shade.

"Hi, Billy," I say.

"Hi," he says, grinning sheepishly.

At twenty, Eddie's youngest brother Billy has barely escaped his teens intact. His sandy hair is tied at the nape of his neck into a tiny ponytail. A tiny skull-head dangles from a pierced earlobe. He's wearing a ripped Grateful Dead T-shirt and jeans. Constantly applying and reapplying cherry-flavored chapstick, he mumbles and stares at the top of his laceless high-top sneakers. I'd like to say that my brother has better social skills, but he doesn't.

"How's school?" I ask.

He mumbles something and appears embarrassed.

"Billy's on a sabbatical," Tim Geary says. "He's thinking things over."

I steer clear of this one.

"Where's Eddie?" I ask.

"He'll be right back," Myra says. "He went to make a telephone call. Teddy was here a few days ago," she volunteered. "He had to go back to Boulder."

"I'm sorry I missed him."

"So, how are you feeling, Tim?" I say, perching myself on the edge of his bed. "You look fine."

He smiles and peers at me from behind half-glasses. "Damn doctors, make life miserable," he complains. "I feel fitter than half of them look. Billy and I are going to the Indy stock car races when I get out of here, aren't we Billy?"

Billy's words dribble onto the floor. I want to give him a good shaking.

"Where have you been keeping yourself?" Myra asks. "Do you still live in New York?"

"Yes. I'm spending part of the summer here. I have a job interview in Philadelphia early next month. Wouldn't it be funny if I wound up back here?"

"You could do much worse," Tim says.

A young pretty nurse enters, laughing. Eddie is close behind. He acts unsurprised to see me.

"Hi, Rebeccah," he says. "Where did you come from?"

"Time for your pill, Mr. Geary," pipes up the nurse.

"Again?" he groans. "I just took one."

"Don't give her a hard time, Dad," Eddie says.

The girl giggles again.

I imagine pulling a lever that opens up a trapdoor through which she and Eddie will fall into a bottomless pit.

"When can I see the doctor?" Tim asks, chasing the pill with a glass of water.

"He'll be by a little later."

"That's what they all say."

"Is there anything else you need?" she asks, but the question is flirtatious, directed more to Eddie than his father.

"How about a new chassis? This one has about had it," Tim says.

She titters and gives Eddie a lingering, come-hither look on her way out.

I refuse to react to this sophomoric display. I refuse to act jealous, or to dignify the situation with a response other than pure indifference. I absolutely refuse.

"Rebeccah," Myra says, for not the first time.

"Excuse me? I wasn't listening."

"We're leaving now. Eddie has an appointment, and is going to drive us home. Would you like to come with us, stay for dinner?"

"I won't be home for dinner," Eddie says.

"I'd love to," I say.

"What are we having?" Billy asks.

"I don't know, dear," Myra says, vacantly. Sometimes the woman who hides inside of her shorts out, leaving the outer Myra to cope on her own.

We all kiss Tim goodbye. He looks relieved to see us going. People in hospitals often feel put upon by their visitors, as though they have to play host.

"Bye, bye Eddie," the nurse calls.

"So long, Connie. See you later."

It occurs to me that the reason he can't stay for dinner is not because I've accepted, and he's loathe to withstand my company, but because he has made a date with this bimbo. I make a clucking sound, like a chicken, signifying his taste for young, nubile girls, but he doesn't get it. Billy, however, does, and grins.

It takes us longer than usual to leave the hospital because Myra will only ride a certain elevator when it is empty, which is nearly an impossibility. Anxiously, we await its arrival and departure like immigrants for entry into the promised land. Finally, one comes, vacated.

Prisoners of Myra's compulsions, none of us dares breathe until we're safely outside the hospital and in proximity of the car.

I follow them home. Eddie drops off his mother and brother, makes a U-turn, and waves goodbye. Maybe I imagined that he had a date with the nurse. And even if he does, so what? Why is theory so hard to put into practice? So much for transcendence.

Myra was never any great shakes as a cook. She serves up overcooked lamb chops, soggy baked potatoes, and frozen peas and carrots. Billy wolfs his food and splits to go to a movie with his friends. That leaves the two of us.

Fascinated, I witness the garbage ritual. I'd forgotten the tinfoil stage which precedes the Ziploc stage. After she carefully wraps everything in tinfoil, it is encased in plastic zipper bags which are deposited into a brown paper bag which she *staples* shut. The bag is then enclosed in large plastic trash bags and *taped*. All that's missing is a big red bow.

"Would you mind?" she asks, handing me the bundle.

I take it across the street to a neighbor's trashcan, hoping no one is looking. What, I wonder, does Myra use her own trashcans for? Most of the Geary's neighbors tolerate her eccentricities because they love her. She's nuts, but harmless, and generous to a fault. Eddie's theory on his mother is that too much yang energy, three boys and a husband, has tipped her off balance. I know she regards me as the daughter she never had, and the subject of Eddie's and my floundering relationship arises like mist before the dawn. Eddie had told her that we were having trouble, but obviously left out the jucier details.

"You're both too young," she says, in the midst of ironing a white cotton glove, which she spritzes with spray starch. "You got too involved at a time when most children your age are experimenting. Eddie is as headstrong as you are. You do what you have to do. I know he will. It'll work out for the best."

Is this wisdom, or lack of interest? I'm not sure.

The Geary's livingroom is off limits. Nobody dares to venture in there. Plastic covers, grandparents of the Ziploc, enshroud the furniture and lamps, line the carpets. The family hangs out in the "family room," where we are.

One of Myra's favorite pastimes is rummaging through flea markets and secondhand stores looking for bargains. She'll buy things in unmarked lots for a dollar or fifty cents. This batch contains soiled white cotton gloves, mostly incomplete pairs. After soaking them in bleach for days, she's dried them out in the sun and is now in the process of ironing them. Each one, or pair, is then inserted into a Ziploc, carefully labeled WHITE GLOVES or GLOVE, and filed away somewhere. Boxes, shelves and storage closets all over the house contain similarly processed used sheets, pillowcases, handkerchiefs, antimacassars, children's clothes and who knows what else. When not shopping, she's cleaning. Eddie once told me that she used to use her tongue to turn on the light switch rather than dirty it with her hand. Her bizarre behavior was diagnosed by psychiatrists as ritualistic, obsessive-compulsive. Mrs. Geary lives by a strict set of rules which, if broken, would send her over the edge. Since there's no known cure, her family has learned to live with it.

"It's better than her being an agoraphobic–alcoholic–diet-pill-freak," Eddie once said, accepting the lesser of two evils as a solution. I can't help but wonder what Myra Geary might have accomplished if this penchant for cleanliness, order and organization had been properly channeled into, say, running a hospital, or a hotel, or a university.

As I'm leaving, she hands me a pair of freshly laundered mismatched gloves that are a size too small. I thank her and drive home with my brain rattling around my head as if too much air has seeped out. Mrs. Geary's life is run by her demons; one of these is kleptomania. Most kleptomaniacs are affluent women who can afford to buy the things they steal. Why do they feel compelled to do it? For the excitement and thrill? To add a little danger to a numb but comfortable existence? I think of Val, and how she copes through drinking and volunteering. That's her way. Deirdre's mother, an ex-alcoholic, gardens and also volunteers. Only the well-heeled can afford to give their time away. I think of my own obsessive-compulsions, although not too deeply. The pendulum swings in extremes. I hear the siren's call, only this time it has changed its tune and is now singing *work, work, work* instead of *sex, sex, sex*. I want to lose myself in it; to merge myself with interior worlds and landscapes where time and space bend into the other dimensions; to grab hold of the tail end of Van Gogh's spiral nebula and go wherever it takes me. Doing work that you love can be as intoxicating, time-consuming and maddening as a love affair.

Last night's fishing gear is strewn all over the garage. Feeling like Myra, I clean up, compulsively putting everything back in its place, fashioning a false sense of order and control out of the chaos of my emotions. I also re-order my priorities, resolving to concentrate on nothing but my design projects until I finish them.

Before leaving the secret place, I wanted to see Tim and Myra one last time. They told me that Eddie had left the day before to return to California. Seeing the disappointment on my face, they each offered excuses for him. We were sitting in the family room, drinking tea and polishing off the rest of the dietetic cookies I'd brought. Tim was half-watching a baseball game on television.

"He was very busy while he was here," Myra said, referring to Eddie.

I thought, "I'll bet."

"Wasn't he, dear?" she asked Tim.

"What's that?"

"Eddie, wasn't he busy?"

"Oh, yes. He said he was checking out the wine situation. I told him it was a waste of his time. This is strictly jug and beer country."

He turned back to the game.

I didn't stay long. Tim still wasn't feeling up to par, and Myra looked like she had enough worries without taking on Eddie's and my romantic problems. Besides I'm restless, and can't sit in one place for very long. I'm anxious to return to civilization, to get on with my life. Something about living alone begins to close in on you after awhile. The solitude I so recently treasured has become ominous, almost hostile. I keep bumping into myself, and I'm not always friendly. The work goes well, but after it's over I always come back to ground zero. Thoughts of Garbo appear less and less in my mind, but every large dose of aloneness I experience reminds me of her. Just how alone is she, really? Joel claimed to know people who knew her; he liked to act as though he was privy to her best-kept secrets. He said that she was much more of a social animal than people realized, with a wide circle of rich friends whom she'd visit whenever the whim struck. Among familiars her morbid shyness dissolved, and she'd talk and laugh and carry on, just like everybody else. But when a stranger appeared, she'd freeze. I read once that Richard Burton, upon meeting her, asked to kiss her knee. She consented. Joel said she'd had many lovers, far more than those broadcast by the press; that it was the interference by the press into her private life that contributed to her early retirement. One of her lovers was an English nobleman who was almost as beautiful as she was. Their romance lasted for a few years.

Still, she never married. She never committed to just one person.

The glimmering of a realization, one of those epiphanous moments that threaten to change forever the way you regard reality, slides like quicksilver in my mind. It's there, just within reach, but I can't quite take hold of it.

After closing up the cabin, I drive Kithy and myself to Philadelphia for the job interview with IKAIA. Gary loves the lingerie washboard and disdains the woman's valet, which she thinks is redundant. Camille loves the woman's valet and snubs the washboard, calling it "too pedestrian." I decide not to show them the sketches for automatic stroller, which needs work, and which I decide to patent and produce independently, if at all.

Gary likes my ideas for the Tools for City Living package I've designed and wants me to do up more models to show her—one for the indoor clothesline as well as the drying rack and porcelain washbasin. She compliments me on the washboard's jazzy colors and the interplay of its geometric shapes.

"I like the triangles encased by the rounded top and edges," she drawls. I place her accent in the Deep South, maybe Mississippi. "It almost looks like a jukebox."

Camille puts the washboard down as being too labor-intensive. It's a throwback. Women won't go for it.

Gary says it has great romantic as well as practical appeal.

Camille asks me if I can make a man's valet to match the woman's? He likens the latter to the female robot in director Fritz Lang's futuristic dystopia, *Metropolis*. Have I seen it? I have.

He nods, like I've passed some kind of test.

Studying the woman's valet, he says, "It's really more like a 'lady-in-waiting' than a valet."

Who am I to disagree? Actually, I'd thought of that before and said so.

"Hmmn," he acknowledges, airily.

Each insists that I do what he or she demands, but neither commits to a job offer. I am reminded of sibling rivalry, or worse, a soured office romance which has turned them into replicas of George and Martha in *Who's Afraid of Virginia Woolf?* Why has fate led me here? I like the place, and its product—quality housewares akin to, if not slightly better than, Conran's—but whoever works for these two would have to possess a higher threshold for migraines and masochism than I have. I thank them for their encouragement, and I explain that I need a job right away.

"The product manager slot is still open," Gary says, leaning back in her swivel chair. I admire her crisp little Chanel suit; she snubs my crumpled-denim elegance.

"I want to design products, not manage their manufacture."

"We could allow you room to do both," Camille says, glancing at Gary, who nods.

Now they're in accord. Neither says "take it or leave it," but it's implied.

"Come back with our suggestions for the new models," they say, "and we'll take it from there."

Feeling like I'm being jerked around, I take my stuff and run.

"Obviously, your destiny lies elsewhere," M'Lou says.

My disappointment is greater than I'd imagined possible. I want instant answers, advice. What should I do next?

"Read me the Tarot," I beg M'Lou.

"Aww," she says, sounding more than ever like Ruth Gordon, "you're still looking for the answers in all the wrong places."

CHAPTER SEVENTEEN

Iam beginning to experience my life as a retro-nightmare: existing in a self-imposed limbo, invisible, forgotten, a cipher of my former lovable, employed and competent self.

When I offered to buy M'Lou's second car, a vintage Volvo, she accepted. Driving back to New York, all I could think of was driving back out again, preferably in the direction of the West Coast. I've convinced myself that my inclination to go to California has nothing to do with Eddie. It has to do with a desire to start all over again, fresh, somewhere else. I had thought it might be in Philadelphia, but my session with Gary and Camille dampened my enthusiasm for looking for more work there. Pennsylvania, like New York, holds too many past associations.

Bucking traffic, I manage to make it to my block in one piece. Mrs. Wallace is on the stoop, schmoozing with the Feldstone-Kleins, whose complexions have the pallidity of an old wedding cake. I want to feed them fresh-squeezed orange juice and take them on long nature walks through the park. Mrs. Wallace told me that *he's* gotten his doctorate in psychology; *she's* still working on hers.

Spotting me, the landlady eyes the car with distrust.

"What are you going to do with *that?*" she asks in a voice that can be heard in the next county.

"Park a lot," I say.

"You planning on moving?" she asks, her eyes registering a rent increase.

"Not immediately."

"If you do," pipe up the Feldstone-Kleins, "we know of someone who'd like the apartment."

Mrs. Wallace is in an uproar. Bruce, sighting Kithkat, who is squirming in my arms, barks. I take to the stairs with the two of them not far behind.

"If you move," she yells, "you'll be breaking the lease. You have to give me plenty of notice. And I don't give security refunds to lease-breakers, and the apartment has to be left in the same shape you found it."

"My air conditioner is broken," I retort, "through no fault of mine. It's an antique. And so is the refrigerator, which is dying a slow, painful death."

"Fixing them is your responsibility. Or buy new ones if you don't like it."

Mrs. Wallace is punishing me for what she considers my profligate ways, and I all but slam the door in her face.

"You've changed," she yells, through the wood, "for the worse. You girls come here, and I don't know what happens to you. You think you can do as you please. Go through one man after another. You should know better." Still yammering, she descends the stairs. It's nice to know that the entire building must think of me as the Whore of Babylon.

One relief is not to find phone messages because I never turned on the machine. Before answering machines, people called back. I'll take my chances. Cara has been collecting my mail, and that too can wait. I've been mentally writing Eddie a letter since our last encounter in the mountains; now I sit down to commit to paper the words I need to tell him. By the time I'm finished it's twelve pages long, double-sided, single-spaced, hand-written. I confess how much he means to me, despite our differences. I ask him to cut the crap and find it in his little black heart to forgive me.

The minute I drop the letter into the mailbox, I think of a thousand other things I want to say, and rush home to write an addendum. It happens this way for nearly a week until every sentiment has been wrung dry. Since the letters aren't returned, I assume that he's received them.

A small package from him arrives, containing a birthday present. He'd dipped twenty-seven garbanzo beans in eighteen-karat gold and had them strung together into a necklace. There is no note, or card. My parents also send me a present from the Florida Keys, where they are still happily sailing around. It's a wall hanging made out of macrame and seashells and embroidered yarn. I hate it. They must be balmy from too much sea and sun.

Eddie's gift, however, mystifies. After playing phone tag for awhile we finally connect.

"Thanks for the birthday present," I say. "What is it?"

"It's a necklace."

"I know that. What does it mean?"

"It doesn't mean anything."

"Damn it, Eddie, you're being so damn cryptic." Then, "Did you get my letters?"

"Yes."

" . . . "

"I've been meaning to write," he says, "but I've been busy. In fact, I started one. It's about fifty pages long. It's turning into a book. Maybe I'll have it published."

"Let me read it first."

"What's it like in New York?"

"Don't change the subject."

"I still don't know where to file us."

I hear a female voice in the background.

"Who's that?"

He covers the receiver with his hand and talks to her. Their voices are muffled.

"Eddie, who is it?"

"A friend. No one you know."

"What friend?"

"Rebeccah, I just said no one you know."

Angry, she's telling him to get off the phone.

"Eddie, who *is* that?"

I hear a crash.

"I have to go. I'll call you."

"Eddie has a girlfriend," I tell Cara.

She shrugs. Cara is a consummate shrugger. I've learned how to interpret them over the years. This one says, "So, you thought he'd live like a monk?"

I'm at her place picking up the rest of my mail. Most of it is junk. A letter from Deirdre Holland is postmarked from Paris. She'll be home soon, perhaps by the time I receive this. I must confess that I haven't thought much about Deirdre lately. When we were kids we spoke religiously on the phone for hours every day, even if we'd spent most of it together. My mother could never understand what we found to talk about.

Cara waves a newspaper clipping in my face and asks, "Did you see this?"

There's a picture of Joel standing inside of his partially reno-vated Upper East Side restaurant, Holdesky's II. Something about the place looks familiar. Looking closer I recognize the sconces, shaped like Art Deco tulips.

"The little bastard stole my interior design ideas," I yell. "I can't believe it."

"Be glad that's all he stole," Cara says.

"I'll sue," I say.

"Write him a letter, on a lawyer's letterhead, just to let him know that you know."

This is a thought, but I haven't got the stomach for any un-dertaking that might mean reinvolvement with him, on any level. Secretly, I'm pleased that he thought the designs were good enough to steal. This is also his way of proving the folly of my trashing the relationship; of rubbing it in.

For my birthday Cara gave me a beautiful silver and turquoise bracelet. I show her the necklace Eddie sent. She laughs, and asks, "What do you think he did with the rest of the beans?"

"I shudder to think."

Some things are better left to be pondered in eternity, and the necklace now heads the top of the list.

Stephen J. Beale calls and invites me to dinner. Cara, bigmouth, must have told him about Joel and the sconces because over the smoked salmon he advises me to sue Holdesky.

"I'd rather have root canal."

"I'd be happy to handle it for you," he says, implying at a lower cost.

"Thanks. I really appreciate it. But it's a closed chapter."

Beale nods, like he understands. A warm and relaxed friendship is developing between us. The sexual attraction is muted by a nonchalance grounded in the fact that we both know the other is in the midst of a shaky, long-term relationship. We're like comrades-in-arms, and it frees us not to take ourselves or each other too seriously. He's gained weight since I last saw him, but is still hands-down the most handsome man in the room.

I shouldn't drink, because it weakens my resistance and opens up valves to my heart and brain and loins that should remain closed. The wine, restaurant and song all conspire to manufacture romance, and no one is a bigger sucker than I am when the mood strikes. Looking across at this gorgeous male, I fantasize about falling in love with him. What beautiful children we could have together. I would spend the rest of my life riding horses, having lunch, and being photographed for Town & Country in designer hostess gowns with borzois at my feet and little Stephen, Jr., and Missy flanking my sides. Catching my mood, Beale orders more wine and stares at me through dark, thoughtful eyes which reflect the candlelight. His eyelashes are so long they cast tiny shadows on his cheeks. We both know that I'll wind up spending the night with him.

He lives nearby, and after dinner invites me up for that night-cap we never got a chance to drink. We're greeted by doormen who resemble Prussian army officers. Everyone bows and scrapes. An elevator the size of my bedroom lifts us to his apartment, which is palatial. A small, timid Oriental woman, who bows her head and smiles a lot, lives in a long, narrow room off the kitchen. She cooks and cleans for him. She's watching television in the dark and jumps when we walk by. The kitchen is the warmest spot in the house, home of two budgies named Jeaves I and Jeaves II. Stephen abhors cats, and thinks the only worth-while dogs are hounds used for the hunt. His family keeps a dozen of them on the Virginia estate. His fondest memories are of the hunt. He has pictures he'll show me later. I think of Deirdre, and how she would eat all this up.

His bedroom contains huge chifforobes and armoirs, and a canopied bed. I've never made love beneath a canopy before. I imagine myself as an abducted princess bride. We undress ourselves and climb into his massive bed. He caresses my breasts, and I shiver.

"Cold?" he says, blanketing me in his body heat. We're both tipsy, and lonely. Ghosts of lovemaking past haunt me, but not for long. Stephen's concentration distracts me from remembering, keeps bringing me back to the present. He doesn't feed me any lines about how much he loves me, or needs me, or how beautiful he thinks I am, although he did say he liked my looks earlier, in the restaurant, over espresso.

"Oh," I said. "What do you like about them?"

"The way you look in pants."

This floored me. I made a mental note of it.

Stephen works hard to please, and is surprisingly adept in the slow, deliberate way he moves, and where he places his hands, and in assessing how ready I am, and in delaying his climax. Then the rubber breaks.

"Shit," he says, panting. "It's the last one."

"What're you doing?"

"Calling Kim. She can run out and get some more."

"Stephen, its 2:00 A.M. Where?"

He groans a laugh.

"Want to get kinky?" I say, not waiting for an answer, Joel taught me tricks, new uses of old body parts, amazing feats of dexterity with hands, fingers, feet, and various joints and makeshift cleavages. Beale is enjoying himself, but I can tell that he's also wondering about me. Where did I learn how to do this, and from whom? If shiitake mushrooms compelled Eddie to beat up trees, how would he react to my new expertise in the bedroom?

The next morning I awake with a headache and stare up at the canopy full of self-recriminations, and the blues. Wanting creates small depressions. The greater the want, the deeper the depression, the more frantic the need to find someone, or something, to assume the shape of the emptiness. We call this the "pursuit of happiness." Janis Joplin said, "It's not the nothing that gives you the blues, it's the wanting."

I don't want Stephen; nor does he want me, and this only creates a hollow drum in which we bang around, trying to make music from the noise. I want to leave without saying goodbye, to disappear; I listen to Stephen's breathing, plotting my escape. I'll leave him a note, saying I had to go and didn't want to wake him. He rolls over, flops an arm over me, cocks open one eye.

"Good morning," he says.

" 'Morning."

I'm afraid he's going to try to make love again, but he doesn't. After splashing about the bathroom, we climb back into his baronial bed and sip the bloody marys Kim had brought us. I could fit my entire apartment in his bathroom. Later, Kim brings us breakfast.

"Do you always eat in bed?" I ask, thinking, "I could get used to this."

"Doesn't everybody?"

Later, I wander around the apartment awed by its grandeur—cathedral ceilings; oil portraits of his ancestors, including an American president on the maternal side; antique furniture; silver; ancient chinoiserie; some fabulous French Impressionist paintings.

Stephen calls the place "the mausoleum" and wants to sell it to buy a loft in Soho, or a condominium in a building with a health club, or a townhouse. His mother won't let him do it and so he feels stuck, trapped.

"Why don't you move out, get your own place?" I suggest. He shrugs.

"How about redecorating, changing it to suit yourself?"

"These are family heirlooms."

I envy Stephen the independence his wealth affords him, but not its duty and obligation. There is about the place, and his life, a feeling of claustrophobia, and the dullness contracted by old money and its rigid behavioral codes.

"Do you want me to call you?," he asks outside. I don't know, and am on the verge of saying that I don't know when he digs into his jacket for a business card. "Here. Why don't you call me."

"Thanks," I say, grateful.

Stephen may be my first one-night stand. I try it on for size, deciding that it has its pros and cons: it's expedient, and satisfies an urgency, but it's lacking. The more men I sleep with, the more I realize how different each one is sexually.

"It would make a fascinating study," I tell Cara. "Imagine the field research!"

We're in her kitchen. She's giving me a manicure.

"So, did he ask you out again?"

"We left it open. We're not really each other's type."

"Hold still," she says.

"We could be friends, though."

"That's how I felt about Shel before I married him."

She looks at me. Her dark eyes are flashing silver patterns and bridal gowns, either in memory of her own, or in anticipation of mine. Married people, even those unhappily wed, aren't content until the world conforms to their own image.

"Another involvement is the last thing I need."

"Involvement is exactly what you need." Then, "Which color nail polish? Red, red or red?"

"I'll take red."

*　　*　　*

After Cara's, I'm not in the mood for a walk, but I don't want to go home. The apartment is full of wraiths. I head down the West Side, all the way to South Street Seaport, which is crammed with Saturday shoppers and tourists. Passing through the West Village on the way back, I consider going to Holdesky's to give Joel a piece of my mind. But I'd probably run into Lori and that deters me. She left a message on the machine suggesting that we do lunch, and I still can't get over it. Am I being ungracious by rejecting her, or is she being insensitive by asking? I can't figure out what I think half the time, let alone analyzing other people's motives. Joel hides behind her, I see that now. She protects him from everyone, including himself. That's why he rebels against her control. I'd be lying if I said I didn't miss Joel, or certain aspects of Joel. It's a funny thing about infatuation. The memory of being in love remains sharp, palpable, but when the infatuation is over, the love dies. Unless the initial passion evolves into something deeper, there's no resuscitating it.

Broadway takes me toward Madison Avenue. As I pass a welfare hotel on East Twenty-third Street, a brick flies out the window, landing a few feet in front of me with a crash. People stare at it dully, like flying bricks are an everyday occurrence. I could have been killed, just like that, and for a few self-pitying moments I imagine the repercussions of my untimely death upon my family, friends, Eddie. At this point, would he care?

I feel more alone than I have in my life; much more than I did in the mountains. I am on the outside looking in, and stare at passersby with envy, wondering where they are going, what appointments they're rushing to keep, with whom?

Garbo has compared herself to a lonely man circling the earth, a good analogy for me as well now. I once saw a color photograph of the earth, and its neighboring planets, that had been taken from a space probe. The earth resembled a giant blue aggie floating in space. The other planets in our solar system looked like mibs, immies, realies, glassies, and stealies which had been abandoned by titanic children in the midst of a game of space-ringers.

The Russian cosmonaut Yuri Gargarin returned from space a

new man, as if he'd had a unifying mystical experience. Whatever he saw, it changed his life forever. You could tell from photographs of his face before and after. Had he heard the music of the spheres? I imagine myself floating high above the planet. A Strauss waltz plays as I drift in orbit, like a satellite. It is very pleasant, and, except for the 2001 sound track, quiet. From up here you can witness the birth of pulsars and the red-death throes of supernovas. You can contemplate forever the eerie capture of light in the aspic of dark.

There she is, just up ahead, encircling the globe.

"How's it going?" I say.

"Ah, it is cold, and monotonous."

"What do you do up here?"

"Nuttin', I don't do nuttin'."

"C'mon down, down to earth."

"I cannot, I have no choice."

Pedestrians jostle me. Momentarily disoriented, I don't know where I am, or which way to turn.

"Trot, don't think," I remind myself, continuing on my walk. There is solace in movement and anonymity. For the first time I completely empathize with Garbo's disdain of celebrity and its unrelenting violation of her privacy.

Storm clouds foretell a summer downpour. Within minutes, small streams and rivulets of water form huge, filthy puddles. I scramble under an awning to wait out the torrent when I hear someone call, "Rebeccah!"

A large man, holding a soggy newspaper over his head, is rushing towards me.

"Larry!" I shout. "I can't believe it! It's so good to see you!"

We give each other big bear hugs. I feel redeemed.

Larry Rumpole was my favorite staff salesmen at my old job. A man of large appetites with a ruddy complexion, sharp blue eyes, and a silver tongue, he was the company's star brush seller, and one of my biggest allies at work. We play catch-up under the awning, and when the rain subsides, he offers to buy me a drink. I hesitate because Larry can pack it away, and I already have a hangover.

"C'mon," he says. "I know a place nearby."

It's a dive with bowls of soggy pretzels on soiled checkered tablecloths. It reeks of stale beer and sour whiskey.

He orders a bourbon on the rocks, and I a light beer. It's good to see him. He fills me in on Magorian and the polymer factory. Soon after I quit, Larry gave notice to take a better-paying position with the competition. His wife has just had her third baby, a girl. His oldest son is dyslexic, and his middle boy hyperkinetic, but outside of that, his baby daughter is a doll, the wife is doing fine, and he's (knock on wood) in good health.

"I can't complain," he says, ordering another round. "What about you? What have been you up to? Are you working?"

I shake my head, and tell him about my desire to break into the design end of the business, and how much more difficult it is than I'd imagined. Listening, Larry's eyes focus inward, like he's mentally flipping through a Rollodex of names and addresses. He comes up with something. He knows of a job with an award-winning design group who are looking for someone with a strong engineering background.

"They want an artist who also knows the nuts and bolts," Larry says, munching on a handful of pretzels. "They want to eliminate the middleman. You know, go from model to prototype to production and all the way to the marketplace with the least amount of hassles. A friend of mine works for them in sales and promotion. It's a class outfit. You interested?"

"Yes, very."

"There's only one hitch."

"What's that?"

"It's in California."

I don't believe my ears. "Where in California? No, let me guess. Santa Monica."

"Close enough. San Francisco."

We talk and drink some more. Larry reaches over and grabs my hand. I pull it away. Is he serious? Does he want to lay the sacrificial bodies of his wife and children at my feet? Even if I was interested in Larry, which I'm not, married men are off limits. Once was more than enough.

"Larry, you've had too much to drink. It's time to go."

"Yeah," he agrees, picking up the check.

Before we part, he gives me the number of his friend, who I call the next day. The friend gives me the number of the California firm. A receptionist with a foreign accent puts me through to the boss's office which tells me to fax my resume, and Fedex the portfolio, any models I want to show, and slides of my work—all of which I do. I call Eddie to tell him about the San Francisco job possibility, then decide against it. I don't want him to influence my decision one way or another. He's loosened up, and now confides details about his private life, which I don't want to hear, but force myself to listen.

He's seeing someone. Her name is Linda, and she hates my guts.

"Why? We've never met."

"She's jealous."

"Does she have any reason to be?"

He doesn't answer.

"Where did you meet her?"

"Cooking class."

Oh, that Linda. "Doesn't she have a boyfriend?"

"Had," he says.

"What happened to Sharon and Karen?"

"They moved."

"What about Maria?"

"What about the Runt?"

"That's finished, long ago, before I went to the Secret Place. I thought you knew that?"

Since he doesn't answer, I go on: "He was like a bad virus that worked its way out of my system."

"Maria and I did get involved. Her old man left her alone while he pushed his music career. We were both feeling pretty low. One thing led to another."

"What happened?"

"Joe, her husband, began to get suspicious. She was never home when he called, and the kids told him she was here. Since

Joe is a physical kind of guy, Maria stopped coming around, even to clean. One day I go to the door and this woman says, 'Hi, I'm Maria's cousin Gina.' "

"What's Gina like?"

"Gina-Gina-the-Cleaning-Machina, I call her. She's about twenty-five years older than Maria, with a moustache. But she packs a mean dust-buster."

I ask him more questions about Linda, trying to gauge just how interested in her he is. From what he says, it sounds like she's feeding into his vulnerability, taking advantage of it. The notion of Eddie's falling in love with somebody else is alien to me. I recalled what he'd said about meeting girls who want to get married. She must be the one.

"I have the perfect person for Linda," I say, aiming for a levity which doesn't ring true. "We could fix them up. His name is Stephen, and he talks like his mouth was shot full of novocaine. 'You know, like this.' " I say in imitation.

The line sounds like it went dead.

"Eddie? Hello? Are you there?"

"I'm here."

"Beale's a nice guy, a friend of Cara and Shel's. He's filthy rich and looks like Mel Gibson in a Brooks Brothers suit."

I'm making it worse, but I can't help myself, because neither Eddie nor I really know where we stand with one another and neither of us has the nerve to bring it up. All this pretense is beginning to wear thin, and is getting on our nerves. But I can't reach him. Emotionally, he still won't let me in.

Eddie cuts the conversation short, like he has a sixth sense about what's coming. The temptation to tell him about my impending San Francisco trip is on the tip of my tongue, but instinct warns me to keep my own counsel for a change. To wing this one on my own.

CHAPTER EIGHTEEN

The plane is late, the cab from the airport gets entangled in traffic, and I curse myself for this little act of self-sabotage.

DQ&Co. is located on Pierce Street in the Pacific Heights section of San Francisco. I spot the modern, glass-enclosed building immediately; situated at the bottom of a steep hill, and surrounded by neighboring Victorian row houses, it looks conspicuous.

The famous San Francisco fog is in full dress, rolling down the hill. Foghorns call to one another like animals in rut. The cab driver explains that the eerie glow emanating from behind the mist is the sun, which is shining over the bay. Ambivalent weather and a city of walkers? So far so good.

The Oriental receptionist greets me with a big smile. No apologies for my lateness are necessary. She's dressed in California-casual, but stylish and chic. As she announces me I pray this isn't one of those small renaissance design companies that thinks it's the best thing since Memphis. I'm hoping for some place with less style and more content.

A secretary, who is also wearing redefined classic but casual clothes, approaches. Maybe I should have worn denim and cowboy boots instead of a jacket over a long skirt and scruffy flats?

I am led down a plushly carpeted mauve passageway to the boss's lair—a large, stark white atelier with a tinted glass atrium.

David Q. Riley and I are introduced. We shake hands, and I notice that mine are slightly sweaty. Strike one.

Riley sits himself behind a huge parson's table that serves as a desk. I am motioned to a one-piece cantilevered chair sculptured from plastic. The chair is more ceremonial than functional, and there is no way to sit on it comfortably, so I perch, with my hands clasped atop my knees, like a penitent novitiate. Riley is an attractive man with a salt-and-pepper beard that matches his hair, dressed in jeans and an expensive open-necked white cotton shirt that hangs on him like silk. He's not quite old enough to be my father, but young enough to swap stories with me about our alma mater, Carnegie-Mellon.

Riley must have read a book about job interviewing. First he tells me about himself, and while he's talking I know that soon it will be my turn. Except for the particulars, I hardly hear a word he says: he earned an engineering degree at Carnegie, and a masters in art at the Art Institute of Chicago, then came west to do a stint in Silicone Valley. After a few years, he started his own company, which designs and produces award-winning high-tech gadgetry. Now he wants to expand into "contemporary renditions of domestic tools from a bygone era."

He thinks my Tools for City Living are interesting.

"Quirky," he says.

Another romantic, I think, feeling slightly more self-confident but nowhere near relaxed. Although friendly, his manner is standoffish, noncommittal. I get no sense of whether his interest in me is enthusiastic or lukewarm. He explains that he's still interviewing for the job, and appreciates the fact that I was willing to travel so great a distance at such short notice for the opportunity to meet.

"I'm happy to be here," I mumble.

I know what's coming.

"Now," he says, holding up the lingerie washboard, "tell me about yourself, and about this."

Everyone knows that the first task of an interviewee is to put the interviewer at ease. Suddenly, I am full of misgivings. I should have offered another design, something high-tech or even low-tech instead of no-tech. But if he wasn't interested, he wouldn't have gone to the trouble of this interview. To keep from hyperventilating, I stare up at the befogged glass ceiling. Have I already reached my limit, before I even begin? My whole work-life is passing before me. Everything I'd rehearsed mentally on the plane now sounds shallow, contrived. I want this job, badly, that much I know.

"I don't know where to start," I say, staring at the top of his head. "My ideas spring out of a basic dissatisfaction with modern household work stations. Ever since I'd started washing out my own lingerie I got in touch with things, feelings and sensations, that were being lost by the distancing of technology . . ."

Riley's facial expression is a mask of disinterest. I have no idea if what I'm saying has hit the mark. Strike two?

"I read a book called *From Hand Ax to Lasers* by John Purcell. In it he talks about the history of tools. My father owns some hardware stores, and tools have fascinated me ever since I was a child. Most girls play with Barbie dolls; I played with pliers and ratchets. Purcell talks about how tools are energy transformers. For instance, a can-opener transforms the chemical energy of the human muscle into mechanical energy. An electric can-opener transforms electrical energy into mechanical motion in another way. Most people prefer the latter. It's easier and quicker. I don't. I think something is lost in the transaction, in the leap from manual to electronic. The things we plug in require a minimum of effort, involvement, and knowledge, and for the most part that's good. It frees us for leisure time and other pursuits. But there's a tradeoff. Instant gratification breeds ignorance, tiny attention spans, high expectations, and growing discontent, not to mention waste. The distance between ourselves and our technology is growing . . ."

I've already said that. I'm repeating myself. I'd swear that Riley moonlights as a Freudian analyst. It's like talking to the wall. I have this desire to shock him, to get a response, positive or negative.

"Take the bra, for instance."

He doesn't budge. His mouth twitches in either a suppressed smile or yawn.

"A French woman invented it to take the torture out of wearing whalebone and corsets, and revolutionized the way women lived and felt about themselves. Whether I buy a bra at a five-and-dime for under five dollars or at a fancy department store for over a hundred dollars, it is still a delicate article of clothing. It can't take the rigors of harsh detergents and washing machines and dryers. And this is ironic, because the advertising for the earliest automatic washing machine prototype promised that machine-laundering would be less hard on clothes, not more. Today, so many clothes instruct handwashing, or dry cleaning. You can even buy a special bra-bag to use in washing machines to help reduce the wear and tear of repeated washings. I'd thought about doing it this way, then remembered the washboard.

"Travelling through India I had an experience I'll never forget. We were staying in a houseboat on Dal Lake, in Srinagar. The mode of transportation there is the *chikara*, the Kashmiri version of the gondola. We took a water tour of the lake's byways and it was like travelling backward in time. Women squatted by the water's edge laundering their family's clothes with washboards. I doubt if any one of those women would refuse the offer of a house complete with electrical can-openers, hot and cold running water and a washer/dryer. But the sight of them washing, talking, laughing amongst themselves, their communality, triggered off something within me. Another place at which I interviewed criticized the washboard as a throwback to a time when women were in purdah. Well, maybe that's true, but it also offers something that we've lost, something that those Kashmiri women, who are still in purdah, experience on a daily basis and probably take for granted, because they don't know any better. But we in the West do, and that gives us an advantage, an edge. We have a choice."

The light in the room brightens. I glance up at the ceiling. The fog is lifting.

"I'm not sure I can explain what we've lost. It occurs to me every time I use the washboard. It involves getting back in touch with touch, with the ability to hold something in your hands and enter into its small world with all your senses; to experience life, not intellectualize it. To focus the eyes so that they work in concert with the rest of you. Handwashing articles of clothing is mindless, like washing dishes or dusting. And it can also be meditative, mindful, even transformational, on both a mechanical and spiritual level. I want to bring the experiential back into living through the mass-produced objects we employ from day to day. What I'm talking about is changing one small facet of the way we experience life through design. I think redesigning antiquated objects goes beyond need or function. It falls somewhere between kitsch and antikitsch, classicism and modernism. It's very exciting, like being present at the creation of a new visual language. As you can see from the model and sketches, I've taken the basic washboard prototype, which is proletarian, and molded it into different forms and shapes, utilizing corresponding materials and colors. The one you're holding, I made myself, and styled in American Jazz Age–Deco. Its shape resembles a jukebox, and the neon colors re-emphasize that. After you use it, you can hang it on the wall in the kitchen, or bathroom, and it's fun to look at. Another favorite of mine is the Ming Dynasty model. I may have gotten carried away with the faux-cloisonne, though. This is one example of how you can visually alter an object and thus, perhaps, the experience of using the object.

"I'm not anti-technology. My degree is in mechanical engineering, with a minor in physics. What we've gained from technology is astounding, but we've also lost a lot, are losing a lot. The washboard in its myriad forms is symbolic of an attempt to regain what's been lost, and even to push beyond it."

I fear I'm running on too much.

For a few agonizing seconds, Riley says nothing.

Strike three?

"Why did you make the corrugated glass ridges in this shape, exactly?" he asks, holding up the model.

"Dennis Quaid's stomach muscles."

Now I know he's concealing a smile, but is he laughing with me or at me?

He asks me a few perfunctory questions about myself, and I volunteer that I am presently without a significant other, although I'm not sure about that, it could change at any moment. To stop from sounding too addlepated I confess my desire to return to school to study other design disciplines.

"I'm thinking about Stanford," I say, cheerfully.

He asks how long I'll be in town, and jots down the telephone numbers of my hotel and home.

We shake hands. "We'll be in touch," he says.

That one belongs with, "I'll call you" or "The check is in the mail."

"Nice meeting you," I say. "I hope you choose me."

As an afterthought, Riley says, "Did you know that this area used to be the communal washbasin for the city's laundry?"

"No, I didn't."

"That was before industry moved in and polluted the lagoon, which had to be filled in."

"Oh."

He smiles, but remains inscrutable to the finish.

So that the trip isn't a total loss, I set up an appointment to see the Stanford campus the next day, and rent a car to drive up the Peninsula.

Whizzing by some of the most magnificent scenery in the world, I question my ability to work or study in such a tropical clime. All I want to do beneath warm, sunny skies is drink tequila on the beach and look for mystery in a grain of sand. You can almost see how millions of years ago different chunks of the ancient earth's granite core tore apart from one another, then floated around for a while before docking along the California coastline to sprout redwoods. You can almost hear the clash of the tectonic plates. Writer-environmentalist Wallace Stegner wrote that California is "America only more so." But the natives pay a steep price for earthly paradise—smog, overpopulation, gridlock, water pollution—and those are manmade. Earthquakes, mudslides and wildfires are some of nature's bounty. Eddie told me there's a crackdown on polluters in L.A. You can get fined for grilling hamburgers or painting with vaporous paint or using underarm deodorant spray. He said he's thinking of going vegetarian and switching to roll-on.

Stanford University is mammoth. Housing seventy departments within seven schools, it looks like a giant Spanish mission. All this adobe grates after a while—too planned, too cute. By trial and error, I locate the Design Yard, a large, new environment composed of professional studio space and well-equipped shops, where I'd work if I got in. By the tour's end, I am impressed with the program, which is shaped to match your expertise, talents, and interests. It's overseen by four graduate faculty who are masters in cross-disciplinary design aspects. Since everyone is on vacation, I am shown around by one of the under-assistants, whose enthusiasm encourages me. She says that, judging from my education and background, my chances are forty–sixty. Even though the percentage of female designers has jumped from 25 to 52 percent nationwide from 1980 to 1985, it's still a male-dominated profession. Eddie told me that Stanford is so conservative that it thinks the Peace Corps is radical. Whether this extends to the graduate design program remains unknown. I had wanted to ask Riley how many women designers he has on staff, but didn't know how to go about it without appearing too aggressive. My sense of him is that gender doesn't matter as much as talent.

More than anything I want to talk to someone about all this, and call Eddie from the hotel room. All he cares about is, why didn't I tell him about the interview before I came.

"I wanted to go through it first. I'm playing a long shot."

Exasperated, he emits a deep sigh. "How'd it go?"

"I think I blew it. I was so nervous I started blathering about bras and Dennis Quaid's stomach muscles."

He laughs. "We'll come back to that. Where are you staying?"

"Some place Cara recommended. The Hotel Berenice, on Sutter Street."

"I know the place. It's near the Vintners Building. I've tasted some mighty fine wines in that building. How long are you staying?"

"I was planning to leave tomorrow evening. Any chance of our getting together before then?"

"Sorry, Rebeccah. I've already made plans for the weekend. You could have given me more notice."

"I'm sorry now that I didn't."

There's static on the line.

"Eddie? Hello?"

"I'm thinking. When's the latest you have to get back?"

"Tuesday."

"It's nuts to start looking for work in August. Everyone knows that. I'm surprised DQ&Co. saw you. They must be desperate. Look, as it turns out, I have to come up there on business. Why not sooner than later? I'll fly up Monday morning. We could spend most of the day together. Have dinner."

"Sounds great."

"What're your plans until then?"

"I don't know. I'll do something touristy, like take a cable-car ride."

"Just being in San Francisco is touristy. The whole city is a tourist agent's wet dream. Go to Chinatown for dinner and try the Dungeness crab, although it's out of season. Delicious. I'll see you Monday, around 11:00 A.M."

"I can't wait."

"Be sure to eat the crab with garlic and ginger."

"I will."

We hang up, and I think, I hate crab.

CHAPTER NINETEEN

Sundays are tough anywhere—like Christmas and New Year's Eve, not a good time to be alone. The day stretches before me like an interstate highway during a fuel crisis. What to do? Tomorrow Eddie comes, and I'd like to look nice for him. He hasn't seen me in a dress since my cousin Lucy's wedding, but where can I buy one on Sunday? Deciding to make this a project, I hit the streets.

San Francisco takes up only seven square miles, and its rolling hills offer breathtaking views. Strolling along, I pass S. G. Gump & Co. and stop to peer at the window display of silver, glass, china and multicolored jade. Cara insisted that I go here with Eddie, and now I see why. Traditionally, it's the place where brides go to register for fine housewares. But I want to redesign housewares, not register for them. Is this a problem?

"Yes," retorts the Cara of my mind, "it is."

"But why?"

"What makes you so special?"

"I'm not special, that's not it. I don't like the package."

"You used to."

"I thought I did, it's hard not to. The idea of not marrying is a new one for me. I don't know, I want something . . . *more*."

I imagine her shrugging. "There is no more. This is as good as it gets, Babe."

"I refuse to believe that."

"You're living in a dream world."

"Maybe."

"I feel sorry for you. You're going to wind up a lonely old maid, like your idol."

"That's exactly my point. Women are defined by their marital status, men aren't. Men can lead single lives of the mind if they so choose and no one blinks. Women can't, or they can, but the whole world judges them lacking. It, in a word, sucks."

Heading south, I hit Market, which is bustling with Sunday brunchers and shoppers. It feels good to mingle with the largely idle crowds. Many of the shops are open, but it is such a gorgeous day I can't concentrate on doing something I basically hate, like trying on clothes. My old green linen shift will have to do. Today is a day for just milling. Up ahead I see a tall, thin boy who looks like Rafael, the beautiful Puerto Rican I used to dance with at the clubs. But it can't be. What would Rafael be doing here? For that matter, what am I doing here? He's walking fast, almost running, obviously late for some appointment. Increasing my speed, I shorten the distance between us, and am tempted to call out his name, but what if I'm wrong?

He catches a bus on Market. I miss it but luckily there's one piggyback to it, which I board.

"Follow that bus," I say to the driver, who doesn't think I'm funny and refuses to make change. A woman, digging into her purse, bales me out. Careening along, the bus swerves around sharp corners and lurches over hills with a panoramic view overlooking the bay. The Rafael look-alike alights at Castro Street, and so do I. At any minute, I expect a loud siren to go off, warning the natives of an alien presence—like in *Invasion of the Body Snatchers*. Castro is crawling with humpy men, most holding hands. The eyes of gays are swift and measuring. A few looks are hostile, a few are not. The boy whom I think is Rafael is sprinting up the block. It's hard to keep up with him, but I'm practically on his back. He enters a bar, and so do I. It's dark, so it takes a few seconds for my eyes to adjust. When I do, I find myself returning the cold, hard stares of a bunch of men in Naugahyde.

THE GIRL WHO LOVED GARBO

"No women allowed," growls one.

Someone bumps into me from behind.

Confused and embarrassed, I turn to leave when I hear, "Leta!"

"Rafael? Oh, thank God. I thought it was you."

"Do you come here often?" he says, laughing, loping toward me.

"I was going to ask you that."

Someone calls him.

"I'll be right there," he yells. To me, he says, "I'm late for work. Where are you staying?"

"Hotel Berenice."

"For how long?"

"Till Tuesday. But I may get a job here."

"Is Joel with you?"

"No. It's over."

He grins. Rafael said it wouldn't last.

He used to tell me that I was too good for Joel. I wasn't too good for him, just not enough for him.

Fumbling for a pen and some scrap paper, Rafael jots down his phone number. "Call me the next time you're in town."

"I will."

He waves, and disappears behind swinging doors.

By now the men have lost interest in my intrusion; it's like I'm invisible. Starving, I grab a hamburger at a crowded joint on Polk Street, which is less macho, more mixed and friendly, then head back toward the hotel by foot.

If Los Angeles is a serial city, composed of over a hundred sprawling partitions, San Francisco is one, large partition encompassing myriad serial neighborhoods which flow from residential to commercial to residential without relief. Many of them remind me of New York on a much smaller, more hospitable scale. Castro is Greenwich Village's Christopher Street, only, in keeping with California, "more so."

Haight-Ashbury is windy and full of young married couples with credit cards. I'm reminded of the West Village, or Park Slope, where Eddie and I used to plan to move, into a brownstone of our own, when we married. We could just as well move into a Victorian row house here, live, work, and raise little garbanzos, but the mere thought arouses the same disquieting resistance and unreadiness that I always feel, no matter where I am. A line from a poem, long forgotten, pops into my head:

> *The mind is its own place, and in itself*
> *Can make a heaven of hell, a hell of heaven.*

The mind is its own place . . . It's from Milton's *Paradise Lost,* and I know all about the loss of paradise; it's the redemption I'm after. Purgatory is a populated place, crowded. I hate crowds, who herd and bray, holding one another back. I always find myself straying, veering off in a different direction, looking for the less trodden and peculiar. What was it Joel had once said to me? He'd called the path I'd chosen singular, narrow, melancholy. How about adventuresome, exploratory, exciting? What did I ever see in the little shit?

I'm not sure how I discovered the Filbert Steps, but a couple wearing plaid who are heading down as I head up smile at me like we've happened on the best kept secret in town. The view from Nob Hill is spectacular, though I think it may be my last: my heart is pounding from the climb and I feel on the verge of cardiac arrest. I take a cable car back down. Like the Eiffel Tower, this is such a well-publicized tourist attraction that I feel like I've done it before. In fact, most of San Francisco strikes me that way.

On my way to the hotel, I wander through Chinatown. The narrow back alleys here—crammed with herb shops, sweatshops, temples, people on puzzling errands—are more interesting than the main strip. I'm tempted to follow one of them to see where it would lead me. This reminds me of something, of someone, and as I stare at a clothesline with fish hanging from it, I remember. In the early days of her career, Garbo and Stiller went to Turkey to make a film. She saw a man on the street who aroused her curiosity, and decided to follow him to see where he lived.

Hours later, she discovered that he didn't live anywhere, but wandered the streets day and night. One can wander or follow; but to be both the wanderer and the follower takes a certain fetish for ambivalence that strains even my talent in that area.

The Chinese Fortune Cookie Factory is a clangorous, mechanical place that smells of cookie batter. I prefer the illusion that the fortunes in the cookies are written by sage old men with long, white beards.

My feet are killing me. By the time I reach the Hotel Berenice, my leaden legs refuse to move beyond the bed. Bumping into Rafael like that is either a stroke of good luck or a bad omen, I can't tell which. He still calls me Leta, but I know that Leta Velveta has sung her swan song. Or is she just getting started? Tomorrow Eddie comes. I cogitate in great detail over how to accessorize, now wishing I'd bought something new and pretty for him.

Eddie is fifteen minutes late, unusual for him. I am about to call the desk clerk when the hotel phone rings.

"Your date is here," I'm told.

I feel giddy and girlish. One last glimpse in the mirror, one last spritz of the hairspray, and I'm off.

Eddie isn't in the lobby. Walking toward the hotel entrance, I see him sitting outside in the car and marvel at the rush of excitement I feel. He's wearing a jacket and a tie. We'd never discussed how to dress, and I'm thrilled that we opted to dress up, not down, for the occasion.

Of all the roles that he could have chosen to play, White Knight was the one I least expected. He's rented a huge, white Chevy Impala convertible. I can tell from his studied nonchalance—his right arm extended over the back of the car seat, drumming his fingers on the leather—that he's making an effort to relax. He sees me and smiles. For an instant we have no past, no future, only the present, pure and uncomplicated, but the instant passes as quickly as Eddie's smile fades.

He leans over and unlatches the door.

"What a great car," I say. "Where'd you get it?"

"From a friend."

He eyes me from head to toe. "Green's a good color for you."

"Thanks."

"Don't mention it."

"Where're we going?"

"You'll see."

For all the display, we're awkward with one another, hesitant and unsure. Small talk was never my forte. Every conversation-starter I think of sounds corny.

"So," I begin.

He doesn't respond.

"Nice day," I continue.

He nods. Two can play this game. I shut up and concentrate on the scenery. We pass through sleepy green hamlets nestling between sloping valleys that look like giant breasts.

"Welcome to the land of the endless grape," Eddie finally says as we enter Sonoma.

Donatello's Winery is located on a hill, and while Eddie is inside negotiating the terms of his career move, I sit contentedly outside on a rock overlooking the grape arbors—rows and rows of viridian scrolls of trees and shrub.

After an hour, he resurfaces looking smug.

"How'd it go?"

"Pretty good. We're still haggling, but they're coming around."

I envy Eddie his self-confidence. Riley and I didn't discuss money, benefits, perks. I feel deflated.

"C'mon," he says, "I'll take you on a tour of the place. In the fall, the time of the grape harvest, you could get drunk from just inhaling the aroma of fermenting wine."

The storage casks are housed in limestone caves that had been carved out long ago by Chinese laborers, I'm told. In his element, Eddie tutors me in the fine arts of wine-making and wine-drinking. We sample some of Donatello's finest, but after three or four tastes, I can't tell the chardonnay from the cabernet sauvignon, or the zinfandel from the pinot noir.

"You never could hold your liquor," he grumbles.

"I'm starving."

"I know a great place," he says, and we get lost looking for it.

"Eddie, anywhere will do. How about that place?"

Desperate, we try a local grill that accepts reservations only, and I glean that beneath the bucolic camouflage of Sonoma thrives the unmistakable California fantasy lifestyle, a merger of hip and yup.

Eddie loves playing tour guide, and while we drive in circles he regales me with the folklore of the Indian tribes who once inhabited the valley, and the Spanish conquistadors who drove them out.

I am ready to scream. He is acting like everything between us is fine, when it's obviously not. If he's going to act like an emotional android, I'm going to be the superbitch, the ball-breaker, who has to ruin everything. Besides, I have to pee, and the growls of my stomach, if measured in movements, would go off the Richter scale.

"Over there," Eddie says, pointing, "look at that hacienda. Isn't it a beauty? You know, there are thousands of acres of grape in this valley, with a hundred and fifty family-owned wineries. One day I'll have my own winery: Geary & Sons."

That does it. I feel bushwacked, beleaguered and furious. Has he always been such a one-way street? Nor do I appreciate the allusions to sons that I may or may not bear him. I open my mouth to complain when he announces, "We're here."

The car rolls up a long driveway to the restaurant which juts out over the valley. The view alone is worth the wait, and the food, I am promised, is better than the view. I run to the john to freshen up, and get a grip. Eddie has ordered appetizers for us both. The waiter returns with two plates of steaming escargot in their shells. I hate escargot, almost as much as I hate crab. Since Eddie's and my separation, the unravelling of my real likes and dislikes is a constant surprise.

"Excuse me," I say to the waiter, "but could I please change my order? I'd rather have the asparagus vinaigrette."

"Very good, Mademoiselle."

"What was *that* all about?" Eddie asks, irritated.

"I don't like snails."

"Since when? We ate them through France, remember?"

"Since now."

He studies me, trying to figure out if I'm being contrary or telling the truth.

The sommelier brings the wine. Ceremoniously, he uncorks, sniffs, and sips it from a silver cup which hangs around his neck. He pours. Eddie tastes, nods approval. The sommelier bows. He is white haired, dignified-looking.

"May I also recommend the *Beau*-jelly and the N*u-it* St. George?" he says in all seriousness.

Eddie and I look at one another, and can barely keep from laughing in the sommelier's face. The comic relief diffuses some of the tension between us, and for the first time we start to enjoy ourselves. We did in fact order some beau-jelly. Eddie mimicked the sommelier's accent perfectly.

"Very good, *mon*-sieur," the sommelier said. "You won't regret it."

This cracked us up more.

"I've got it!" Eddie exclaims. "The guy thinks he's saying it right. I mean, nobody tells him, and everybody mocks him, so he doesn't get it. He thinks that that's the way it's pronounced."

We dwell on this for awhile. It's like old times, except that there's a lot of sediment in the bottom of our glasses which we're reluctant to stir up. We talk about safe things, or rather Eddie talks. I listen. After a while it all sounds familiar. It's not what he's saying, but how he says it: Eddie is doing Fallingwater. Only instead of architecture, it's oenology; and we're not in western Pennsylvania, but northern California. He's transferred his grand populist vision from one profession to another. Once he yearned to house the masses in styles to which they'd never been accustomed, now he aspires to educate their sensibilities and taste buds to the grape. To hear him speak, he will produce the finest affordable wine the world has known and plant it on every dinner table across America before he's thirty.

In the background, I hear not the sonorous sounds of the waterfall, but the popping of corks and the plopping of wine as it pours from bottle to glass. Eddie is either completely full of shit or he's going to accomplish great things one day, I can't tell which. I start to laugh. Tears come to my eyes, and I have a coughing fit.

He looks irritated, then alarmed. Solicitous, he pats me on the back, offers me a glass of water.

"I'm fine," I say, "really."

"Don't go hysterical on me. Lay off that stuff for awhile."

He asks me about the job interview with DQ&Co. One word leads to a verbal flood. As it spills out, I appreciate how much I've missed talking to him. How the best part of our cohabitation was the shared confidences, the pillow talk, the bond of intimacy made up of genuine affection, familiarity, respect. That was in the first few years of our living together. Gradually, without realizing how, we became two people who'd lost touch with each other; who'd grown to want and expect too much from one another, and to resent the disappointments for which we'd lay blame at each other's feet. He sought to break the stranglehold by moving out here, I see that now. But we've almost thrown the baby out with the bathwater.

I want to share my revelations with him, but don't know how to switch gears. So I'm trying to work them in while babbling about events that have led me here—the disappointing interview at IKAIA, the chance meeting with Larry, the interview at DQ&Co., the Stanford campus tour. It comes out garbled. I sound like I am rubbing his nose in my independence, like I am moving to California to spite him. That's not what I mean at all.

Eddie's face pales. Before my eyes he is transformed from jolly human to monster worm, lost in his circuitous wormhole of jealous rage. What led me here has nothing to do with him, and he can't stand that. He used to encourage my work, my projects, my ambition, even act like he admired me, but no longer. I want Octaman back, not this slippery, serpentine monster sitting across from me with flaring nostrils and narrowed eyes.

"You think you got the job?" he asks.

"It's hard to tell. Riley never let on how he . . ."

He doesn't let me finish.

"Ha!" he says, tossing his head. "You kill me, Rebel, you really do."

"What's that suppose to mean?"

"Nothing. Let's get the hell out of here."

He's silent on the ride back, closed in on himself, shutting me out again. His mood swings are extreme, and I'm sick of them.

"Look, I just wish you'd just get it all off your chest."

He ignores me.

"Stop acting like a pecker."

He gives me a takes-one-to-know-one look.

We pass the Golden Gate Bridge, which is magnificent all lit up at night. I'm thinking of what a marvel of engineering it is when he says, "Eight hundred and twenty-two people have jumped from here since 1937."

"Thanks for telling me."

We head for the hotel, and double-park.

"You really plan on moving out here?" he asks.

"Does that bother you?"

"Just answer me."

"I'd be willing to give it a try."

"That's not the impression you gave me in Santa Monica."

"A lot has happened since Santa Monica."

"Don't remind me."

"Look, just say what's on your mind. I hate all these innuendos. Tell me exactly what's bothering you."

"A lot of things are bothering me. You, for one. I don't know how I feel about you anymore. I want to forget you, to erase you from my mind, but I can't. I just can't shake you."

"I know. I feel the same way about you."

"Do you? I don't think so. I don't think you have a clue about how I feel. You don't know the hell you've caused me."

"Yes I do, I do know."

Eddie turns and asks, "Look, what the hell do you want from me?"

"What we had. Friendship . . ."

"Friends don't do to each other what you did to me."

"You keep talking about what I did to you. I didn't do anything *to* you, Eddie. Why can't you get that? You're so bogged down in male pride, and protecting your honor, that you can't see anything else. What I did, I did *for* me, not *to* you. And it's a mistake I keep paying for over and over again. Did you read my letters? I said it all in my letters."

"Of course I read your letters. Do you think that saying you're sorry is going to make it all better? Now who's the pecker?"

"I carry this thing everywhere I go," I say, pulling the gold-dipped garbanzo-bean necklace from my purse.

"You like it? There's plenty more where that came from."

"Were you awake that night?"

A horn honks from behind us.

"Look, it's late. Overall, it's been a swell day. Why don't we leave it at that."

Neither of us could have figured on the airport scene.

I went to bed thinking, *It's over*, tossed and turned thinking, *It's over*, and awakened from a fitful sleep, thinking, *It's over*, like I was trying it on for size.

This recurring theme accompanied my packing. At any minute, I expected Eddie to call and cancel his offer to drive me to the airport. Our differences seemed irreconcilable. All night long I examined our relationship like it was a big rubber ball with stations of our life together painted onto it. I had to turn the ball over and over again in order to delineate the boundaries of one phase from another. A lot of the lines had blurred, and the ball was getting too heavy for me to carry with all my other baggage.

The desk clerk called up to tell me he'd arrived.

Barely civil, he grunted a hello and threw my luggage into the back seat of the car.

He wore a Dodgers baseball cap, which he hid beneath and

kept realigning on his head, as though it didn't fit right. I felt like Barbara Stanwyck in a Forties *film noir*—fatal, lethal, tragic, the cause of not only my own ruination but of my man's. Eddie's feeling of betrayal runs deep—too deep for words or apologies or explanations. How could one act of infidelity, of transgression, make null and void all of the good years we've had? Before last night I had believed in the resurrection of our love, a phoenix rising out of the ashes, but now I'm not so sure.

I crossed and uncrossed my legs and wished I smoked.

Eddie fiddled with the radio dial but couldn't catch a good station. He began to beat the steering wheel with the palms of his hands in time to some melody in his head. Then he started telling jokes, including some tasteless ones about Polish people and dead babies.

"Just stop it!" I yelled. "Don't do this to us, to me!"

Peeved by my outburst, he quieted down and relapsed into silence. I didn't know which was worse. Numbness had set in at this point. I just wanted to escape.

We checked our baggage and walked together as far as possible. This is it, I thought, *It's over.*

We loitered together, awkward and sullen. I looked up at him, one of the few men I can do that with. He looked awful, like he'd slept in his clothes; unshaven.

Reading my mind, he said, "I really tied one on after I left you last night."

I was reminded of a guilty school boy—the boy I had met and fell in love with; of the man he'd grown to be, and was still in the process of becoming.

"Octaman," I said, reaching out, touching his face.

He recoiled, as though the tips of my fingers would singe his skin, then relaxed, covering my hand with his own, leaning into it, closing his eyes, and giving in to it. And I knew what was wrong between us, just like that, like I'd never not known except for thinking that I did. Blind faith is for fools and children. Eddie and I can't go back to the days of innocence, but we have to get on with the rest of our lives. Part of me wanted to cling to him, to submit to and be subsumed by his male authority, but another part wants just the opposite. Real commitment involves surrender, and you can't surrender without trust, and trust will not be compromised.

The energy between us changed; we could both feel it happening. According to the Heisenberg uncertainty principle, nothing is as it seems, not a thing. Eddie's and my ideals about each other had been shattered into millions of subatomic particles. Who knew how or where they'd reassemble?

"Beam us aboard, Scottie," I said, and he laughed. His stooped shoulders straightened, and his face brightened. We gazed into one another's eyes. The quixotic smile on his face would haunt me for a long time.

I don't know how long we stood there, or what words we said, or if we even spoke at all. Our emotions looped around us, like string twisting into various shapes and configurations: now love, now hate, now anger, now pain, now loss, now gain. In the end what's left is two people saying goodbye in an airport, for however long it takes.

Our leave-taking was wrenching. I don't know why I didn't surrender to him on the spot, I came so close, we both did, then we each pulled back and parted. All this time I'd thought that that fin in the water belonged to a shark. But it doesn't; it's a dolphin splashing and playing around me, making great spiraling leaps into the air, tempting me to follow.

I can't remember boarding the plane, and throughout the entire flight back to New York I prayed it would remain aloft for at least ten thousand years, so that I could figure out what had happened.

CHAPTER TWENTY

I returned home a basket case. I knew that I had to get out of New York, and decided to pack and drive to San Francisco to look for a job, any job at this point, as soon as possible. It seemed that the minute I'd made the decision, everything fell into place. Dave Riley called to offer me the designer's position at DQ&Co.

"Are you interested?" he said.

"Are you kidding?"

We talked about salary and benefits. The pay was half as much and more as Magorian had offered me. Riley said that he liked my ideas, but that I was on the wrong track. We'd talk about it in greater detail when I got there.

"I want to see you here at 9:00 A.M. sharp the day after Labor Day," he said. "Can you handle that?"

"I'm halfway there."

He gave me an assignment, which I was puzzling over when the phone rang. Deirdre Holland is in town. I love Deirdre—she's my oldest and dearest friend—but I don't have the time right now to entertain her.

"Not to worry, mon amie. You'll hardly know I'm around."

The least of my worries was Mrs. Wallace and the breaking of my lease. After I explained that I'd found work in California, she

drew her own conclusions: I was chasing after Eddie, desperate
for him to forgive me and take me back. In Mrs. Wallace's
opinion, moving so far away from family and friends for anything
less was worse than *messugganah*.

"You think it's going to be better out there," she accused. "I
hope for your sake it is."

I didn't bother to argue with her. Eddie's and my reconcilia-
tion may or may not be written on a fortune cookie. Anything is
possible, but it's none of her damn business. I almost said so, but
I can't afford to alienate her further. Who says I don't know how
to compromise?

Deirdre arrived with enough luggage for a six-month stay.
Cara, as usual, saved the day by throwing a small going-away
party for me to which Deirdre is invited, and where I introduce
her to Stephen Beale. Standing on the sidelines, I watch Deirdre
flirt outrageously with Stephen, who doesn't seem to mind.

"If this is your best pal," Cara says, "I want to meet your worst
enemy."

"She has a lot more in common with him than I do. They can
compare trust funds."

"They're both beautiful," Cara agrees. "In fact, they could be
related."

"Her five o'clock shadow is darker."

"Meooow. I thought you didn't care about him?"

"I don't. Not in that way."

"Here," she says, handing me a plate of cheese straws, "pass
these around."

"I'm the guest of honor," I protest, "the soon-to-be godmother
of your unborn child."

"So? That doesn't make you a Jewish princess."

Cara is pregnant. A cousin of hers, who claimed that Cara's
doctor was a quack, persuaded her to seek a second opinion from
a fertility expert. The expert told them that there was nothing
wrong with Shel's sperm that a little boosting wouldn't help.

"What kind of boosting?" I ask.

She shrugged. This one means "I'll never tell, but at least try."

"C'mon," I coaxed, "What did you do? Put a little Spanish fly in Shel's coffee?"

"I took him off caffeine, alcohol, and sugar. And we're learning to do more with less."

"You mean. . . ?" I wasn't sure I understood.

"I had a pelvic infection, low-grade, and we were doing it too much anyway, trying too hard."

"So now, you. . . ?"

"Quality, not quantity."

Knowing too many sexual secrets about your closest friends breeds embarrassment. Changing the subject, I asked, "Is it a boy or a girl?"

"It's too soon to tell. We don't care as long as it's healthy."

"If it's a girl what are you going to name her?"

"Rebeccah."

"Really?" I squealed, my voice rising an octave.

"Uh-huh."

"And if it's a boy?"

"Burgess."

"Burgess?" Up another octave.

"Burgess Sheldon Shelstein."

"It has a certain cachet. Wait'll I tell Mom."

The happiness I feel for Cara and her pregnancy is muddied by the sadness I still experience from the memory of the forced termination of my own. I'm going to miss Cara terribly, and by the end of the evening everyone knows it, *ad nauseum*. Deirdre has to drag me away. She's got Beale on the brain.

"I can't believe you're leaving lui behind," she says, repeatedly.

In high school Dee and I used to spend hours fantasizing about being grown up and sophisticated and French. We invented an Anglocized French patois that we still use, and which only makes sense entre nous.

"Did he ask tu out?" I ask.

"Don't worry, not that I didn't try. What's l'histoire on you two?"

Rarely do Deirdre and I like the same type. It happened once in grammar school, I think. Memory serves up a picture of a rangy little boy with freckles and a cowlick. She thought my first boyfriend, Jay, was a superjerk, and Eddie is a close second. The men she likes are all stuck-up, like her.

"There's not much to tell. We've gone out a couple of times, that's about it. What if I told you that I was toujours l'amour with him?"

"Are you?"

I shake my head, "Non, mon amie." Then, "I'm taking a sabbatical from the love market for a while. To show you what a big sport I am, I'll give you Stephen's carte de business."

She inserts it in her Filofax under THINGS TO DO.

The next day I let her talk me into going shopping. She's staying at the Wyndham Hotel, where I pick her up. Her father keeps a suite there for business purposes. My parents and hers are good friends, although the Hollands are much richer and snootier than we are. I loathe shopping, but decide to humor Deirdre who insists that we go in search of some new boutique in the East Fifties that a friend of her mother's told her about. But first we make pit stops along the way. In Ann Taylor's, Deirdre announces that she's seriously thinking of joining the Peace Corps.

Rolling my eyes, I say, "Get a job."

"No, Rebe, I mean it."

She selects a bright red cashmere jacket and examines it.

"Deirdre, pourquois?"

"I think this would look nice with the skirt I bought at Bergdorf's."

"Not why the jacket, but why the Peace Corps?"

"Why not? I mean I've been around the world several times, done everything. I feel purposeless."

"What about the art gallery? Remember? You were going to open one up in Baltimore, or someplace?"

"The world doesn't need another art gallery. It needs people relating to other people in caring ways."

My poor-little-rich girlfriend, who is decked out in her designer clothes and two-hundred-dollar haircut, is either putting me on or deluding herself.

"I'm serious, Rebe. I've never been more serious."

"Will you be taking the jacket?" a salesgirl asks.

"Yes."

"Will that be cash or charge?"

"Cash. Do you take traveller's checks?"

The girl nods.

"But you can't go shopping in Mauritania, or wherever they send you," I insist. I don't know why I'm carrying on so.

"Believe me, you can shop quelque part if you have the means. None of this matters," she says with a sweep of her gold-braceleted arm. "This is like le dernier Binge before le grand Diet. I've shopped from here to Zanzibar. I'm bon marche-ed out—all shopped, lessoned, schooled and traveled out."

The salesgirl exchanges a look with one of her colleagues. Very few people sympathize with Deirdre's problems. They think she's a rich, spoiled bitch, and she'd be the first to admit it. But I know Deirdre better. In her case, what you get is so much more than what you see—if she so elects.

Out on the street, she says, "Let's skip Hermes. Their stuff bores moi."

"Deirdre, how can you spend two years in some third-world country where they don't have indoor plumbing if all that inter-ests you in New York is looking for a new place to shop?"

"That's not fair. You're hitting below the belt. I could ask how you can think about stealing ideas from the poor people of third-world countries to provide products for the rich who have no real use for them?"

"That's unfair!" I feel misunderstood.

"See what I mean?"

"Yes, unfortunately."

"Nobody takes me seriously," she says, and the way it comes out, like all the air has been let out of her balloon, makes me feel sorry for her.

"I do, mon amie," I say, "I think you are tres serious."

241

She starts sniffing. I'm afraid she's going to cry.

"Do you have one of those ridiculous, oversized hankies you always carry?"

I don't, but extract some moldering Kleenex from the bottom of my purse. She blows her nose. Several times in my life I've seen Deirdre Holland drop her guard to reveal just how vulnerable she really is. She has the toned body of an aerobics fitness freak, but the soul of an anorexic, and suffers from all the fears and insecurities intrinsic to the disease.

Laughing, arm-in-arm, we rove around the East Fifties in search of the shopper's Shangri-la. We never find it, and don't really care. Hot, exhausted, hungry, Deirdre treats us to lunch at an overpriced French restaurant. I order the French equivalent of a hamburger. She orders something that looks like throw-up, and I say so.

"You still eat like a teenager," she says.

"Well, it does."

"How're your folks taking your move to San Francisco?" she asks, eager to change the subject.

"Don't you know? Didn't your mother tell toi?"

"She's in Europe, remember?"

"Oh, that's right, Val is miserable that I'm moving so far away. She called and said, 'Your father and I have been talking, and we don't want you to move to California.' Then, when that didn't work, she called and said, 'Your father and I have been talking, and we don't want you to drive out there alone.' Poor Val. She never stops being a mom. But she's thrilled that Eddie and I will be in the same state, maybe even in the same city again. To them it all augurs well."

"And to you?"

"Who knows, mon amie, who knows? Life is like connect the dots. One dot is over here, and another is over here, and another is here."

By the time I'm finished, the whole table is rearranged.

"I get the point."

"Well, the choices you make are the lines that connect the

dots. And you don't know what the big picture looks like until the end."

"You always were full of merde, mon amie."

"Pense-tu?"

On our way home, we walk pass Joel's apartment building. The doorman recognizes and nods at me. I pray Joel doesn't emerge and I mentally rehearse how I'd react if he did.

"Do you miss him?" Deirdre asks, reading my mind.

"Like strep throat."

But I think about it, and cast an unwavering gaze within, searching for pangs, twinges, all and any signs of feckless yearning. They're all there, running on automatic, but growing weaker and weaker like the gravitational pull of an ever-more-distant star.

"We did it on a park bench at the end of one of these streets," I say.

"Who was it who said that the older you get, the more life is like high school?"

"Sounds comme Jerry Garcia."

"No, je pense that it was Janis Joplin."

"Jamais! It was Frank Zappa."

"Zut alors! Andy Warhol."

"Sacre bleu! Madonna."

"Non, non, non. It's Frank Zappa."

We're arguing in this fashion, bumping into ourselves on the street, not paying much attention to the other pedestrians.

We pass Riverhouse, where Deirdre says she'd like to live if she moved to the city.

I notice them over a block away, heading south.

Two old women, one with a cane, holding onto the arm of the other, but it doesn't register, not until they're about twenty yards away. The one with the cane murmurs to the other from time to time, but mostly they walk on in a dignified silence. She is dressed in a beige, oversized man's shirt and brown slacks. Her hair is colorless, bleached by age, and hangs limply over her shoulders in a style reminiscent of her youth. Her hair is the giveaway, and I wonder if it's real, if it's not a wig? Once she wouldn't have considered leaving the house without her mascara in place. Once she dreaded old age, rued its inevitability, and here she is held in its clawlike clutch, sporting the signature hairstyle of her youth. The pathos of this makes tiny stabs at my heart.

Darkly tinted glasses cover her eyes. Her mouth is set in a determined frown. The invisible barrier she's erected around herself seems impenetrable. She stares straight ahead, not at people, never at people. But people stare at her, and the excitement generated by their recognition creates a stir, a rippling effect that undulates in waves of passersby whose faces log expressions of surprise, awe, gaping curiosity, as she passes.

Garbo, in life, is as ephemeral and unassailable as the celluloid from which her movies were made. The shock of her reality, of her frailty, of the fact that she's mortal, jars me. My goddess sits not on a pedestal, but walks with a cane. Her feet are shod in men's bedroom slippers. Her companion is wearing moccasins. Did they buy them together, giggling like girls?

Without realizing it, I'm squeezing Deirdre's wrist so hard that she says, "Ooow," and pulls it away.

"What's gotten into you?"

I can't answer. My tongue is glued to my brain, which is ready to spill all over the sidewalk. My eyes are riveted to Garbo, computing, How can one person embody human vulnerability, divinity and myth all at once? Even beside a companion, she appears to be all alone.

Women aren't suppose to be alone. Her mystery resides in the fact of this solitariness, this pathological singularity. Without it she would be just another aging movie star, venerated for longevity and her contribution to the art of film, but without the mystique, the enigma. Seeing her in the flesh, I realize how heavy is the mantle of responsibility her celebrity has imposed upon her. Her worst detractors criticize her for shirking the responsibilities of her fame, but I feel the opposite is true. Her whole life has been her greatest part, providing us, her public, with endless speculation and entertainment.

She considered her years in Hollywood a form of prostitution, yet behaved with laudable professionalism, always putting the work first, diligently rehearsing, giving and demanding perfection. Clarence Brown, her director, when asked what Garbo was thinking about during her greatest close-ups, said, "Absolutely nothing." Brown attributed her ability to convey emotion with a minimum of facial expression to the intelligence behind her eyes. She could launch turbojets of feeling—love, hate, desire, jealousy, rage, despair—through the focus of her gaze. Or in the way she moved. But now the hand that she once placed over a bony hip in a perpetual slouch, or to brush back the hair from her forehead, is veined and gnarled and grips the handle of a cane.

She never intended to retire at thirty-six. Her last picture, *Two-Faced Woman*, bombed at the box office in 1941.

"They've dug my grave," she said of MGM, and wisely withdrew until a more propitious time. She never made another picture, yet she is still Garbo. She did not compromise herself for anyone, at anytime her entire life. How I envy her that—her ability, throughout it all, to be unequivocally herself, to have a self to be.

Garbo disdains her public, and I think of how we must be relentless reminders to her of a career she has had occasion to denounce, a past she condemns, a life she regrets, a beauty and talent that have faded except for what is preserved on celluloid and videotape. She once said that she gave all of herself on screen, there was nothing else left. She asked, "What do people want from me?"

I want to present her with bouquets of pansies, or violets, her favorites. I want to call out her names and peudonyms—Miss Garbo, Geebo, GG, Flicka, Harriet, Miss Brown, Brownie, Gussie Berger, Karen Lund, Mary Holmquist. Her closest friends create around her a protective circle, guarding the mystery like sworn disciples, keepers of the flame. Those who break the trust are excommunicated.

Garbo walks right by us without looking, as though we're invisible. I know she knows that I recognize her, and feel oddly hurt that there is no sign or acknowledgment. In rendering us invisible and inconsequential, doesn't she invalidate a great part of herself? Or am I to assume reciprocity from the stoniness of her reception?

There's an unofficial code among Garbo-watchers: look, but leave her alone. Not everybody obeys. We all twirl our invisible lariats, hoping to capture her attention, to be the object of her thoughtful gaze, to possess her, if only for a millisecond. Somebody with a camera snaps her picture. She doesn't flinch. In fact, she and her companion, who calls her M'Lady, treat the whole thing like a giant nuisance. The star ages, but the legend lives on.

I watch her walk away. "Farewell," I think, full of sorrow.

"What was that all about?" Deirdre asks.

"Greta Garbo."

"The woman whose picture is hanging on your wall?"

"Yes."

"You could have fooled me."

I had debated about whether or not to cart the large film still with me to California, and know now that I'll either give it away or leave it behind. How many hours had I stared at it, struggling to crack its complex equation? Who in the photograph is holding onto whom? Who holds sway? Is Garbo leading Barrymore, or is Barrymore leading Garbo? The thrust of her head, the challenge in her eyes as they gaze at one another, the set of her mouth and jaw, all indicated challenge. Rather than surrender, her character seems to meet Barrymore's on an equal footing. Yet their ardor for one another is enhanced not diminished by her independent stance. To me it was always a portrait of true love and grand passion, and something more. To say equality is misleading. It is commitment without subjugation, passion without abandonment, surrender that is both mutual and consummate.

The awful, magnifying power of the projected image, especially one frozen in the blowup of a 35mm still, is such that I'd never questioned its reality, not until I'd seen Garbo in person. Have I misinterpreted a collector's item, a relic of an old movie— a make-believe moment in the lives of two actors, a man and a woman fixed in a posed embrace, who will never let go, grow old and die—in some impossible romantic delusion?

I feel like the top of my head has blown off and hundreds of little chirruping birds have flown out. Until now, I only partially understood why Garbo always referred to herself in the masculine gender. Nothing in the feminine embraces the kind of enigmatic journey that she has travelled her whole life. I imagine her following the wandering Turk, impassioned and rootless, each looking for a place to rest. I imagine Garbo's astonishment to discover many years later that she is and always has been that which she seeks.

The eccentric California artist and M'Lou had both told me as much, but I never listened. I turn to Deirdre anxious to share with her what I am feeling, and how funny it is, really, the way that imagination shapes us and where it leads us, all of us on our own peculiar journeys, but there are no words to describe the experience. My arms flail. My mouth is moving, but, except for stuttering fits and starts, no words come. My eyes feel like they're spinning in their sockets like Roger Rabbit after he's sipped some whisky.

"You quit that this minute, mon amie," Dee says, looking nervous.

This makes me laugh, but it is the laughter of the fanatic and she's not sure how to react.

I now know why certain movie stars always conceal their eyes behind dark glasses. I used to think it was to hide, to prevent disclosure, but it's also because the rich and famous can neither contain nor withstand, full-blast, the false reflection of themselves mirrored in the hopeful, preying eyes of those they hold captive.

BOOK
THREE

Deirdre cut her visit short, and I was devastated to see her go. She left early partly because I had to hit the road, and partly because Stephen Beale had rejected her. She called him up and asked him out. He said he was busy. Cara explained that his girlfriend had returned from Sardinia, or wherever she was spending the summer, but that didn't appease Deirdre, whose crushed feelings emerged in acid sarcasm and feigned indifference.

"You wouldn't have liked him anyway," I said. "He's stuffy."

"Not too stuffy to fuck."

Pain makes Deirdre, all of us, cruel. I shrugged it off. Sometimes I could hate Dee if I didn't love her.

We said our fond farewells in front of my building under the nosy gaze of Mrs. Wallace and her drooling dog. While waiting for the taxi, I presented Dee with a Swiss Army knife full of useful gadgets, including a tiny magnifying glass.

"In case you have to build a feu in the desert, or the jungle, or wherever the Peace Corps sends you," I said.

I was also happy to give her the Garbo still, which she said that she wanted, and had had crated and shipped to her home in D.C. To me, the passing on of the photograph is like the passing on of the sacred mysteries of Ephesus, temple of Artemis, Goddess of the Hunt.

I've outgrown my need for the talismanic. The obsession has abated, shifted, and is veering off in other directions.

"What're you going to do avec that in Mauritania?" I asked Dee, alluding to the giant still.

"I haven't a clue. But tu never know. It sure gave you something to think about."

With the help of the driver, we stowed her Louis Vuitton luggage in the cab.

"Be sure to write, mon amie," she said, hugging me.

"I will, I promise. I'll send you my new address toute de suite."

"Au revoir."

"Au revoir."

"That's nice," Mrs. Wallace commented, as I climbed up the stoop.

"That's none of your damn business."

There goes my apartment recommendation, I thought, but I'd wanted to tell her that for years. For once, Mrs. Wallace was at a loss for words. Instead of angry, she appeared hurt, and I felt not triumphant, but lousy.

Dee gave me a carrying case for Kithkat for the cross-country drive. Both the cat and I hate it, but I use it to blackmail her into occasional docility. Kithy is a travelling animal. Like her mistress, she loves the existential life of the road.

I called Eddie somewhere outside of Chicago to tell him that I was on my way, again. Dave Riley had insisted that I fly back out to San Francisco to meet his staff and become more acclimated, all expenses paid, before my final move. I liked everyone I'd met—and I'd met everyone except one guy who was on vacation.

After the DQ&Co. business was over, Eddie and I had agreed to meet. He said he always had business to do in San Francisco. I was surprised when he offered to help me scope out the apartment scene. We'd been in constant telephone contact since our last parting, at the L.A. airport. Neither of us mentioned what had transpired between us, but whatever it was has reforged a newer and stronger link between us.

By the third apartment look-see, I'd despaired of finding a decent place to live in San Francisco.

"It's just like New York," I complained. "All the nice places are too expensive, and all the affordable ones are crummy."

"There's one last place," he said, "in Fillmore. Let's check it out."

Grumbling, I went along, and the place was perfect—a sunny, clean, one-bedroom—similar to our New York apartment minus the fireplace. But we'd arrived too late, and it had been taken. Eddie was more upset than I was.

"Don't worry," I said. "Riley offered to contribute towards a hotel until I find a place."

He was staring out of a tall window which overlooked a row of backyards.

"What are you looking at?" I asked, peering over his shoulder.

Down below an old man was puttering around a garden, tending to his oleander vines and hibiscus.

"Where do you think his wife is?" I asked.

"Maybe he doesn't have one."

We had turned toward one another and were holding each other's upper arms in an embrace that had stalled midway between a hug and pulling apart. It was as though we'd become frozen in a film frame whose images were being superimposed on those of Garbo and Barrymore in the photograph. I tilted my chin with the same teasing defiance that Garbo gave Barrymore. Grinning a lopsided smile, Eddie locked his eyes on mine. Neither of us moved. I could feel the hardness of his biceps beneath the material of his jacket, smell his aftershave, feel his warm breath upon my face, see the tiny prisms of gray and green that make up the color of his eyes. He tightened his grip, as I did mine. We stood that way, neither coiling nor recoiling, bearing equal tension and weight, for what seemed like a long time.

I was the first to relax, I think—it no longer matters. Eddie emitted a long, plaintive sigh, one part relief, one part resignation, one part desire. His arms dropped to his side, and I moved into them. He held me close, as close as two people can physically get outside of sex. The memory of that moment lingers and taunts. I long to relive it and like to imagine that he does too. I must ask myself what still keeps us apart a hundred times a day? Now Eddie claims that *he's* the one who needs the break.

"I want time out on the field," he wrote.

His letters have been long, and tortuous to read. He rages at me, and I encourage him, because at least it's a way for him to exorcize his emotions which have become impacted deep inside of him, like an infected tooth. He says he feels like a pitcher in a world series game. It's the ninth inning, a full count with a runner in scoring position, and he doesn't know whether to throw the batter a fast ball or a curve.

I make a mental note to read up on baseball to improve my communication skills with Eddie.

He's decided not to take the Donatello job offer, and I'm not surprised. He said that being an executive, a desk-jockey, was about as exciting to him right now "as modern Chinese architecture."

I told him to take his time. Cara will never give up her conviction that Eddie and I are Plato's original twin souls who were separated before birth. I tell her we're more akin to the "superpartner" aspect of the "superstring" theory of physics: every particle has an antiparticle—quarks have squarks, leptons have sleptons, and Eddie has Rebeccah. It's understood that if we so choose, we'll see other people. But I don't believe that either of us wants to, really—and besides, there's always the fact of our echolocation. No matter where Eddie goes on a date, I'll hear him.

For the first time in ages we've agreed on something. In a funny-peculiar way this agreement to leave one another alone has brought us closer together.

"I hope the Lindas of this world don't steal him away from you," Mom said.

"Nobody can steal somebody," I said.

"You have a lot to learn, honey," she said, sighing.

I always found the analogy of people owning or stealing other people offensive. It makes us seem like private property. When I marry I want to give myself away, but I didn't bother to tell Val that. She has enough troubles with me as it is.

Mom said that Granny Peck offered to pay for one of those male dummy torsos to put on the passenger seat to deceive people into thinking that I'm not a woman traveling alone. I prefer to take my chances. So far nobody has bothered us, except for the weird send-off I got on the outskirts of Chicago. A black Trans-Am blaring Madonna's "Express Yourself" over a two thousand-megawatt car stereo system trailed me for a while. Her warning not to settle for second best struck me as apt. I can still hear the words, and feel the throbbing vibration of the bass.

I'd promised I'd stick to the main highways, but it's off the beaten path that magnetizes.

"Let's face it, Kithy," I say, pulling over and studying my map, "you and I are good and lost."

She doesn't seem to mind, and neither do I. I wanted to get lost—it's my last gasp of Garbo, of transience, of drifting from place to place like a wind-swept sand dune. Dave Riley expects me bright and early the day after tomorrow, and here I am lost in a red-dust desert, staring at rocks that look like they've been carved by space aliens. Riley called my design ideas unsophisticated, but "full of potential." I was tempted to argue with him, to tell him that according to Paul Theroux's *Riding the Iron Rooster*, the only people who will survive if the plug is pulled are the Chinese. For infathomable reasons of their own, they continue to build train engines that run on steam, washboards and other seemingly outdated and useless objects, hand-operated and made to endure. Maybe they know something we don't? But I bit my tongue, which Dad said was wise.

"It's too soon to disagree with the boss," he said.

My father is pleased that I've rejoined the ranks of the employed. He listens now with less impatience to my plans.

"I want to own my own design company one day," I said, and he offered encouragement, but no promise of financial assistance.

Riley gave me an assignment. "I want you to redesign an eggbeater."

"Electronic or manual?"

"Be inventive. Stick to the principles you outlined in my office. Think about it. Do some sketches, and show them to me when you get here."

Watching people pump gas from Newark to Denver has given me an idea, which I've etched out on paper napkins pilched from truck stops and diners along the way. The gas-pump handle is shaped like a gun. Why not design an eggbeater with a trigger that activates a rotary blade? I've seen screwdrivers constructed on this premise operate as well, if not better, than their cordless, battery-run counterparts.

Deirdre was astounded to learn that a return to manually operated kitchen tools would probably result in the loss of ten pounds or more a year. Cara had heard this argument from me before. Dee went out and bought herself a vegetable peeler, swearing to forsake her Cuisinart forever.

"Don't overdo it, mon amie," I said.

Preoccupied by the ergonomics of the eggbeater and the handgun, I am too busy making up slogans—

Make cookie dough, not war.
Make batter, not strife, save life.
Save watts, conserve energy, lose weight

—to pay much attention to where I am going. I've wound up somewhere in the canyonlands of Utah.

"I'm also running out of gas," I tell Kithkat. "We're in big trouble, my friend."

By sheer luck we find a ramshackle gas station in the middle of Nowhere, Utah. It appears to be working, but is momentarily abandoned.

I get out to stretch my legs.

"Me, too," mews the cat.

I put her on a leash. I refuse to cage her, but I don't want her running wild either.

We're surrounded by sandstone mountains with rounded tops. I unfold the map to ascertain exactly where we have stumbled when a woman appears from out back. She's sporting a two-foot-high pompadour. If Deirdre were here she'd snap her picture as anthropological proof of the existence of the beehive hairdo in the late twentieth century, U.S.A. All that's missing is the bow.

"Howdy," she says.

"Hi."

"What can I do for you?"

"I need gas, water, oil, the works."

She pulls a white, grease-stained T-shirt from her back pocket and opens the overheated hood. "Nice car," she says. "Good condition. You don't see many of these anymore. How is it on gas?"

"Thirsty."

"You're lucky you found us. Car's low on water, and oil, too. Where're you headed?"

"San Francisco."

Since this elicits neither guffaws nor ridicule, I ask, "How do I get back on the main drag?"

It takes awhile, but over a couple of Cokes and bags of potato chips, she gives me directions, laced with a little local history.

I pay and thank her.

"You have a nice day," she says, "and keep an eye on them oil and water gauges."

"Thanks. I will."

The farther away from New York City, the more civil people are. Slowly, my own manners are returning.

The woman told me that I'm in the waterpocket fold in the heart of the Capitol Reef National Park. The white sandstone mounds on top of the fold resemble capitol domes, which explain the park's name. The Fremont River nearby parallels the highway, which is what I want to get onto and head due west.

This land is pockmarked by eerie eruptions of rock—mountains and mesas, plateaus and cliffs. I pass walls of stone colored in pigments that defy description. The Navajos used to call this "the land of the sleeping rainbow." What would happen if the rainbow awoke? The stone glows with an inner illumination, as if powered from some elfish magic.

While we were chatting, the gas lady had peered up at the gathering thunderclouds and predicted that it would rain soon. If it did, I should pull over by the side of the road until it passes.

"It don't last long," she said, "but it's mighty powerful."

I have trouble finding the highway. Darkening clouds continue to amass overhead. Electromagnetic energy from storms ionizes the atmosphere, and electrifies me. I feel not fear but awe, reverence, primal connection. The whiplash of lightning, the low, rumbling roll and clap of thunder, evoke atavistic memories of the human need to name Names, to tame the raging elements. The downpour falls in sheets of chain mail, rendering the windshield wipers useless.

"Guess we'd better do as the lady said."

I pull over. The cat's ears are pricked, alert. She starts when a flash of lightning cracks nearby, but not from fear. One paw is raised as if to strike out at it if necessary.

The storm passes in time, leaving hundreds of waterpockets in the canyon floor. The gas-pump lady had explained that the thin bottom layers of the moist sand shelter eggs which hatch tiny creatures, including fairy and crab shrimp.

"Life is short," she said, "only lasts a matter of days for the little critters."

The eggs will mature and mate, and more eggs will be deposited in the sand. Eventually, the water will dry up under the blazing heat of the sun, leaving hundreds of tiny corpses to quilt the land. The few eggs that survive sometimes wait years for another rain.

"You're going to witness the miracle of life," she said.

I think of Cara and her happiness at being pregnant. I'll miss being there for the birth of her baby, but she told me not to worry. Shel bought a video recorder and is planning to videotape the birth, which is going to be at home. Cara is gung-ho on this Russian method of having the baby underwater so that the transition from womb to world is as stressless and painless—for both mother and infant—as possible. They're going to rent a jacuzzi and install it in their living room. She was in the process of interviewing midwives when I left. Her mother and sister, who think she's crazy, are coming up from Florida for the event. I could come too if I wanted. I said I'd have to think about that one.

I recall my own untimely pregnancy and the unhappiness it caused. Regret is a form of self-torture, I'm convinced, and I try hard to keep it at bay. But too often I think of things like if I'd had the baby, Cara and I could have shared the experience of pregnancy, birth and motherhood together, and feel a pang. Life hits you like a flash flood sometimes, and you have to scramble around like the tiny fairy shrimp, trying to survive in the best way you can.

On the surface, you'd never know that the water pockets are teeming with life. They remind me of the pocket water of Jake's run where I fished for the odd trout. Incubating in secret, hidden places—that could describe Eddie and me.

I wish I could stay to watch the frenetic mating dance of the water pocket's miniscule denizens. At three weeks the human embryo resembles a fish; by six weeks, it's amphibian, and supposedly the whole ontogenetical chain is re-enacted. Hundreds of millions of years of evolution, recapitulated in our mother's womb in nine months. Humans are supposed to be at the top of the food chain, top of the line, but I wonder. At times, like now, I imagine that we're being watched by intelligent creatures from another galaxy who observe our mating rituals with the same hushed curiosity that I reserve for the teeming life in the wet sand. What a tremendous affirmation: to gestate in the hot, arid earth, perhaps for years, awaiting the next rainfall, to release us from the slumbering shell of our existence.

The sky clears. I drive on.